TOBY GOLD
AND THE SECRET FORTUNE

CRAIG R. EVERETT

FISCAL PRESS

AN IMPRINT OF WYATT-MACKENZIE

Copyright © 2012 by Craig R. Everett.
Illustrations copyright © 2012 by Jessica Ellen Lindsey.

Fiscal Press
an imprint of Wyatt-MacKenzie Publishing
Visit FiscalPress.com
bulk discounts are available

Publisher's Cataloging-in-Publication Data
Everett, Craig R., 1965-
Toby Gold and the Secret Fortune / by Craig R. Everett
p. cm.
Summary: Toby Gold discovers he possesses amazing powers with money, which pull him into a very dangerous financial conspiracy.
ISBN 978-1-936-21495-2 (hardcover)
978-0-9882374-0-7 (eBook)
1. Magic—Juvenile fiction. 2. Money—Juvenile fiction.
3. Bullying—Juvenile fiction.
I. Everett, Craig R., 1965- II. Title
Library of Congress Control Number: 2012946359
[Fic]—dc22

Printed in the United States of America.

Information about Toby Gold and about scheduling the author
for school visits is available at TobyGold.com

This book is dedicated to my beloved wife and companion Sandee, and to my five incredible children for all their love, support and overall awesomeness.

CHAPTER 1

The Man in the Italian Suit

THE MAN IN THE Italian suit reached the train platform in New Haven just in time to hop aboard the last car of the *Vermonter*, a silver-gray Amtrak train en route from New York City to Burlington, Vermont. He was still fuming. His target had eluded him at Penn Station in Manhattan, forcing him to request an emergency chopper flight to Connecticut to intercept the train there.

Out of sight with his back up against the wall of the vestibule, he popped the ammo clip out of his nine millimeter handgun and replaced it with a fresh one. There was *no way* she would get away from him this time. There's simply not that many places on a passenger train that a woman with a baby can hide.

He closed his eyes and took a deep breath. *Try to relax.* It was a very dangerous situation and he knew he would not survive it if his heart rate exceeded ninety beats per minute. He needed his powers intact in order to shield his mind from her as long as humanly possible. An elevated pulse would severely limit his ability to do that. If his target had been anyone else, he would have just cast his mind over the train and known instantly where she was hiding.

1

But he knew that taking that approach against Marie would be suicide. Reluctant as he was to admit it, her powers were easily ten times more powerful than his. Using his mental ability that way would leave him vulnerable to counter-attack — she could effortlessly crush his mind like a grape. He liked his job, but not well enough to risk spending the rest of his life as a drooling idiot. He also knew to *NEVER* underestimate the ferocity of a frightened mother protecting her young.

"Well, I guess I'll just have to do this the old-fashioned way," he said under his breath as he holstered his weapon and checked his reflection in the window. He buttoned his jacket and frowned. He really hated how the shoulder holster ruined the lines of his Armani suit. He made a mental note that as soon as this mission was over, he needed to find a good mafia tailor. "Those guys know how to wear a gun with style." He placed his fingers against the side of his neck to quickly double-check his pulse. Seventy beats per minute. *Excellent.*

He made his way from the rear of the train toward the front, meticulously checking every potential hiding place along the way. In the third car from the rear, he encountered an occupied bathroom. He gave three firm knocks on the door, then stepped back into the adjacent vestibule. There was no answer. Careful to avoid the direct line of sight of the other passengers, he removed his gun from its holster and took a deep breath. He could have easily jimmied the lock, but if Marie were in there, that approach would sacrifice the element of surprise. On the other hand, kicking in the door would maintain the element of surprise, but would also alarm the passengers, whose responses could be annoyingly unpredictable.

Figuring that the latter was the less risky option, he released the safety from his weapon and kicked in the door, eliciting shocked gasps from nearby passengers. The only occupant of the bathroom, however, was a startled baby lying in a large open green leather handbag. "Well, *there* you are, little guy," the man in the Italian suit said in his most reassuring baby-talk. "Where's your mommy?"

The baby, apparently unconvinced of the man's attempts to be soothing, started to fuss.

The man backed out of the bathroom and turned toward the passengers, some of whom were already pulling out their cell phones and dialing 911. "It's alright, everyone. My name is Agent Faux, with the FBI," he lied. "I'm pursuing an unarmed female fugitive, so there's no danger to anyone here, but it's very important that I apprehend her. Did anyone see the woman who last used this bathroom and where she went?"

An expressionless old lady two rows back sheepishly pointed toward the door of the next car, but said nothing.

"Thank you ma'am." He poked his head back into the bathroom and said, "I'll be back for *you* in just a few minutes, sport." The baby just frowned, lower lip protruding as if preparing to quiver.

▲ ▲ ▲

Marie was two cars ahead, standing in the vestibule of the dining car trying to gather her thoughts and calm down. She watched the smooth blur of trees flow past the train in the darkness, hoping that it would help her relax. It didn't. Like the man in the Italian suit, her powers were rendered useless by an excessively rapid heart rate. Despite her best efforts, she had been entirely unable to regain her composure since her husband's assassination back in New York just two hours earlier. Unarmed and without her abilities, she was a sitting duck, nakedly visible to her enemies, yet unable to defend herself or her child in any meaningful way.

As a consequence, minutes earlier she made the heart-wrenching decision that keeping her infant son with her was putting him in too much danger. Her enemies would be drawn to *her* location, not his. As soon as the immediate danger had passed, she would go back for him.

Without warning, she felt the sharp prick of a needle in her neck. Her eyes bulged. From behind her, she heard a familiar voice.

"Hello Marie."

She spun around to face her attacker, holding her hand against the spot on her neck where the needle had entered. "What have you done to me?"

The man smiled, holding the empty syringe with one hand while pressing his gun to her forehead with the other. "Don't worry, my dear. It's nothing nefarious. Just a little shot of adrenaline to make sure your heart rate stays nice and high while I ask you a few questions."

"I still can't believe *you* of all people are involved in this," Marie said. "We trusted you. Why on earth…" Marie's voice caught in her throat. It was all she could do to hold back tears, but she was determined not to give him the satisfaction of seeing her cry.

"If you don't mind, I'll be the one asking the questions here, my dear, not you," the man replied with sweet over-politeness. "You say you trusted me, yet clearly not quite enough. You led me to believe that your Wall Street facility was the headquarters of the Order. Tonight's events have clearly demonstrated that is *not* the case. So where are the real headquarters? Where is your *father?* Why won't he face us like a man?" He pressed the barrel of the gun harder against her forehead.

Marie felt the adrenaline injection start to kick in with two immediate effects. As expected, her heart rate accelerated, making it impossible to use her abilities. But it also gave her a sudden burst of explosive physical energy, which she directed into a full-force kick to his groin.

The sound of the gunshot was muffled by the roaring drone of the train's wheels on the track. Since Marie had already dropped into a three-point crouch on the floor, the bullet flew harmlessly past her through the open doorway and into the trees blurredly whizzing by. Without hesitation, she executed a flawless sweep kick against the legs of her attacker. His feet promptly popped up in the air and his body crashed to the metal floor, the back of his head taking the brunt of the impact.

Taking advantage of her assailant's temporary disorientation, Marie walked over and stepped on the gun, still held loosely in his right hand. She reached down, picked it up and pointed it at the man, who was still looking quite baffled by what had just happened. The adrenaline still surging in her veins, she picked him up by his shirt collar and leaned him over the safety bar. The fifty mile-per-hour wind finally messed up his hair, which up until now had stayed perfectly in place.

"Now it's my turn to ask the questions," Marie said. "How many other thugs from *Legio* have infiltrated the Order? There's no way you could have pulled this off alone."

The only response to her question was the muffled crack of a gunshot. The sensation was strange. She felt no pain at first, just a sickly warm feeling in her chest. She stumbled backwards and looked down at her blouse, which was steadily turning from white to crimson. *He shot me.* She dropped the gun and fell to her knees.

The man in the Italian suit picked himself up off the safety bar and walked over to Marie, holding a small shiny revolver. He dragged her over to the windy doorway and unlatched the safety bar. "You didn't actually think that I would come on a mission like this with only *one* gun, do you?"

5

She turned her head to look up at him, trying to focus. Her vision was becoming darker. "Please don't hurt my baby," she whispered.

"That's no longer your concern. I'm truly sorry it had to come to this. Good-bye, Marie." Already too weak to cry out, she fell silently from the train.

▲ ▲ ▲

The Vermonter's horn gave a long toot and a voice came over the speaker announcing the next stop. *Wallingford, Connecticut.* The man in the Italian suit leaned out into the darkness and saw the blue and red flashing lights of several police cars already waiting at the station.

"Crap," he said out loud. He spun around and burst into the dining car, knocking over the snack lady and her cart. He held his gun in the air, which elicited several screams from the crowded car. "Everyone just sit back and relax. Don't do anything stupid and I promise everything will be *just like it never happened.*" Toward the rear of the car, he found an empty table with a copy of the *Wall Street Journal.* He sat down, took out his comb, and fixed his hair in the window reflection. Reasonably satisfied with the results, he opened the paper and did his best to relax and slow his breathing. He knew he had less than a minute to take control of his metabolism — and the situation. It was going to be close.

▲ ▲ ▲

The police had received several 911 calls from the train about gunshots and an abandoned baby in a handbag in the bathroom. They stormed onto the train as soon as it arrived at the tiny Wall-

7

ingford Station, weapons drawn. Checking the bathrooms first, the baby was quickly discovered and removed from the train.

They interviewed all of the passengers in the dining car, as well as the passenger cars fore and aft. No one, not a single person, had noticed the baby, or who had put him there. This was odd, because there were clear indications of a struggle. The safety bar in the vestibule was unlatched, the snack cart had been overturned nearby and the snack lady had a black eye and a small cut on her left hand. Yet she had absolutely no recollection of what had happened. No one else did, either. In fact, none of the potential witnesses on the dining car remembered seeing any struggle or seeing the snack cart crash, even though it had clearly happened right in front of them. Likewise, as the police interviewed the passengers in the other cars, none of them could even recall what they had been doing at the time of the incident. Although several emergency calls had been received, no one could remember calling 911.

Captain Sullivan was the police officer in charge at the scene. He was the no-nonsense type, large and gruff, and was quite intimidating until you got to know him. That's the way he liked it. There was absolutely no advantage in a perp knowing that deep down, this oversized scary cop was actually a big friendly teddy bear who loved playing "peek-a-boo" with his fourteen month-old niece in New Haven. His friends and superiors called him Sully. Everyone else called him Captain.

Sully interviewed the passengers on the dining car, while the other officers each took one of the remaining passenger cars. They all came up empty. No one could remember seeing anything, and the passengers were becoming increasingly agitated that the train was not being allowed to continue. The exception was one particular passenger in the dining car. He was a good-looking man with slick black hair in his mid-twenties, who sat at the last table, legs crossed, calmly reading the *Wall Street Journal.*

As he walked toward this passenger, Sully couldn't help noticing that the man's expensive dark gray Italian suit had a small tear in the shoulder, where the seam looked as though it had recently popped. Both of the man's hands were in view, since he was holding the newspaper, revealing that his left cuff link was missing, leaving one French cuff on his shirt dangling open. This guy's clothes cost more than Sully's entire salary for two full months. That was one of many reasons he hated these Wall Street types.

"Excuse me, sir, do you mind if I ask you a few questions?"

"Not at all," replied the man in the Italian suit. "Go right ahead." As the man set the newspaper down, Sully noticed that the man's one remaining cuff link was perfectly circular and silver, with a fancy "L" on it. The L design was somewhat similar to the symbol for British money.

"There appears to have been a struggle down at the other end of the dining car. Can you remember seeing anything?"

The man smiled, looked at Sully's name tag, then up into his eyes. His left hand moved smoothly down under the table into his coat pocket, where he silently removed the safety from his handgun, still hot from being fired just minutes earlier. He didn't think he would need to use it again, but better safe than sorry. "No, Captain Sullivan. I've been sitting here the whole trip, ever since Penn Station. I didn't see anything. *Nothing happened here.*"

A blank look washed across Sully's face as he tried to remember the next question he was going to ask. It had been on the tip of his tongue, but now it was gone. *Think Sully. Something about a baby.* He looked around, hoping to see something that might jog his memory. No luck. He turned back to the man in the Italian suit. "I'm sorry sir, what were we talking about?"

The man smiled, clicked the safety back on, and removed his empty hand from his coat pocket. "You were asking me the time. *It's very late, and it's time to let the train get moving again. Noth-*

ing happened here." After a brief pause and the hint of a crooked smile, the man added, "*and these are not the droids you're looking for.*" Sully was a huge *Star Wars* fan and would have immediately recognized that line if he hadn't been under the influence of a mind trick himself. But he didn't. His thoughts were now completely under the control of the man in the Italian suit.

"Oh yeah. Of course. Thank you for your time." Sully turned and started walking back to the other end of the car. He pushed the little "talk" button on the police radio clipped to his chest. "Okay, men, it's late and time to let this train get moving again. Nothing happened here. These are not the droids we're looking for."

"*Uhh, could you repeat that last part, Captain?*" asked a voice from an officer on the other end of the radio.

"I said that nothing happened here," repeated Sully. "Let's clear out so these nice folks can get on their way."

Sully notified the conductor that the train was free to leave. Within a few seconds it was pulling out of the station and away from Wallingford. The man in the Italian suit smirked and nodded at Sully from the window of the dining car as it passed the spot where the patrol cars were parked, blue and red lights still flashing. Sully politely nodded back, wondering where he had seen the man before.

The ambulance had already rushed the baby to the nearby Masonic hospital, which was the closest medical facility. Being a hospital for the elderly, they weren't quite sure what to do with a baby in a handbag. Nevertheless, the attending doctor examined him and he was judged to be in perfect health. By the doctor's measurements, he was estimated to be approximately six months old. The nurses were quite heartbroken when the county authorities arrived in the morning to take him to a more suitable place.

There was absolutely nothing to identify the baby, except for the word "Tobias" on a slip of paper at the bottom of the handbag. Ultimately, it was discovered that the slip of paper was completely unrelated to the baby. It merely referred to a handbag factory quality inspector named Ernest Tobias. By then, though, it was too late. Toby had already been named.

"Baby Tobias," as he was called in the local newspaper, needed to find his parents, but his parents apparently did not want to be found. So Toby was placed temporarily into foster care until his parents could be located. *Temporarily*, in Toby's case, turned out to be twelve and a half years and counting.

CHAPTER 2

Toby Gold

WITH CAT-LIKE STEALTH, TOBY peeked his head around the door of the office, hoping that he would find it unoccupied. No such luck.

"Happy birthday!" Mrs. Stephens exclaimed with a plastic smile.

Toby let out an audible sigh. With a shrug, he maneuvered his rolling suitcase through the door of her office at county social services.

"Thanks, but we both know it's not my real birthday. And changing foster families sort of spoils the celebration anyway." Toby slouched into the chair facing her desk.

Toby had just turned thirteen…sort of.

No one knew his true name or date of birth, so the birthday he celebrated every year was just the one selected by Mrs. Stephens, loosely based on the doctor's estimates of Toby's age when he was found. Ever since that night he was pulled off the train, she had been his county caseworker. Unfortunately, she hadn't shown much skill in choosing foster homes. They had all ended more or less badly for him. With every passing year, Toby's hope of being adopted and actually *belonging* somewhere slowly slipped away.

Just minutes earlier he had left his ninth foster home, forcing Mrs. Stephens to scramble to quickly find a new one for him. "So what was the problem this time, Mr. Gold?" she sighed.

He hated when she called him that. She did it to sound formal and official, but the last name Gold was just as fake as his first name and birth date. Mrs. Stephens had invented all of them years ago in order to complete the paperwork for his first foster placement. She picked the name Gold because his right eye, otherwise crystal blue like his left eye, had a thin ring of amber-gold coloring on the innermost part of the iris, next to the pupil. It wasn't really noticeable from a distance, but most observers couldn't help seeing it if they were up close. Adults called his blue and gold eye "striking" or "unique." Kids, on the other hand, usually just called it freaky.

"Honestly, I'm not sure. I actually thought things were going okay," Toby replied.

"Then why do you think they asked us to find a new home for you?"

Toby scrunched his eyebrows for a moment. "Probably because if I had stayed just a few more hours, they would have had to bake a cake and buy me presents for my birthday."

Mrs. Stephens ignored Toby's last comment, instead focusing on the open file folder on her desk. "Fortunately, I've found a new home for you — the Jones family. They only have one child, a seventeen year-old junior in high school. They've had foster kids before, but none recently."

"Where do they live?" Toby asked with a worried tone.

"Don't worry, Toby. It's the same side of town. You won't have to change schools."

Toby was relieved. The only thing worse than changing foster homes was changing schools, too.

The phone rang, interrupting their conversation. "Janet Stephens," she answered. "Oh, yes. Send them up." Mrs. Stephens hung up the phone. "Well that didn't take long. The Joneses are here for you."

Mr. and Mrs. Jones seemed nice enough. Mrs. Jones was the chatty one, making small talk and asking lots of pointless questions. Mr. Jones kept pretty quiet. He was a big guy. Big shoulders, big neck, and big gut. On his big head he wore a faded New England Patriots cap. Fortunately he also had a big smile, which made him a little less scary.

After the required introductions, small talk, and signatures on government forms, they escorted Toby out to their car. Mr. Jones offered to carry the suitcase, so Toby just stuck his hands in his pockets and jingled the change. *One dollar and thirty-seven cents*. He could tell just by the feel of it.

▲ ▲ ▲

Ever since he could remember, Toby had an unnaturally good head for numbers. He always knew exactly how much money was in his pocket at any given time, and ever since the first grade he had been able to calculate sales tax instantly in his head. He really should have been at the top of his math class, but he wasn't. He aced the tests, but more often than not, forgot to turn in his homework, or had citizenship points taken off for not paying attention in class. It wasn't that Toby didn't like math — he loved it. Math was like breathing to him, effortless and hardly requiring any real thought. Thus, math class gave Toby the chance to think about other things, like his true talent, which was his amazing ability to make money.

In second grade, he became known around school as the *Fruit Snack Tycoon*, due to his prosperous underground snack trading business in the school cafeteria. The first fifteen minutes of his half-hour lunchtime overlapped with the first grade, and the final fifteen minutes overlapped with the third grade. This allowed Toby to buy snacks from the first graders for twenty-five cents and then sell them a few minutes later to the third graders for fifty cents.

"That's a quick and easy 100% profit!" he would brag to his best friend Marc Lopez.

"Yeah, you're a regular Donald Trump," Marc would reply, rolling his eyes.

Calculating profit margins isn't something that typical second graders do for fun, but back then, Toby wasn't like most second graders. He read *The Wall Street Journal* every day and zoned out most afternoons watching the financial news channel — mostly because he found it relaxing.

At the time of his reign as Fruit Snack Tycoon, Toby was in foster home number five. For some bizarre reason, he always seemed to get stuck with foster parents that insisted on buying him dorky clothes at the Goodwill thrift store, feeding him macaroni and cheese every meal, and then pocketing the savings themselves. That was his situation in the second grade. His big mistake back then, though, was telling his foster dad about his lunchroom profits at dinner one night.

"I made thirty-five bucks this week selling snacks in the cafeteria at school," bragged little Toby between mouthfuls of macaroni and cheese. "With the rest of the money I've made this month, pretty soon I'll have enough to buy that new bike!"

Foster Dad #5, affectionately known to Toby as FD5, looked up from his perfectly grilled steak and, squinting his eyes ever so slightly, replied, "That's a lot of cash for a kid so young. I hope you're keeping it in a safe place."

"Oh, sure, don't worry about that!" said Toby, "I keep it in an old sneaker in the back of my closet. No burglar would think to look there!"

"That sounds like an absolutely perfect hiding place," said FD5, smiling to himself as he took another bite of his steak. "You're a very clever boy."

Not clever enough, apparently. Within a few days, Toby noticed ten dollars had disappeared from his hiding place. *Maybe I counted wrong last week,* he thought briefly, though not quite convinced. He *never* counted wrong. But when twenty dollars went missing the following week, he knew for sure that FD5 was stealing from him. So he moved the money to a new hiding place, under his mattress. What Toby didn't know, of course, that this was the most completely obvious hiding place that could possibly exist in a kid's bedroom.

Within a week, his entire life savings was gone.

Toby ran into the living room, where FD5 was watching the news and admiring the brand new watch on his left wrist. "Why did you take my money?" Toby brushed his curly blond hair out of his eyes, exposing the fresh tears still streaming down his face.

"The *nerve* accusing me of such a thing! Is this the thanks we get after all we've done for you? Go to your room immediately. No mac and cheese for you tonight!"

Toby did as he was told and shuffled with wet eyes down the hallway to his room. It felt so unfair. The next time that Toby met with his social worker, he told her that FD5 was stealing from him. FD5 denied it, of course, and demanded that Toby be removed from his house at once. He could not bear to have such a dishonest and ungrateful child living under his roof.

It seemed as though wherever Toby went, someone was always trying to steal from him. Adults just couldn't be trusted. Every attempt to set things right only seemed to result in Toby getting into more trouble and being sent to a new foster home.

This time, though, things would be different. If only he could figure out a plan to deal with his latest nemesis, Eddie Jones.

▲ ▲ ▲

Unfortunately, in addition to his role as nemesis, Eddie also happened to be Toby's new foster brother. He was a junior at Lyman Hall High School, while Toby was just a measly seventh grader at Dag Hammarskjold Middle School. Over the years, Toby had accumulated such a dizzying array of past and present foster family members that he devised an abbreviation system for keeping them all straight in his mind. The letters in the beginning stood for the type of relative. *FD* meant foster dad, *FM* meant foster mother, *FB* meant foster brother, and so on. The number that followed stood for which foster home it was in Toby's long series of foster homes. In this case, "10" meant that it was Toby's tenth foster home, so Eddie was FB10.

Eddie made it clear how things were going to be when Toby first arrived home that day from social services. "Eddie! We're home! Come meet your new brother!" yelled FM10, as she, Toby and FD10 came through the back door into the kitchen from the garage, carrying Toby's suitcase.

"Hey, buddy! Let me help you with that," Eddie said with a big warm smile as he put down the carton of milk he was drinking from and wiped his mouth on his sleeve. He grabbed Toby's full-sized suitcase and tucked it effortlessly under his massive right arm as though it were full of marshmallows. "Come this way, dude. I'll show you where your room is." Eddie put his other arm around Toby's shoulder like they were long lost pals and escorted him down the hallway to the second door on the right.

Toby walked into the room and took a quick glance around. The room was smallish, but more than adequate, especially because he would have the room all to himself. It was a lot better than his room at foster home number nine, which he had to share with a five-year-old named Oliver, who had the unfortunate tendency of prolonged night-farts. This room had a big window that overlooked the back yard with lots of trees. In front of the window was a small desk with a computer. Toby smiled and immediately went over and turned it on. It wasn't state-of-the-art or anything — probably a hand-me-down from Eddie. That was no big deal, though. An old computer was a heck of a lot better than nothing. In his last foster home, Toby wasn't allowed to use the computer at all, so this was a big step up. *Yup,* Toby thought, *I think I'm going to be happy here.*

Eddie came into the room behind him, quietly shut the door and set the suitcase down. Toby turned around to thank Eddie for helping him with the suitcase. But before Toby could even speak the "th" part of "thank you," Eddie placed his left hand firmly on Toby's right shoulder, holding him steadily in place while he landed a powerful sucker punch with his right fist into Toby's unsuspecting stomach. He even pulled Toby toward him with his left hand during the punch to increase its effectiveness.

Pain shot across Toby's abdomen as he doubled over, his hands clutching his stomach. He dropped to his knees and curled up into a quivering ball on the floor of his new comfortable, yet smallish, bedroom. Eddie had knocked the wind out of him, so he couldn't scream, despite the intense pain that he was feeling. With Toby still gasping for air, Eddie grabbed the back of his new foster brother's belt, picked him up off the floor with one hand, and tossed him unceremoniously onto the bed like a rag doll. Turning Toby face up, Eddie sat down on him, with his right knee on Toby's chest and his left hand over Toby's mouth to keep him from yelling for help. Toby had never been more frightened in his life than at that moment. Terrified, he stared into Eddie's smirking face.

"Listen to me, you little twerp," Eddie hissed through his still-smiling teeth, "because I'm only going to tell you this once. You're on *my* turf now. You do exactly what I say, whenever I say, and you might not get hurt…much. Did my little love tap a second ago get your attention?" Eddie tapped him on the stomach with his free hand as a reminder, as if he needed one.

Toby nodded.

"Good," said Eddie, "It's just my way of saying hello and welcome to the family. It also won't leave a mark, so don't even think about telling mom and dad. They won't believe you anyway. You're not going to tell, right?"

Toby shook his head.

"Fantastic. Here's the deal. Whenever we have a foster kid in the house, mom and dad usually give them five dollars a week for an allowance."

Five dollars! thought Toby, his face lighting up for a brief second until he remembered that he still couldn't breathe. He had never had a decent allowance before.

"Don't get excited, because it's mine now," said Eddie. "In fact, a good way to look at it is that, as of right now, *everything* that's yours is mine. So this is how it's going to work. Mom and dad usually pay allowances on Friday mornings. Put yours in my top dresser drawer. If it's not in there by the time I get home from football, I'll kick your butt a LOT worse than I did just now. Are we clear, dirtbag?"

Toby nodded again, now unable to control his sobbing. He couldn't believe this was happening to him.

Then as quickly as it began, it ended. Eddie jumped up off the bed, and with that big warm smile of his, continued exactly like nothing had just happened, "…and over here is your closet. You gotta be careful of the left sliding door, because it can pop off its track if you open it too quickly. Here, let me help you put your stuff away."

What a total psycho, thought Toby, *an evil, inconceivably strong psycho that happens to live in the next bedroom and hates my guts. Great.*

Toby's instinct was to tell his foster parents what happened, but he had to wait until Eddie wasn't around. Breakfast would be the ideal opportunity, since Eddie left the house thirty minutes before Toby. The high school was on an earlier schedule than the middle school.

"So, Eddie's on the football team?" Toby began.

"Oh yes!" replied FM10 enthusiastically. "He's one of the team captains. Everyone just loves him!"

Well, not everyone, thought Toby. "Yeah, he certainly has a good build for football." Toby reflected on Eddie's two-hundred twenty pounds pressing down on his chest yesterday. "Has he gotten along well with the previous foster kids?" Toby asked, hoping for a history of trouble to boost his case.

"Oh, Eddie's been a wonderful foster brother. There's never been even one complaint about him from any of the other foster kids."

Toby knew exactly *why* there had been no complaints. It was clear that direct-tattle approach wasn't going to get him anywhere. Eddie was the unquestioned pride and joy of FD10 and FM10.

▲ ▲ ▲

Despite being the devil incarnate, in his parent's eyes Eddie could do no wrong. According to Toby's research over the next few days, Eddie had only been in trouble once, when he got into a fight with a bunch of Choaties over a plate of french fries at the Half Moon Café, a restaurant in town that happens to have the best fries on earth. "Choaties" is the nickname of the students at Choate, the ultra-prestigious private high school in town. The police were called to break up the fight, but no one was arrested.

FD10 had pretended like he was mad at Eddie about the french fry incident, but since he had also grown up hating Choaties, Eddie only got a one-day grounding. FD10's reasoning for the light sentence was because the Choaties probably had it coming. At the Half Moon, they always acted like they owned the place.

That one incident with the french fries was, in fact, the only time in his life that Eddie had ever been grounded. It wasn't that he never did anything wrong, he was just clever enough to never get caught. Eddie took particular pride in secretly terrorizing the foster kids. It annoyed him that his parents kept taking in foster kids, despite his protests. The extra bedroom would have been an ideal weight room — much better than the dusty basement where his weights had been forced to reside. There were spiders down there. Spiders were the one thing in the world that Eddie hated even more than foster brothers.

Eventually, Eddie figured out that his parents weren't going to stop taking in foster kids, and that he needed to at least *pretend* to play nice in order to maintain his privileges as favorite son. So Eddie made darn sure that he was always the perfect foster brother whenever his parents were watching. But when they weren't watching, it was an altogether different story.

▲ ▲ ▲

Friday rolled around, and true to Eddie's prediction, FM10 took Toby aside and handed him a five-dollar bill. Smiling, she said, "Toby, you've been really good at doing all your chores this week." It was true. Toby had taken out the trash every day and

21

kept his room clean. FM10 continued, "In this house, kids who take their responsibilities seriously get a five-dollar allowance." Toby, to be polite, tried to act surprised, happy and grateful. In reality, however, the moment was quite bitter for him since he knew that he wouldn't be able to keep the money.

Obedient to the instructions of his nemesis, Toby put his entire allowance into Eddie's top dresser drawer. It really wasn't the end of the world, though, since Toby could always figure out other ways to make money. He just had to keep it a secret from Eddie. As long as Eddie thought Toby was broke, he might leave him alone.

Toby needed a way to earn money that Eddie wouldn't find out about. Since moneymaking ideas flowed like a river into his brain on a regular basis, this task wasn't difficult at all. He decided to give dog-walking a try. Using his 'new' hand-me-down computer, he printed up some flyers advertising his availability to walk dogs. Since the flyers had his name and number on it, he decided to distribute them in a richer neighborhood across town so that Eddie would be less likely to find out. In that part of town, there were a lot of commuters to New York City, which was nearly two hours away by train. This resulted in lonely dogs that needed to be walked in the afternoon so that they didn't poop in the house before their owners got back at night.

Within twenty-four hours of passing out the flyers, Toby received his first call from a customer.

"Hello. May I speak to Toby, please?"

"This is Toby."

"Hi. My name is Jack Leonard. I saw your flyer about walking dogs. Are you still available?"

"I sure am," Toby replied, barely able to conceal his excitement.

"Great. We have two golden retrievers. They're very friendly. Can you start on Monday?"

"Absolutely, Mr. Leonard. I charge twenty dollars per week, per dog. Is that okay?" Toby asked sheepishly. He was embarrassed to be asking for forty dollars per week, when his allowance was only five.

"Your price is fine, as long as we can depend on you."

"You can totally count on me, Mr. Leonard." Toby's grin was so wide his lips hurt. "Where do you live?"

"We live in the next to last house on Stonybrook Road."

Toby paused for a second. He hadn't passed out any flyers on Stonybrook Road. "How did you get my name, then? I didn't do any flyers in your neighborhood."

There was a short pause. "Umm, a friend of mine across town got your flyer and mentioned it to me. Is there a problem for you getting to my house?"

That wasn't the problem at all. The house was, in fact, a little *too* convenient. He was just going to have to be careful about staying out of Eddie's way. "No sir, that won't be a problem."

"Great. Then we'll see you on Monday. What time is good for you?"

"For me, it's best if I come straight there after school, like 3:30." Not coincidentally, this was the same time of day that Eddie was at football practice.

"Can you stop by this Sunday so that we can meet you and introduce you to the dogs? We don't get home until much later on weekdays, so we need to show you beforehand how to get into the house. We'll be home all day on Sunday, so just stop by anytime."

▲ ▲ ▲

On Sunday afternoon, Toby biked over to the Leonards' house. Mrs. Leonard answered the door with a warm smile and invited him in. She was a small and friendly woman, similar to Toby's new foster mom — but more stylish. As they walked to the study, she explained that she was a lawyer and that her husband worked at an investment company on Wall Street. Both of them commuted to New York City every day and arrived home around nine o'clock every night, which was too long to leave the dogs alone in the house.

They stopped at the doorway of the study. Mr. Leonard was sitting at his desk talking on the phone. He had black hair, neatly slicked back, with some gray hair on the sides, above his ears. He was meticulously dressed in what appeared to be a very expensive business suit, like the Armani suits that Toby frequently saw advertised in the *Wall Street Journal.* On his blue and white striped shirt sleeve, Toby noticed a round silver cufflink with a fancy "L" engraved on it. *Must stand for "Leonard,"* Toby thought.

Mr. Leonard, finally noticing the visitors standing in the doorway, cut his phone conversation short. "He's here," Mr. Leonard said into the phone. "I'll touch base with you later, sir." Mr. Leonard hung up the phone, plastered a big smile on his face, and jauntily strode over to where Toby was standing.

"A pleasure to meet you, son." He offered his hand, which Toby shook as firmly as he could. "I've been looking forward to meeting you. Let me introduce you to our dogs."

They walked through the kitchen and out the patio door into the backyard. Two large golden retrievers, Max and Ginnie, came bounding toward them to greet their newest visitor. After a few minutes of intense belly scratching and hand-licking, the Leonards took Toby back inside, where they demonstrated how to disarm the security system and showed him the garage where they kept the leashes. At the far end of the three-car garage, residing in the third and final bay, was a silver 1955 Porsche 356 Speedster, in mint condition with cherry red leather interior.

Toby's heart jumped when he saw it. He had never really experienced love, but he figured that it must be something like what he instantly felt for that car. *Cars are so much better than girls*, he thought. He gave an audible sigh. *Someday*. Of course he knew that someday was a long time off. It would take a whole lot of dog-walking to be able to afford a classic sports car like that, especially when there was a bully taking his money on a regular basis.

"Yeah, I know exactly how you feel," Mr. Leonard said, noticing Toby's admiration of the car. "You want to take a ride?"

"Seriously?" Toby asked, hardly believing his luck.

"Sure," Mr. Leonard replied. "Markets are closed today, so I've got nothing to do. Hop in."

Toby ran around to the passenger side of the car and got in.

"Top up, or top down?" Mr. Leonard asked, referring to the convertible top.

"Down, please!"

"Now, how did I know you'd say that?" Mr. Leonard smiled while he expertly popped the latches and folded the convertible top down toward the back. He sat down in the driver's seat and pressed the button on the remote garage door opener.

"Be sure to buckle your seat belt," he said to Toby.

Toby reached down and pulled the vintage seat belt across his lap until it clicked into place.

Mr. Leonard turned the key in the ignition and the speedster roared to life. Toby felt his heart beating faster as they backed out of the driveway and sped down Stonybrook Road. Toby tilted his head back and enjoyed the feeling of the wind whipping his hair around. This car was awesome! He looked over and Mr. Leonard was smiling broadly, his black and gray hair somehow remaining prefectly in place.

Starting the very next day, rain or shine, Toby showed up every afternoon at the Leonards' house to walk Max and Ginnie. Mrs. Leonard always left him a snack, and every Friday Mr. Leonard left him an envelope with forty dollars. Though he was always disappointed that Mr. Leonard wasn't home to offer him another ride in the Porsche.

▲ ▲ ▲

For the time being, Toby kept his dog-walking money a tightly held secret. But the cash was starting to add up, so he needed to find a good hiding place. This was a problem. Previous experience had proven that hiding money in a shoe or under a mattress were bad choices. He briefly considered opening a savings account at a bank, but when he went to the closest branch to try to open one, he discovered that the bank required a parent or guardian to be a co-owner of the account. Toby just didn't trust any adult nearly enough for that.

Where would Eddie NEVER think to look? This was a tough question, since Eddie routinely searched Toby's room for anything of value. Then the perfect idea hit him. *I'll hide it in Eddie's room!*

Eddie's room was a pig sty. It was amazing that he could ever find anything in there at all. Toby went in and started looking around for potential hiding places. He slowly gazed around the room, and looking past the piles of dirty cloths, sports equipment, and the unmade bed, Toby's eyes lighted upon Eddie's massive bookcase that took up an entire wall. 'Bookcase' may not be exactly the right term, since it contained mostly trophies and just a sprinkling of books, apparently as an afterthought. What books he had sat on the bottom shelf, gathering dust from lack of human contact.

Perfect, Toby thought, as he knelt down to examine the neglected books. *Which one of these is Eddie least likely to ever look at?* This question was tougher than it might seem, since Toby had never seen Eddie touch any book, ever. Then he spotted *The Comprehensive History of Iceland.* Eddie's family was of Viking heritage, which explained his passion for going berserk and pillaging foster brothers. The book was dusty and clearly untouched by Eddie. *Yup, perfect.*

Toby flipped through the pages of the thick book, placing a twenty dollar bill every thirtieth page or so. In total, he hid two hundred and sixty dollars in the book that day, and then carefully placed the book back on the shelf, exactly where he found it. Just as he began to get up from his kneeling position on the floor, he was startled by a loud *tap tap* on Eddie's window. Toby spun around to see who was there. He was relieved to discover that it was only a crow standing outside on the window ledge, tapping with its beak.

"Stupid bird," Toby said as he walked toward the window, waving his arms threateningly. The crow, still staring at Toby, cocked his head to the side for a moment — as if fully aware that there was really no danger. Then it lazily jumped off the ledge and glided to a nearby tree.

▲　▲　▲

For the next several weeks, every Friday afternoon, Toby went into Eddie's room, placed his required five-dollar tribute payment into Eddie's top dresser drawer, and then hid his *real* weekly income in the book. Periodically, Eddie searched Toby's room for hidden booty, but there was none to be found. It was a perfect plan.

One fateful Friday afternoon, Toby had just delivered his five-dollar tribute and was kneeling down in front of Eddie's bookcase, flipping through *The Comprehensive History of Iceland*, looking for some new pages to stash his real cash.

"What the heck are you doing in my room, dipwad? Eddie yelled. There was no one else home at the time, so he didn't need to keep his voice down. Toby's heart raced as the adrenalin rushed into his arteries.

"Nothing, Eddie. I was just putting my allowance in your dresser like I always do on Fridays," Toby said. His voice was noticeably shaking and his ears turned bright red. They always did that when he was lying.

"So then what are you doing way over there?" Eddie scowled.

"I was just looking at this book about Iceland. It has some pretty cool pictures of glaciers." Toby was thinking as fast as he could. If Eddie bought the story, there was a chance he might still get out of this with his life and fortune intact. "Do you mind if I borrow it for a while?" Toby asked.

"Whatever," Eddie grunted, "it's not mine anyway. Just get out of my room. If you ever touch my stuff again, you're *dead.* Got that?"

"Got it," replied Toby as he slid past Eddie toward the door. "It won't happen again, Eddie." Toby was feeling an awesome wave of relief flow over him as he left Eddie's room and started down the hall toward his own.

But then Toby felt a hand grabbing his shirt collar from behind. "Wait just a sec, dirtbag," Eddie snorted, "I don't remember that book having any pictures of glaciers. Give it here."

Toby's heart sank as he handed Eddie the book. Eddie opened the book and a crisp twenty-dollar bill fell out and floated gracefully to the ground. There was something truly beautiful about the way new bills caught the air as they fell, but under the circumstances, Toby wasn't able to enjoy the sight the way he normally would have. Eddie's eyes grew wide as he started flipping through the pages. "What is this?" Eddie snarled, "Are you stealing from me?"

"Give it back, Eddie. It's *my* money!"

"My room, my money, dude," chuckled Eddie as he slammed Toby against the wall. "You've been holding out on me, bro. What are you, selling drugs or something? Jeez, there's gotta be five hundred bucks in here."

"I'm not selling drugs. Nothing like that. I've been working extra jobs because I need money and you take my whole allowance every week. Gimme a break, Eddie, you know I've never missed a payment."

"True that," Eddie replied. "But that doesn't change that you've been holding out on me. Worse, you've been messing with my room. You know that I can't just let this one go." Eddie leaned in close to Toby's face, the effluvia from his fuzzy yellow teeth reeking of partially decomposed school cafeteria burritos.

Toby tried not to breathe. He closed his eyes and braced himself for the gut punch that he figured was coming at any moment. He had discovered that if he clenched his stomach muscles really hard, the pain didn't last as long. This time, however, the punch never came.

"But I'm feeling generous today," continued Eddie, "so I'm not going to kick your butt like I should. I'll just take this five hundred bucks you were trying to steal from me and let you go, as long as you promise not to do it again."

Toby was distraught. It had taken him months to save up that money and now, suddenly, it was gone. His instinct for self-preservation, however, told him at that particular moment his life was worth more than the money. He couldn't risk going to his new foster parents about it, since long experience had taught him that parents will take the word of a *real* son over the word of a foster son every time. So Toby had no choice but to nod in agreement.

Eddie released him from against the wall. "Oh, and one more thing. Since you broke our little agreement, we need a new one. Instead of five dollars every Friday, it's now forty."

"WHAT!" protested Toby. "That's not fair!"

"Hey, obviously you can afford it, being such a hard worker and all!" Eddie chuckled as he went back into his room with a newfound interest in Icelandic history.

Toby ran into his own room. He was too mad to cry. He threw himself onto his bed, cursing Eddie every way he knew how, and trying to come up with a way to get revenge. Within moments an idea came to him out of the blue — a wonderfully cruel and brilliant idea.

CHAPTER 3

Operation Pantalones

"**O**PERATION *WHAT?*" ASKED MARC, folding his arms contemptuously and looking annoyed. Toby had been describing the basic details of his plan to Marc and Bidge at lunch the next day. This would be the first of five lunchtime planning meetings.

Bidge and Marc had been Toby's best friends, off and on, since his two full years in kindergarten. The "off" times were the couple of years when his foster home was in different elementary school boundaries. Now that the three friends were in middle school, it was unlikely that they would be separated again.

"Pantalones," responded Toby. "*Operation Pantalones.* It's Spanish for pants."

"I *know* what pantalones means," Marc retorted, rolling his eyes. "My last name is Lopez, remember? It's just that it's hard to take anything seriously that's called *pantalones.*"

"It sounds kinda dangerous," added Bidge, cocking her head to one side and brushing her bright red hair behind her ear with her fingers. "Are you really sure you want to do this?"

Bidge Donnelly had recently made the mysterious transformation from tom-boy jock to strikingly pretty teenage girl. Not that Toby had officially noticed. He couldn't think romantically about someone who routinely punched him in the arm at every real or imagined offense. She had been Toby's best friend since his first year in kindergarten, after which she moved on to first grade, while Toby moved on to a new foster home where the dad made him repeat kindergarten so he'd be "bigger for sports." It didn't help. He was now a year behind in school but was still embarrassingly terrible at sports. The only bright side of being held back a year was meeting Marc, who was in Toby's second kindergarten class.

"It's not dangerous if we all work together," Toby answered, trying to sound reassuring. In reality, he was not nearly so sure. "...and it's the only way to solve the problem permanently. Eddie always keeps all his cash in his pants — every dime he owns," he continued. "That's the only place he thinks he can protect it. So that's exactly where my five hundred bucks is right now."

"But why can't you just steal it back at night, when he's asleep?" asked Marc. He obviously still hoped for an honorable way to back out of this.

"No, he'd know it was me," Toby replied, "plus, I really NEED him to be totally humiliated. The plan will only work if all three of us do it together. So what do you say? Are you guys — "

"In or out?" Bidge interrupted, a devious smile drifting across her freckled face. She was always finishing Toby's sentences, which Toby found exasperatingly annoying, especially when she got it right, which was pretty much every time.

Toby looked at Bidge, scowled and nodded in the affirmative.

"I'm in," Bidge said without hesitation. Toby had already figured as much. He had never known her to pass up a chance to cause someone pain and humiliation.

"Yeah, I guess I'm in, too," Marc added, not sounding quite as enthusiastic as Bidge.

"Awesome," said Toby. "This is going to be great! Okay, so Operation Pantalones —"

"I wish you'd stop calling it that," interrupted Marc.

"…is officially a 'go' for Friday night after the game." continued Toby, trying to ignore Marc's negativism. "Let's get together a few hours earlier for a practice run. We can all meet at Bidge's house at 5:00. Marc, you bring the rope. It needs to be at least one hundred feet long and preferably a dark color. Bidge, you bring your video camera and your brother's walkie-talkies. I'll bring the duct tape …"

▲ ▲ ▲

The first official practice run of Operation Pantalones didn't go so well. They had to repeat it, start to finish, two more times before getting through the whole plan without any serious mistakes. One thing that they figured out was that they needed the duct tape pre-cut into two-foot lengths. There just wasn't time enough to tear pieces off the roll individually during the action.

It was the end of October and the leaves had already turned their brilliant New England autumn colors and fallen to the ground to be raked into big piles and sucked up by big orange vacuum cleaner trucks. High school football in Connecticut was rapidly approaching the end of its season. The game on this particular Friday night had ended nearly an hour ago. Eddie and his buddy Vance had a tradition of taking a short cut through one particular back street after every game to work out some of their post-game energy by busting out windows in a vacant warehouse along the way. They had never been caught because it was dark and also because this part of town was pretty much deserted at night. Their boisterous voices echoed through the empty streets.

▲ ▲ ▲

Toby crouched in the darkness behind a rusty dumpster and brushed his hair away from his eyes. Taking a deep breath, he slipped the black ski mask over his head. The moonlight sparkled like silver glitter on the wet pavement as he peeked around the corner to look down the deserted street. He pulled his head back out of sight behind the corner of the building and started breathing again. He was starting to wonder if he was going to regret this plan.

"Hey Bidge," Toby whispered. "Tuck your hair into the back of your shirt or something. It practically glows in the dark." In reality, her bright red hair actually looked more like brown in the dark, but Toby couldn't resist any opportunity to tease her about it, even though he was fully aware that he would pay the price. Bidge could hit really hard — for a girl.

"Ow!" Toby grunted under his breath. He grabbed his shoulder with his left hand, attempting to soothe the pain of the impossibly fast punch that Bidge had just delivered.

"My hair does NOT glow in the dark, you jerk!" said Bidge, glowering at Toby as she crammed her hair up into the back of her ski mask.

"If you two love birds could just shut up and keep your hands off each other for a few minutes, we might get through this thing alive. OVER," said a muffled voice over their walkie-talkies. Marc was already in position and was watching them from his hiding place across the deserted street.

With his curly blond "surfer" hair and piercing blue eyes, most adult women immediately noticed how handsome Toby was. But since he wasn't interested in sports, girls his own age never paid much attention to him. Except Bidge. They had been practically inseparable since kindergarten. It bugged Toby in a big way, though, whenever anyone assumed that Bidge was his girlfriend. They just hung out a lot. Toby knew that Marc needled him about it just to get under his skin, but it still annoyed him.

Toby pressed the talk button on his radio. "Shut your face. I repeat, shut your face. Please advise if you require assistance in shutting it, as I would be happy to come over there and help shut it for you. OVER."

Bidge rolled her eyes. "Idiots," she muttered, just loudly enough so that Toby could hear, as she moved into her lookout position above him on the fire escape. She settled into a seated position where she and Toby could see each other clearly. Peering down at him, she smirked and pressed the talk button on her radio. *"You know, sometime you guys might want to try acting like seventh graders instead of cranky kindergarteners who missed their afternoon nap."*

Just as Bidge began her all-too-familiar lecture on how much the universe would improve without boys in it, a burst of laughter echoed in the distance. A few hundred yards away, she could see two alarmingly large high school boys rounding the corner and heading toward them. *"Guys! The targets are in sight. I repeat, the targets are in sight!"* Bidge whispered into her walkie-talkie.

"Roger that," replied Marc, closing the cover of his notebook computer, his second-best friend next to Toby. Bidge ran a close third.

The laughing voices reverberating off the wet pavement and buildings, getting steadily stronger as they got closer to Toby. In his unusual mind, a formula instantly appeared for the relationships between the loudness of the voices, the timing of the echoes, the walking speed of the targets, and the exact amount of time it would take the targets to reach them: 8.3 seconds.

"It's showtime," answered Toby over the radio. "Operation Pantalones is a GO!" He tightened his grip on his end of the black rope stretched across the pavement, and waited.

▲ ▲ ▲

Three blocks in the opposite direction, a gray-haired man in a blue jumpsuit sat quietly in his pickup truck and watched the unfolding scene, completely unobserved by its participants. He casually reached over to the passenger seat to grab his night-vision binoculars, but to his annoyance, they had fallen to the floor and were now out of easy reach.

"Criminy!" he said under his breath. He looked first to the left and then to the right in quick succession. Confirming that no one was around, he reached toward the binoculars and twitched his pinky finger slightly toward himself. The binoculars promptly leapt from the floor and flew into his open hand. He brought the binoculars up to his eyes, made a few minor adjustments to the night vision settings and continued his surveillance.

▲ ▲ ▲

Toby adjusted his grip on his end of the rope, which was lying loosely across the alley. The other end was tied to a metal pipe that ran up the front of the building on the other side. Marc was standing in the shadows of a deep doorway in that same build-ing, with several long pieces of black duct tape hanging from his left arm, ready to use. In Marc's right hand was a plastic cup full of chocolate pudding. Toby had considered using pepper spray to disable their targets, but after painstaking deliberation, decided to use pudding instead. Not only was it less dangerous, but it was also just funnier. After careful research, he also figured it was less likely to get them into trouble. Although pudding attacks, in fact, are illegal in all fifty states, he discovered that those cases are rarely prosecuted. Prosecutors just can't get juries to stop laughing long enough to pass a guilty verdict.

Eddie and Vance walked side by side, laughing and shoving each other as they approached. Looking up at the fire escape, Toby saw the little red light on Bidge's video camera switch on. That was the signal that the targets were fewer than five seconds away.

Toby waited for the perfect moment, according to his precise mental calculations of speed and distance. This had to be timed right, or it wouldn't work. Eddie and Vance were now only two feet away from the rope. Suddenly, at exactly the right time, Toby yanked the rope tight, so that it was suspended about twelve inches off the ground.

"WHAT THE….!" Eddie exclaimed, as he and Vance both tumbled face first to the ground.

According to plan, Toby and Marc leapt into action with their duct tape. Toby was on top of Eddie, and Marc took Vance. It took Eddie a couple seconds to recover from the initial shock of the attack, but when he did, he twisted his body around so that he was facing up and took a swing at his masked attacker. Toby dodged the blow and responded with a handful of chocolate pudding plopped into each of Eddie's eyes. Vance received the same treatment of chocolaty goodness at the hands of Marc.

"Aaaarrrgghh!," screamed Eddie as he instinctively brought both hands together to cover his face. Toby had been expecting this hand position and used the opportunity to quickly wrap a piece of duct tape around Eddie's exposed wrists, followed by a second piece of tape over his mouth.

Toby pulled the shoes off Eddie's feet, and then with one smooth graceful motion, yanked off his pants. Marc, having already finished the job with Vance, had another piece of tape ready to wrap around Eddie's hairy ankles at the moment the pants came off.

"Let's go!" Toby barked to his two accomplices and the three of them took off down the street, pants and all.

A look of puzzlement crossed Eddie's face. "I KNOW THAT VOICE!" he said in incoherent, muffled tones due to the tape over his mouth. Still immobilized on the ground, he reached his still-taped hands up to his mouth to rip the tape off.

"Yoww!" Apparently removing the tape stung a bit more than he expected. "TOBY GOLD, I KNOW IT'S YOU, AND YOU'RE DEAD! YOU HEAR ME, DIPWAD?" Eddie yelled.

Toby heard it all right. Once they reached the end of the block, Toby, Marc and Bidge split up and went in three different directions, exactly according to their well-rehearsed plan.

▲ ▲ ▲

Within ten minutes, Toby had already covered the distance to his house, which was completely empty as usual on a Friday night during football season. His foster parents always went to dinner after the game with friends from the football boosters.

Toby was in his room feverishly packing clothes and other personal belongings into a large duffel bag, when suddenly the door burst open. Standing there in the doorway like a rabid go-rilla was Eddie, still in his underwear and with traces of chocolate pudding dripping down his face. For a second, Toby even thought he could see puffs of smoke shooting out of his nostrils, like an angry cartoon bull. It was probably just his imagination, though.

"Dead," said Eddie, still catching his breath and pointing at Toby.

"Hey, Eddie," said Toby, attempting to hide his fear. Gorillas can smell fear. "Why are you in your underwear?"

"Don't bother playing innocent," snapped Eddie. "I know it was you and your dorky little friends."

"I don't know what you're talking about."

"Yeah, right," Eddie said. "First things first, give me back my money…"

"You mean the money you stole from *me*?" replied Toby, "I still don't understand why you had to do that to me. Wasn't taking my allowance every week enough for you?"

"I think I made myself totally clear, you little twerp," snorted Eddie. "This is my turf, and everything that's yours belongs to me. Now hand it over." With that, Eddie walked over and delivered one of his famous sucker punches into Toby's stomach.

Jeez, I forgot how much this hurts, thought Toby as he lay doubled up on the floor in pain.

Eddie stepped forward in order to follow the punch with a kick to the gut, as was the style at the time among Wallingford bullies. Before he could deliver, he was interrupted by the closet door opening. Out stepped Bidge, holding her video camera and smiling broadly. She popped out the memory card and held it up where both Eddie and Toby could see. "Well, that was a really beautiful family moment. Aren't you glad I was here to capture your violent confession for posterity?" snickered Bidge.

Eddie wasn't exactly the brightest bulb in the room, so it took him a full three seconds to realize what was happening. The confused look on his face melted into one of pure malice. He turned and advanced toward Bidge, his eyes focused on the memory card she was holding. Before he reached her, though, she shrugged and tossed the memory card out of Toby's window into the backyard.

"Got it!" A voice came from outside. It was Marc. Eddie rushed to the window just in time to see Marc hop on his bike and take off toward the street.

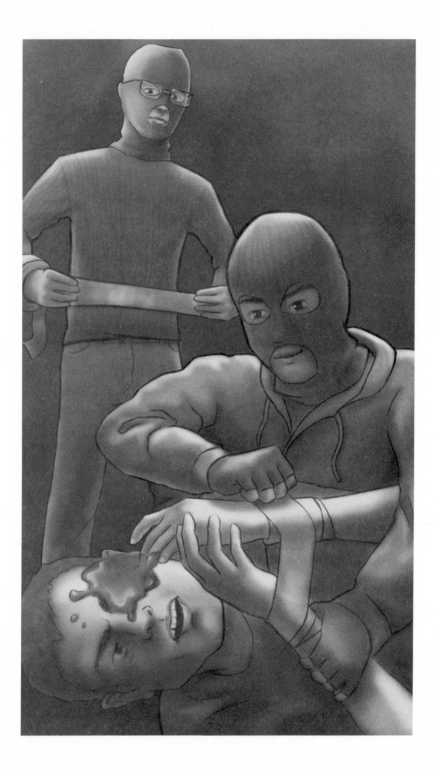

"Dang it!" Eddie exclaimed, and he was out the bedroom door in a flash. Bidge and Toby followed behind him to the front door, which he had left open in his rush to catch Marc while still in the yard. But Marc had a headstart and was already out of reach, heading at top speed down the street.

Bidge's bike was the only one readily available, so Eddie grabbed it and took off after Marc in hot pursuit.

"Man, I wish I had gotten a shot of that," Bidge chuckled. "A picture of Eddie in his underwear on a girl's bike. The football team would have LOVED that one…"

Toby laughed, "Yeah, that was classic, especially with the facial pudding." They both had a good chuckle, then Toby, getting serious again, continued, "Okay, it's time for Phase III. You got the *real* memory card?"

"Right here," Bidge pulled an identical memory card out of her pocket. "I made the switch before I stepped out of the closet."

"You rock. Let's get going on my computer upstairs. We still have a lot of work to do before Eddie gets back." Toby put his arm around Bidge's shoulder and they headed back inside to begin Phase III.

▲　▲　▲

Marc started with nearly a full two-block lead, exactly how they had planned it. He found that he had to slow down a little before rounding the first corner to make sure that Eddie saw him and could follow. On the other hand, for his own safety, Marc also had to make sure that Eddie didn't actually catch him. Unfortunately for Marc, Eddie was quickly closing the gap. Marc just needed to stay out of reach for a couple more minutes.

"C'mon Marky-boy," Marc said to himself. *"Feel the burn!"* Marc stood up on the pedals and pumped as fast as he could. He

was indeed feeling the burn. He wouldn't be able to keep this pace up much longer.

As he blasted around the corner onto Elm Street, the predetermined finish line came into view. The fluorescent glow of the 24-hour convenience store was a warm and welcoming contrast to the dark streets of the bike chase. Marc swung into the parking lot, riding up to the store while simultaneously starting his dismount. Ditching his bike on the sidewalk by the door, he walked into the store and, as calmly as he could, ambled over to the soda machine and pulled a 64-ounce cup off the stack.

Good, there are other people here, thought Marc. It would probably have still been okay if the only other person had been the cashier, but it was better to have as many potential witnesses as possible. Toby had promised that Eddie probably wouldn't get violent if there were others around. Marc was counting on that, even if he hadn't liked the sound of the word *probably*.

Marc was still filling his cup with root beer with his back to the door when he heard the little bells on the door jingle, indicating that someone had just come in. It was Eddie. The heavy breathing was a dead giveaway.

"Uh, sir…" the well-pimpled attendant said to Eddie, avoiding eye-contact. "We have a strict store policy requiring that our customers wear pants."

"This'll only take a second," Eddie mumbled, looking very self-conscious as he pantslessly crossed the floor toward Marc.

"Oh. Hi, Eddie," said Marc lightly, as he took a sip of his root beer, "You want a drink?"

"You and I both know what I want," hissed Eddie in a harsh whisper as he held out his open hand. He didn't want the attendant to be included in this conversation. "Hand it over."

"Or what?" replied Marc. "Are you planning to assault me right here in front of all these witnesses and that security camera up there?" Marc pointed up at the camera mounted near the ceiling behind the front counter.

"Of course not," Eddie smiled. "Not here, anyway. I can be very patient when it comes to revenge."

"Fair enough," said Marc matter-of-factly. "Here you go." Marc pulled the memory card out of his pocket and tossed it to Eddie. Eddie caught it in his outstretched hand and just stared at it for a second. He seemed a little disappointed that Marc didn't put up more of a fight.

▲ ▲ ▲

"We have to work fast," Toby said to Bidge. "Marc will only be able to keep Eddie occupied for fifteen minutes max. Here, let me see that memory card."

Bidge handed Toby the card. He inserted the card into the computer and immediately started uploading the evening's footage.

"Nice work, Bidge," Toby laughed as the raw video images danced across the computer screen. "Some of this stuff is pretty amazing!"

Bidge, who was standing behind Toby at the time, leaned in over his left shoulder to get a better look at the screen, placing her right hand on his other shoulder for balance. This made Toby a little uncomfortable. He had recently watched in horror as other boys his age had, one-by-one, become interested in girls. What were those guys thinking? Everyone knows that girls are the preferred breeding ground for cooties. But her hair *did* smell good — almost like a fruit salad.

Fortunately, Bidge broke contact of her own accord and grabbed the extra desk chair that sat against the opposite wall. Phase III was going to take a while, so she might as well get comfortable. She placed the chair next to Toby's, punched him really hard on the arm, and then sat down.

"Ow!" *How can a girl that small hit so freaking hard?* Toby turned to face Bidge. "What was THAT for?"

"That's for smelling my hair," replied Bidge. She was smiling a little so it wasn't clear if she was truly mad about it or not.

Rat Snacks, she noticed! thought Toby, blushing a little as he turned back to the computer and pretended to concentrate on organizing the video clips. "Don't worry, Bidge, it won't happen again," Toby said. "It actually stinks pretty bad. You really should shower more often."

The second punch didn't hurt nearly as much, since Toby had already braced himself for it.

"If you're done assaulting me, let's get back to work," Toby said, trying to sound annoyed. "We need to edit this down to Eddie's most highly embarrassing moments during the pantsing and then add the footage of his confession that you shot from the closet."

In preparation for tonight's operation, Marc had taught Toby some basic video editing skills on the computer, which enabled him to complete the whole process in just under ten minutes. Toby and Bidge reviewed the final product and were satisfied. Then they reviewed it again just for laughs. And then one more time for no particular reason.

"Okay, looks like we're ready," Toby said. "Let me just attach this video to an email and I'll send it to Eddie, Marc and you. We need to make sure he knows there are multiple copies around, just to be sure he doesn't try something."

Toby had just dragged the video file onto a new email with those three addresses, when a big hairy arm reached past them to the computer and popped the memory card out of the slot.

"I'll be taking that, thanks," Eddie said with a smug grin, shoving Toby out of the way as he took the card and snapped it into two pieces. He was now standing between Toby and the computer. "I gotta hand it to you, punk, sending me off after your dorky friend on a wild goose chase was a nice touch. Until just this second, I had no idea that the memory card that I took out of Marc's cold dead fingers was a fake."

"You *killed* Marc?" Toby's gasped.

Eddie just shrugged.

Toby thought it was highly unlikely that Eddie had actually murdered Marc, but knowing what a neanderthal Eddie was, he couldn't be 100% sure. Toby glanced at the computer screen out of the corner of his eye. He hadn't hit the send button yet, so the email was still just sitting there.

If Eddie deletes that email, we're totally hosed, thought Toby. He glanced over at Bidge. She was looking at the computer monitor and was clearly thinking the same thing. Since Bidge was the closest one to the keyboard, she was going to have to be the one to go for it. The problem was that she weighed only about seventy pounds and Eddie was more like two-twenty, so there was no way she could get past him using a direct attack. They needed a diversion.

"Hey, guys!" said a cheerful Marc as he walked through the door. Seeing Eddie standing there with the two memory card pieces in his hand, though, took the smile immediately off his face. Toby, on the other hand, was quite happy and relieved to see Marc both alive and providing the required diversion.

"You!" Eddie exclaimed, and took an aggressive step toward Marc — and away from the computer.

This was the opening that Bidge was waiting for. She jumped to the keyboard and hit the send button. The video file was so large that it didn't get completely sent at once. A window popped onto the screen that said, *Sending…14%*.

So Bidge kicked Eddie in the shin to buy some time, while Toby fumbled for something in his jacket pocket. He found it.

Sending…33%.

They just needed a few more seconds. With his teeth, using grenade pin-pulling style, Toby peeled back the foil lid on his backup chocolate pudding cup and flung the contents into Eddie's eyes.

"Aaaahhrrr!" Now Eddie was *really* mad.

Sending…84%.

"Well, *that* was unexpected," noted Marc, still standing by the door — conveniently away from the action. What were the chances being involved in two pudding attacks against the same guy on the same night?

Sending…91%.

With his vision still pudding-impaired, Eddie turned around and felt for the computer keyboard.

Bidge, having run out of other options, kicked him again on the shin, in the same exact spot as before.

"OW! Jeez Louise!" Eddie yelled. "Stop doing that!"

Sending…98%.

Eddie started banging on keys in a desperate and blind attempt to stop the email.

Send Complete.

"Yes!" Toby and Bidge yelled simultaneously. They gave each other a high-five, followed by a joyful embrace that almost immediately became socially awkward. Feeling left out, Marc joined the embrace, making it a group hug and tipping the scale into full social awkwardness.

Eddie gradually ceased pounding the keyboard. "So who did that get sent to, anyway?" His meek tone of voice indicated that he was now a broken man.

Toby tossed him a towel. "Clean yourself up a little, Eddie," said Toby with a mildly gloating tone. "We have something to show you." He opened up his *Sent Mail* folder and double-clicked the attached video file.

Eddie wiped the pudding from his eyes. Some remnants remained, making him look not entirely unlike a stunned raccoon. He watched in silence as the video played.

When it was finished, Toby simply said, "I really don't see any reason why your parents *or the football team* ever have to see this. It can totally remain our little secret. All I ask is that you leave me, my friends, and my money alone."

"Deal," Eddie replied. "But if this ever gets out, you know what will happen, right?"

Toby swallowed hard. "Yes, Eddie. We have an agreement." Toby wondered if Eddie was even capable of honoring such an agreement. He knew he'd find out soon enough.

CHAPTER 4

Save Half

I T WAS QUARTER PAST ten on a Friday night and Operation Pantalones had been a wild success. Revenge had been served cold — cold like a pudding-covered pantsless football player on a girl's bike. Toby's foster parents still weren't home, but it was far too late at night for a bunch of middle school kids to go out and celebrate. Exchanging one last round of high-fives, the three pudding warriors went their separate ways for the evening. They agreed to meet at noon the next day for pizza at Christos and then a movie. With Toby's newly restored wealth, he was more than happy to treat.

▲ ▲ ▲

"So, are you guys excited for the big game against Moran?" Bidge asked the next day as they were waiting for their pizza at Christos.

"Isn't that in two weeks?" Toby asked. "A little early to be getting excited, don't you think?"

Bidge glowered.

"You know that you're too short to play basketball, right?" Toby added casually.

"Gee, I never thought of that," she said with a sarcastic tone. "I guess I'll just have to tell them I can't be team captain anymore."

Toby would have been disappointed if his comment had not resulted in a Bidge-punch. He was *not* disappointed. Despite her diminutive stature, Bidge was the star of the team. She had a killer outside jump shot and awesome defensive instincts. Toby assumed that all the arm-punching over the years had given her superior upper body strength. Unfortunately for Toby, Bidge's impressive athletic talent meant that she no longer had time to hang out after school. She always had practice or games to attend.

But now that Toby had his dog-walking duties every afternoon, Bidge's basketball practice and Marc's computer club meetings had become less of an issue for him. Toby was content spending his afternoons walking dogs and watching the stock market. And now that he no longer had to hide his extra income from Eddie, he didn't have to skulk around while he was walking Max and Ginnie, worrying about who might spot him. The five-dollar allowance every week was just icing on the cake.

The whole allowance concept increasingly occupied Toby's thoughts. He had never before had an allowance as high as five dollars. Now that Eddie's tyranny was at an end, he was finally able to collect it and keep it. He liked the idea of having a steady income so much that he put his brain to work trying to figure out a way to *never* lose his allowance again. In fact, the concept of being able to permanently provide himself an allowance of five dollars a week became an obsession. Five dollars per week times fifty-two weeks in a year equals two hundred and sixty dollars per year. He found a bank in town that advertised a money-market savings account that paid a four percent annual rate. In order to figure out how much money he would need to save in order to generate interest income of $260 per year (or $5 per week), he simply divided $260 by 4% in his head, for a grand total of $6,500.

So Toby needed to invest six thousand, five hundred dollars in order to finally achieve his goal of financial freedom. Then he would get an income of five dollars per week forever, without ever having to withdraw any of his principal savings. Unfortunately, the success of his plan required opening an interest-paying account, which could only be done by an adult. This meant he would have to trust a foster parent or guardian enough to have them co-sign on the account with him. Based on Toby's bad experiences with foster parents, he wasn't likely to trust his life savings with an adult anytime soon.

At the rate he was saving, Toby knew that he would reach his financial goal in less than two years if he could add a couple more dog-walking customers and if he strictly followed his *Save Half* rule. The rule was pretty simple. Any time he received money, he set aside half of it to invest for the long term in order to produce more income. The remaining half was for himself, to spend now or save up for a bigger purchase later. It was out of this remaining half that he would also do things like buy pizza for his friends, or give to charity. Even at his age, he had noticed that generous people were happier than selfish people. He wanted to be one of the happy ones.

Toby couldn't help noticing that FD10 was always worried about money. Each month he just barely paid his bills, sporting a scowl on his face whenever he thumbed through the pile of mail each day. A guy like that would have a hard time getting started with the Save Half rule, since he never had any extra money available to invest each month. Toby promised himself that he would try to never get in that kind of financial position, but if he did, he would slowly work toward saving half. Even if he could only invest one dollar per month, he would invest that dollar and then completely freeze the rest of his spending. That way, whenever he got a raise he would dedicate all that extra money toward investment. He'd keep doing that every time he got a raise until he one day reached the goal of saving fifty percent.

Everybody's income *eventually* doubles, even if it takes many years, so there's no reason why everyone can't eventually follow the Save Half rule as long as they have enough self-discipline and patience to freeze their spending. Anyone living by the *Save Half* rule for about fifteen years should be able to live permanently off their investment income.

Toby's savings increased quickly because he was working furiously toward his goal of $6,500. As a kid, he had minimal expenses, so he was actually able to invest much more than the fifty percent required by his rule. With hard work and self-discipline, he knew he would reach his goal in no time.

Every day after school, he rode his bike over to the Leonards' house to fulfill his dog-walking duties. Before taking the dogs out, he spent a few minutes plopped down on their couch in the family room to watch the financial news channel. He figured Mrs. Leonard wouldn't mind, but he had never actually asked permission. Toby didn't realize how little he really knew about his employers.

CHAPTER 5

The Secret Message

OST OF THE TIME Toby didn't even listen to what the anchors were saying on the financial news channel. He just zoned out watching the stock ticker scrolling from right to left on the television screen. He didn't really pay attention to the information in the ticker itself, but just found it relaxing to watch the stock symbols and their price changes flow by. The patterns of letters, numbers and colors were almost like visual music to him.

The timing of buying and selling events came in green and red waves, which Toby could see in the stream of data that danced across the bottom of the television screen. Green was when most people were buying and red was when most people were selling. Toby instinctively knew, in advance, when the green and red waves would happen.

At first, Toby just assumed that everyone could see these flows and patterns in the data, because they seemed so obvious. One time he and Bidge were hanging out in the family room of his ninth foster home when the financial news was on in the background. He mentioned the beautiful patterns in the financial data. She just raised one eyebrow and looked at him like he was nuts, but at least she didn't punch him in the arm. After realizing that no one else could see what he could see, he stopped mentioning it. Watching the ticker just became his own private way of relaxing at the end of each day.

One Friday afternoon just a few minutes before the markets closed at 4:00 p.m., Toby was sitting on the couch watching the ticker when he saw something different. *That's weird. The last seven ticker symbols all started with the same letter. I don't think I've ever seen that happen before.*

But what was even stranger was the pattern he saw in the symbols immediately *following* those seven symbols with the same first letter. He leaned forward in the chair, staring at the television screen, as the ticker continued to scroll by. Thinking that he must be seeing something important, he paused the DVR, reversed for a few seconds, and then wrote down the ticker symbols as they passed the second time.

IDTC 8.2K@13.34 ▼0.37 FDG 9.4K@20.31 ▼0.15
MWV 4.9K@30.38 ▼0.48 KMB 2.0K@68.38 ▲0.40
NHP 3.1K@30.41 ▲0.15 AGN 9.8K@119.26 UNCH
STD 3.2K@19.46 ▲0.35 PII 1.7K@47.41 ▼0.43
CTX 0.2K@54.28 ▼1.48 ZNH 2.2K@22.51 ▼1.91

Toby stared at the symbols and numbers. Something was weird about this, but he couldn't quite see what it was. Suddenly, Toby felt goose bumps on his skin as the patterns and symbols resolved themselves in his head. It was just too bizarre to be true. It was an ingeniously clever, yet simple code. Once he visualized the decryption algorithm in his mind, the message in the ticker data was both crystal clear and quite disturbing:

"HELLO TOBY"

Toby sank back on the couch. His heart was pounding. "That's just not possible," he said aloud. He picked up the remote and clicked the rewind button. Maybe he wrote it down wrong. He pressed play and verified each character as it scrolled by. It all checked out.

"Okay, maybe it's just a coincidence. A random sequence that just happens to say hello to me." Toby was trying his best to convince himself that the stock market ticker was not talking to him. It was 4:02 pm and the market had just closed for the weekend. Toby would not be able to watch for more messages until Monday.

The digital video recorder on top of the TV only kept the most recent hour of video in memory, unless you specifically told it to record the program. Toby rewound back to the beginning of the last hour and then started watching the ticker at double speed. If the ticker was sending him messages, then there may be more than one. At the time in the recording that corresponded to 3:07 p.m., he spotted the same telltale sign of seven stocks in a row with the same first letter immediately followed by:

GPX 7.6K@8.34 ▲0.09 DIS 2.2K@34.31 ▲0.07 MDS 9.7K@22.38 ▼0.16 MET 7.0K@60.38 ▼1.14 NP 3.8K@35.41 ▲0.35 MO 8.7K@86.26 UNCH UST 5.8K@58.46 ▼0.16 NCR 3.7K@43.41 ▲0.25 CEM 3.6K@9.28 ▼0.06 X 4.7K@71.51 ▲1.83

Toby quickly did the decryption in his head. It was an entirely different set of symbols, numbers and arrows than before, but the translated message was exactly the same:

"HELLO TOBY"

Once again, he sank back on the couch and stared at the screen blankly for several seconds. There could be no doubt now.

This was no coincidence. Someone was communicating with him through the stock market ticker!

CHAPTER 6

The Watchers

I N A WINDOWLESS OFFICE located ten floors below ground level on Wall Street, a small red flashing box popped up on a computer screen. The room was dimly lit, presumably to let its occupant clearly see the television and computer monitors that filled the far wall. Mounted in the exact center above the door to the hallway was a curious gold symbol of an equilateral triangle, pointy end up. Inside the triangle was the dotted outline of an open hand with a symbol in the center of the palm that was shaped like a coin, but with sun-like rays emanating from coin's edge.

The woman sitting at the desk glanced up from her work, and seeing the flashing box, smiled thinly. She picked up the phone on her desk and jabbed the first speed-dial button with her index finger.

"It's me," she said to the person on the other end. "He's deciphered the messages from *Legio*."

"Are you sure?"

"Quite sure. They've been sending messages for months now, but today is the first time he's noticed. They sent a message at 3:59 and he rewound and watched it three times."

"Amazing kid to have broken the code this quickly. Okay, now that contact has been confirmed, this project is your top priority. I don't have to tell you how important he is to us — the very survival of the Order is at stake."

"Of course. I understand completely," she replied.

"Start intercepting their messages before they hit the ticker and add our own messages using the encrypted piggyback protocol. We can't show our hand too early."

"Already on it." The sender hung up her phone.

CHAPTER 7

Tell No One

ALTHOUGH IT WAS UNDENIABLY unsettling that someone or something was sending him secret messages on a national cable news broadcast, Toby was simultaneously basking in a newfound feeling of importance. Very few adults in his entire life had ever cared anything about him, but now somebody out there knew who he was and thought he was consequential enough to send him secret messages — somebody influential enough to have access to the stock ticker on a national news channel.

At first he thought it might have been Marc playing a practical joke. Toby had witnessed him hacking into some pretty sophisticated systems before. But Toby quickly dismissed that idea. Gifted as he was, Marc lacked the imagination to do something this weird.

Toby was on pins and needles all weekend. With the markets closed, there was nothing to do but wait until Monday. He stumbled through his dog-walking duties on Saturday in a daze, wondering who could be trying to communicate with him and why. When he stopped at the Leonards' to pick up Max and Ginnie, he was so lost in his thoughts that he almost forgot his passcode for their alarm system. Sometimes they were actually home on Saturdays, so he rang the bell first. Toby liked it when they weren't home, because then he got to use the keyless entry system, which was tremendously cool. As soon as he shook off the fog in his mind, he remembered his passcode. Taking off his right glove and looking around to make sure no burglars were watching, he punched the number into the keypad and pressed his right thumb onto the fingerprint scanner. After a brief pause, the red light turned green and the door lock clicked open.

Max and Ginnie were happily waiting on the other side of the door. "Just a second, guys," Toby said. He kicked off his boots and went into the kitchen to see if Mrs. Leonard had left him a snack. Indeed she had. Toby popped one of the cookies into his mouth while he poured himself a glass of milk.

Toby leaned back against the kitchen counter to enjoy his snack. He looked around the kitchen and out into the family room. He was always amazed at how clean their house was. Having grown up in foster homes where there were always kids around to mess up the place, Toby had never before experienced a truly clean house. The Leonard's house looked more like an art museum, or maybe a fancy hotel lobby. Everything looked like it had been designed for the very spot that it inhabited. Family homes never look like that.

It was clear from the lack of personal keepsakes and photos that the Leonards had no kids, not even grown ones. "Too bad," thought Toby as he horked down the last cookie and headed to the garage to grab the leashes. It seemed a shame that such a huge beautiful house was wasted on just two people. Max and Ginnie, who had been waiting patiently by the door this whole time, didn't seem to mind that the house was so lonely.

▲ ▲ ▲

Toby was dying to tell Bidge and Marc about the messages in the ticker. He agonized about it all weekend. Should he tell anyone? Would they even believe him? Would they think it was cool or would they think it was scary? Toby decided that he should at least wait until he could tell them in person, for the sake of security. Anybody with the ability to send secret messages over the television could easily bug a phone.

After a weekend that seemed like forever, Monday finally came. At lunch, Toby tried to tell Bidge and Marc about the message he received through the television.

"So, what you're saying is that you want us to believe that the TV is talking to you?" Marc laughed across the table. "How about the toaster? Do any other household appliances seem chatty lately?"

"I'm being serious," Toby insisted. "It's totally like a secret code based on the first letter of the stock symbol…"

Bidge and Marc's eyes immediately glazed over, as they always did whenever Toby started talking about the stock market. Marc took off his sneaker and lifted it to his ear, nodding intently as if listening to a voice giving him instructions from the shoe-phone within.

Toby's voice trailed off to nothing, but his face darkened as he reached for the pudding cup on his tray, never taking his eyes off Marc. He slowly peeled the foil lid back.

Marc, sensing that he was in imminent pudding-related danger, did his best to diffuse the situation. "Whoa there, Tex," Marc chuckled. "No need to bring out the big guns. I was just yanking your chain a little."

Toby slowly loosened his grip on the pudding cup, dipped in his plastic spoon, and put it in his mouth. "Dude, I'm already freaking out about this. I don't need you telling me I'm nuts," Toby said, finally breaking eye contact and looking down at his tray. "It's just…"

"It's not that we don't believe you," Bidge interrupted. "It's just that we don't get it. Who would be sending you a message over the TV like that? Why not just pick up the phone or send an email? Wouldn't that make more sense? Maybe the message you saw was just a coincidence."

She had a point. There were much easier ways to communicate. Encrypting a message to a kid and inserting it into a financial data stream seemed really far-fetched and bizarrely unnecessary.

"You're probably right," Toby said. "I must be hallucinating."

Toby didn't want to talk about it anymore, but he *knew* he wasn't hallucinating. He had already done the probability calculations in his head for fun. It was pretty straightforward. The message had nine letters plus a space. Counting the space as an additional letter, there are 27 possible letters in the alphabet. So the odds of any particular ten letter sequence, like HELLO TOBY, showing up because of random chance was exactly one in twenty-seven to the tenth power, or approximately 206 trillion. At those odds, there was just *no way* it could have been a coincidence.

The stock market opened as usual at 9:30 am. Since Toby would be in school at that time, he programmed the Leonard's DVR to capture the financial news all day long. He didn't want to miss any new messages. After school he went straight there and started watching the day's recording at triple speed. One hour, two hours, three hours of recording flew by. Nothing.

"Maybe they were right. Maybe I was just imagining it," Toby said to Max, who was chewing a tennis ball at his feet. Max looked up briefly when spoken to, but immediately turned his attention back to the increasingly slimy ball.

Then at 3:55 pm, five minutes before the closing bell, he saw that familiar string of seven stocks starting with the same first letter. Then came the encoded message. By this time, he was so familiar with the encryption technique that he didn't have to write it down. He could just translate in his head as the symbols marched across the bottom of the screen.

UN 6.3K@27.28 ▼0.18 FUN 2.8K@27.31 ▼0.09
KFI 0.6K@23.26 ▲0.29 MTL 7.0K@25.29 ▼0.07
AMG 6.8K@105.27 UNCH MPX 4.1K@11.44 ▲0.09
PNK 9.3K@33.31 ▼0.14 ACV 3.6K@22.32 UNCH
NNN 6.7K@23.47 ▲0.06 MRO 4.9K@87.38 ▲5.15
FPL 0.4K@55.26 ▼0.68

"TELL NO ONE"

A feeling of panic descended upon Toby, for more than one reason. First, the message was no longer just a friendly greeting — it seemed like a direct order. The mystery messenger, or M^2, as Toby had already nicknamed him, clearly wanted the one-way conversations to be confidential. Second, if M^2 was giving Toby an order, what were the consequences for disobeying? Toby had already told Bidge and Marc, so technically he was already in violation. Toby took comfort in the realization that his friends hadn't really believed his story anyway.

Thankfully, the topic of secret TV messages did not come up on Tuesday at lunch. Bidge chatted non-stop about her big basketball game this Friday against Moran Middle School, their arch-rival. Moran's point guard was rumored to be the best in the division. Bidge had seen her play before, though, and was confident that with the right strategy she could hold her to fewer than sixteen points.

Toby nodded at all the appropriate times to show interest, but his mind was elsewhere. Would there be another message today? What was all this leading to, and why was it such a big secret? Who *was* M^2 and what did he want with him? One thing was sure — without your best friends to share them with, secrets are lonely things.

CHAPTER 8

An Afternoon Rally

IF ANOTHER SECRET MESSAGE was coming today, Toby wanted to make sure he didn't miss it. He went straight to the Leonards' house again after school in order to get the dog-walking out of the way as soon as possible so he'd still have time to watch the day's stock ticker recording. He recorded the ticker both at home and at the Leonards' house so that he could be certain not to miss it. He arrived at the Leonards' at 3:15 pm. Pressed for time, Toby skipped the snack and went straight to the garage to get the leashes. Today, he would only have the chance to give a brief, but loving glance at Mr. Leonard's classic Porsche. As he headed back inside to hook up the dogs, still waggingly waiting for him, he passed the open French doors of Mr. Leonard's study.

"Hello, Toby. How are you today?"

Toby just about jumped out of his skin. He had no idea that Mr. Leonard was home. He was sitting behind his desk, dressed like before in an expensive-looking suit and tie. Even though it was mid-afternoon, his blue and white striped shirt was smooth and crisp, like he had just put it on. His cuff links were just visible beyond his coat sleeves. They were the same silver ones Toby had seen him wear before, with a fancy but somewhat strange "L" design. Toby thought the design looked a little like the symbol for the Pound Sterling, the money they use in England, except the "L" had three crossbars. "Just fine, sir, and you?"

"To be honest, I've had better days." Mr. Leonard glanced over at the television set, which was turned at an angle on the credenza in the corner of the twelve-foot square room. It was tuned to the financial news station. The sea of red numbers on the stock ticker told the whole story. "When you're in my line of work, son, a bad day like this on Wall Street makes for a long line of angry customers calling. I've been hiding out here all day."

Toby nodded. He was still studying the rhythms of the ticker scrolling across the bottom of the TV, trying to catch the mood of the market. Once he was in tune with the ticker, he spoke. "I wouldn't worry too much, Mr. Leonard, things seem to be turning around and I'll bet the market finishes in positive territory before the closing bell."

Mr. Leonard, who had been looking at the TV rather than at Toby during this exchange, quickly snapped his head around and looked Toby directly in the eye. For a few uncomfortable seconds, he just stared, saying nothing. Finally, his stern look softened a little. "I hope you're right, Toby."

"Me too," Toby said. "Now if you'll excuse me, I need to take the dogs out for their walk."

"By all means. Nice seeing you again, Toby."

Toby felt Mr. Leonard's eyes on the back of his head as he put the dogs on their leashes and hurried out the front door. He took them for an extra long walk that day. When he got back, he was relieved to find that Mr. Leonard had left the house. He couldn't put his finger on it, but something about the way Mr. Leonard had looked at him made him feel strangely uncomfortable.

As Toby was hanging up the leashes on their hook in the garage, he saw a yellow sticky note on the wall just above the hook:

Toby,

    As you predicted, the market closed higher today. It didn't turn out to be such a bad day after all. Are your guesses always this lucky? See you soon.

Jack Leonard

Toby raced home after finishing his dog duties to see if there were any new clues in the recorded ticker data. It was just under a mile from the Leonards' to his house. He alternated between jogging and walking on the way home, since he couldn't run full-speed on the icy sidewalk. It had been a really good day on Wall Street. The Dow Jones Industrial Average had rallied two hundred points in afternoon trading.

Toby arrived home well after the closing bell, but on the video recording, he was able to watch the ticker representing the last half-hour of trading, the period between the time he talked to Mr. Leonard and the end of trading for the day.

"Nothing sweeter than an afternoon rally," Toby thought. There are undoubtedly lots of investors that would agree with Toby on that point, but for different reasons. Investors usually make a lot of money when the market rallies, so they have an obvious reason for liking it. For Toby it was different. The market data swirled past him like melodies and harmonies, flowing in a special type of song. The mood of the *rally song* was filled with hope and joy. It was especially relaxing and put Toby in good spirits.

Once the market closed and the song had stopped, he re-played the ticker data at high speed all the way from 9:30 a.m. until 4:00 p.m. to see if there was another message.

Nothing. Toby went back to the beginning and played it again a little slower. *Maybe I missed it.* Still nothing. The anxiety and exhilaration that he had felt all day about the prospect of getting another secret message from M² had quickly turned into disappointment. In the same way that getting the messages made him feel important, *not* getting a message made him feel just a little *less* important. He didn't like feeling unimportant — that was how he had felt his entire life. Of course, feeling important has its limits. A deer probably feels very important while being chased by guys in orange vests during hunting season. Toby had a feeling deep down that being important might do more harm than good.

CHAPTER 9

Use Your Gift Wisely

A S TOBY AND THE other students filed into Social Studies class the next day, Mr. Sanborn completely ignored them. He was too busy hunched over his computer, checking the balance of his retirement account. After a few moments, a smile crept across his face, indicating good news.

"Good morning, class," Mr. Sanborn said, finally breaking his attention from the account balances. "If you're wondering why I'm in a good mood, it's because there was a stock market rally yesterday — very good for my retirement account."

The class fidgeted uncaringly in their seats.

"I'm trying not to get too excited though," Mr. Sanborn continued. "What goes up always comes back down."

"But not today," said Toby off-hand.

"Did you say something, Mr. Gold?" asked Mr. Sanborn.

Toby had been simply thinking out loud, so he was a little surprised that anyone had heard him. He looked around, somewhat embarrassed. Mr. Sanborn was staring at him with raised eyebrows, waiting for Toby to respond.

"Oh, I just said 'not today.' The market won't go down today," Toby replied matter-of-factly. In reality, he didn't know for an absolute surety. Although he was usually right, the market still surprised him sometimes. The mood of the market had been bright and sunny at the closing bell the previous day. It didn't betray any sense of gathering darkness, nor did it have an irrationally positive exuberance. Those were the two things that usually meant that a rally would soon end. Yesterday was neither. The market was just calmly happy, which meant that the upward movement was likely to continue the next day.

This was not an exact science, just a feeling, so Toby wasn't always correct about it. Sometimes the mood of the market song told Toby to expect a rally, but then some unexpected bad economic news came out that resulted in a sell-off, forcing the market down. He just couldn't predict when that kind of thing might happen.

But if he told the class about the market song, they would think he was nuts, and wouldn't believe it anyway. "I don't know, Mr. Sanborn, it just seemed to me like the rally would continue. It might just be wishful thinking, though. We like it when you're happy, because you give us less homework."

The rest of the class laughed, along with Mr. Sanborn. "I can't argue with that logic," he said. "I'll tell you what. If the market is still in positive territory by the end of class, there will be no homework tonight." The class cheered. Then Mr. Sanborn added, "But if it ends up negative, I'm giving everyone five extra homework questions to answer."

Toby didn't look around, but he could feel the other students glaring at him.

Mr. Sanborn kept the TV news channel on during the remainder of the class, with the sound turned down. It had a stock ticker, and Toby couldn't help glancing up every few seconds, hoping to see a secret message. None appeared. The market had remained fairly stable and positive up until about ten minutes left in class, when it suddenly took a downturn into negative territory. Mr. Sanborn looked at Toby with a frown, then turned around and started writing extra homework questions on the board. A crumpled-up piece of notebook paper hit Toby on the back of the head. He didn't know who had thrown it, but he didn't want to turn around and find out, either.

But then the market song suddenly changed its mood and the market started turning around again. By the end of class, it was up 150 points. The cheers from the class were deafening, and Toby got lots of friendly no-homework slaps on the back as everyone filed out of the room to their next class.

▲ ▲ ▲

That afternoon, when Toby performed his daily ritual of scanning the ticker data at high speed for hidden messages, he found one.

**VHI 9.3K@24.51 ▼1.00 TEN 1.0K@24.41 ▼0.06
FCH 7.0K@21.47 ▼0.36 AT 6.2K@61.44 UNCH
XJT 2.4K@8.26 ▲0.25 PTP 2.1K@31.32 ▼0.14
VVI 6.9K@41.27 ▼1.14 QTM 9.5K@2.46 ▲0.01
AGU 8.4K@32.34 UNCH FA 9.2K@2.31 ▲0.06
JOE 2.1K@53.44 ▼0.33 GNI 9.9K@117.26 ▼2.44
SAM 6.3K@36.35 ▲0.18 AYR 2.9K@29.45 UNCH
VDM 8.1K@6.26 ▲0.22 HDL 0.1K@6.30 ▲0.05
TIF 9.1K@39.31 ▼0.16 DT 5.9K@18.27 ▲0.24 KFI
9.6K@23.30 ▲0.29 XRX 3.1K@16.26 ▲0.05**

"USE YOUR GIFT WISELY"

Toby stared at the screen blankly for a few minutes. *My gift?* he thought. *What exactly IS my gift, anyway?* Toby reflected on this message while he zoned out and watched the remaining few minutes of stock trading for the day. The market had been up most of the day, but he was sensing a mood change for the worse.

Good time to sell, he thought casually. As if on cue, the market started to tumble into negative territory. It was weird that others couldn't see these big movements coming, he thought. To him, it really couldn't have been more obvious.

Then it hit him. *Maybe this is the talent that M² is talking about. I can see patterns and trends in the financial data that others can't see!*

Toby hadn't told many others about the song of the market, mostly because everyone so far just didn't get it. They looked at him like he was crazy. He always figured it was because *they* were weird, or maybe because they were just kids. He always assumed that there must at least be some adults that saw financial data the way he did. He had never considered that he might be the *only* one that could see the music.

Toby knew that one thing was certain. If he was truly the only one that could see the song of the market, then M² was right — he probably shouldn't be casually bragging about it in Social Studies class. What Toby didn't understand is how M² could have possibly known about that. The idea that he was being watched at school gave him the creeps. Toby shuddered as a cold chill ran down his spine.

CHAPTER 10

The Big Game

FRIDAY CAME AT LAST — a day that Toby had been looking forward to all week. It was the day of the big basketball game against Moran, so maybe Bidge would finally shut up about it. She hadn't been able to stop talking about it all week. Lunchtime conversations had all revolved around what strategies would work best against a larger team, and which plays she would be calling as team captain. Toby pretended to be interested, of course. In truth, he couldn't care less about basketball, so while Bidge babbled on and on, Toby just calculated compound interest in his head to pass the time.

That same afternoon, Toby received his next secret message while enjoying a cookie and watching the stock ticker at the Leonards' house. This had become a daily ritual for him, but the messages were becoming more spread out. Sometimes several days would pass without so much as a peep from M^2.

HS 4.9K@20.51 ▲0.20 KAR 4.1K@27.41 UNCH LEH 2.6K@78.47 ▼0.51 ORI 9.9K@23.44 ▼0.23 NSR 4.1K@32.26 ▲0.44 VC 4.9K@8.39 ▲0.03 AXA 3.7K@41.41 UNCH XNR 1.7K@4.46 ▲0.09 PJC 4.6K@67.34 ▼2.20 TBH 9.2K@30.31 ▲0.25 QI 2.2K@17.44 ▲0.06 AFN 8.2K@10.26 UNCH QTM

7.4K@2.45 ▲0.01 FRE 5.4K@67.46 ▼0.01 ZNT
6.2K@47.35 ▲0.49 KEA 9.0K@12.38 ▲0.20 AYR
3.9K@29.38 UNCH OII 7.9K@36.26 ▲2.79 ZMH
2.7K@77.38 ▲1.28 SQM 5.2K@134.35 ▼0.58 DNR
1.7K@26.48 ▲1.05 OXM 5.0K@50.31 ▼0.70 SLE
1.9K@16.45 ▲0.14 RLH 1.0K@12.26 ▲0.12

"I KNOW YOUR REAL PARENTS"

Toby stopped eating his cookie. Several crumbs fell from his gaping mouth onto the otherwise spotless sofa. He reversed the recording and watched the message again to make sure it said what he thought it said. No mistake. Toby felt a chill rush through his body. *Is this possible? Does M² really know who my parents are, or is someone just messing with me?* At that moment, it seemed horribly cruel to Toby that M² hadn't provided a means for two-way communication. Toby had so many questions, but no way on earth to ask them.

He checked the black digital watch on his left wrist. There were only two and a half hours until Bidge's game. He still had homework to do and dinner to eat before going to the game, yet he still hadn't walked the Leonards' dogs. He'd never hear the end of it from Bidge if he missed even one minute of the big game. He quickly grabbed the leashes from the garage — foregoing his daily admiration of the Porsche — and took Ginnie and Max out for a quick run around the block. It was a shorter walk for the dogs than usual.

"I'll make it up to you guys with a longer walk tomorrow," he said to the dogs as he put them back in the house. Ginnie gave a quick bark, indicating that she intended to hold him to that deal. The agreement with the dogs firmly in place, Toby re-engaged the security system and headed home.

▲ ▲ ▲

As usual, Toby's math homework took less than a half hour to complete. It might have taken less, but the latest secret message was churning in his head, making it even more difficult than usual to concentrate. The assignment should have taken only five minutes, but Toby's math teacher had started taking off points when he didn't show all his work. Why show work when the answer was totally obvious? So now Toby couldn't just write down the answers, he had to make up a bunch of steps between the original question and the final answer, which he already knew in the first place. It seemed silly.

He looked at his watch again. Only an hour until Bidge's game, and he still had to finish a book report for language arts. Toby loved reading, but he hated writing. Not just dislike, actual honest-to-goodness hatred. It was such a painfully slow process. In math, he could go at supersonic speed — he pretty much knew the answer to any question before it was even asked. It was the same thing for science. If he heard the teacher say something, he'd remember it. Or if he read it in the textbook, he could repeat it back on the test. But writing was slower than death compared with reading or math.

It wasn't that he couldn't think of things to write. That wasn't the problem at all. The problem was that his brain went full speed at a thousand words a minute, but he could only physically write at about fifteen words per minute. It was so frustrating that it made him want to scream. Toby sat down at his desk and started writing, but then his head began to get ahead of his hands, so he had to slow down his brain so that his hands could keep up. It was like damming a river of thought. Pretty soon, as if the dam in his head were overflowing, he started making mistakes that he'd have to repair, which made the writing process even slower. Inevitably, his left leg started bouncing. This may have been due to the excess brainwaves spilling over the dam in his head, flowing down his body, and settling like a pool of energy in his butt muscle, making his leg twitch.

"Argh!" Toby jumped out of his chair in frustration and paced around his room for a minute, shaking his arms and hands to work the excess energy out. He looked at his watch again. "Okay, I gotta get at least two more paragraphs written before I go." He sat down again at his desk to painfully grind out the rest of the page.

Putting his still unfinished book report away in his backpack, Toby looked at his watch again. It was getting close to game time and Marc and his dad would be here to pick him up any minute. No time to eat. Toby threw on his bright red Dag Hammarskjold Middle School Panthers sweatshirt and headed for the kitchen to grab something for the road. FM10 was there, still making dinner.

"I'm going to the game," Toby said, as he poked his head in the refrigerator.

"Dinner's almost ready," FM10 said. "Can't you just wait a few more minutes?"

Just then they heard Marc's dad's car turn into the driveway followed by a quick double-toot on the car horn. Toby looked at FM10 and shrugged his shoulders. "I guess not."

FM10 opened her purse and pulled out a five-dollar bill. She gave him a kiss on the forehead. "Here, sweetie. You can get a hot dog at the game or something."

Toby quickly glanced around the room to make sure Eddie didn't see him receiving the money. Eddie had already been tamed, so there was no real danger. But he was still instinctively uncomfortable receiving cash around Eddie. Toby put the five dollars in his pocket, gave FM10 a quick hug, ran out the door down to Marc's car and hopped in the backseat. Marc was there, wearing a red sweatshirt identical to Toby's. Sitting in the middle of the backseat was Marc's precocious nine-year old sister, Trista, wearing square glasses and her hair in two black pigtails protruding straight out from each side of her head. Like her brother

Marc, Trista was intelligent far beyond her age — and unfortunately far beyond her maturity.

"Oh. Hi Trista. I didn't know you were coming tonight," Toby said.

"Mi nombre no es *Trista*. Me llamo *Maria Trista de los Dolores Lopez*," she replied indignantly.

"Huh?" Toby asked blankly.

Marc came to his rescue. "Just ignore her. She's gone all Latina on us recently. We're not quite sure what brought it on."

"What did she say her name was again?" Toby asked.

"It's actually her real name. Maria Trista de los Dolores Lopez. It means *Sad Mary of the Pains*."

Toby raised one eyebrow.

Marc quickly added, "Don't even ask. It's a Catholic thing — you wouldn't understand."

"What do you mean? Did you forget that I'm part Catholic?" Toby tried his best to appear offended.

Marc snorted. "Jeez, for the last time, living with a Catholic foster family for one year when you were four does *not* make you part Catholic."

"It was a year and a half," Toby replied sullenly.

"Hey, I can tell there's a lot of Panther Pride back there!" Mr. Lopez interrupted from the driver's seat. Marc's dad was a teacher at Dag Hammarskjold and he attended pretty much every game for every sport for both the boys' and girls' teams. For this reason, Marc ended up going to a lot of games. Not because he liked sports, but because it was the only regular way to spend time with his dad.

"You betcha!" Toby replied, trying to sound sincere with limited success. He liked the school all right, but honestly wasn't heavily into the whole Panther Pride school spirit thing. He went

75

to Bidge's games, though, to be supportive and to avoid arm-punches.

Tonight was truly the big game of the season. They arrived 30 minutes before tip-off, and the bleachers were already mostly full. The home side was awash in red and black. The visitors' bleachers on the other side of the gym were a sea of blue and gold, supporting the Panthers' vilest enemies, the Moran Mustangs.

The two teams were already on the court, in their warm-ups, doing lay-ups and some passing drills. The Mustangs were clearly the taller team. They looked more like a *high school* girls' team than a middle school team. They played like it, too. They were undefeated coming into tonight's game and were heavily favored to win by most reasonable observers. Panther fans, though, had no intention of being reasonable, so they held out hope for a decisive victory. What the Panther students also held out were big hand painted signs indicating their feelings on the matter — with slogans such as "Go Home Little Ponies" and "Smell that Mustank." As Toby and Marc passed that section, the principal was in the process of confiscating those particular two signs.

"Now kids, we don't want to display poor sportsmanship, do we?" he said to them as he collected the signs. He immediately turned and carried the signs toward the double doors without waiting for a response.

Bidge was impossible to overlook on the court. She was by far the shortest girl out there and her bright red ponytail bounced energetically whenever she ran, like a big orange rabbit's foot tied loosely to the handle of a pogo stick.

The team was still warming up when Bidge spotted Toby and waved enthusiastically, grinning from ear-to-ear. A couple hundred basketball fans turned their heads toward him to see who the jaunty little redhead was waving at. Toby nodded back at her, embarrassed at the unexpected attention, and then slunk off to the concession stand to grab a hot dog while Marc went to save him a seat high up in the student section.

Because of the capacity crowd, the line for food was longer than usual. Toby made it back just as the starting players were announced over the PA system. When Bridget Donnelly was introduced as the Panther starting point guard and team captain, Toby couldn't clap because of the hot dog in one hand, and a bag of popcorn in the other, so he just yelled "Go Bidge!" really loudly, but just a little bit too late, after the applause had already started dying down. Bidge's face and Toby's ears both went Panther-red simultaneously, but Bidge smiled and waved again anyway. She had always been much more comfortable with public attention than he was.

▲ ▲ ▲

Each team's starting five took their places at center court for the tip-off. *Okay, this is it!* thought Bidge with butterflies swarming in her stomach. She always had a brief moment of extreme nervousness just before games began. The starting guard for the Mustangs, Amanda Pummelshrimp, stood a full head taller than Bidge. It became clear that it was going to be nearly impossible to hold Amanda to sixteen points, as Bidge had promised herself she would do.

The starting center for the Panthers was Janice Dewey. Unlike Bidge, she was quite tall, even taller than the Amazon women on the Mustangs. Unfortunately, though, she was the *only* Lady Panther that could be considered tall. She controlled the tip-off, flipping the ball to Panther power forward, Tammy Johnson. Tammy immediately chest-passed the ball back to Bidge, who hand-signaled a simple give-and-go play. She brought the ball down to the three point line and passed it laterally to the left to the other Panther guard, Jolene Weymouth. As soon as the ball left her hands, Bidge deftly cut toward the lane. Jolene quickly whipped the ball back into Bidge's hands, just like they had practiced hundreds of times. Taking advantage of her momentum, Bidge brought her trailing right foot up even with her left foot and sprang into a graceful, picture-perfect jump shot. As she released the ball gracefully from her right hand — with the ideal amount of spin — Bidge knew the basket would be good.

And that would have been true, except that Amanda Pummelshrimp was guarding her. Out of nowhere, Amanda appeared in front of Bidge, just in time to jump, cup the ball with her freakishly large right hand, and slam it down with contempt onto Bidge's left foot, sending the ball careening out of bounds.

"Jeez Louise. There's no way I can get any shots off with this chick guarding me," Bidge thought. "Nice block, Amanda." Bidge said, relunctantly mustering her best sportsmanlike smile.

Amanda just grunted in reply.

Bidge shook it off and took her position on defense. The Mustangs were bringing the ball inbounds. Amanda got the ball and slowly brought it down the court. Bidge covered her tightly, trying not to let her set up any easy plays. When Amanda reached the top of the key, she casually popped a jump shot good for the first two points of the game. Bidge tried to block it, but Amanda was just too tall.

Toby groaned and turned to Marc. "This is going to be a long game."

Marc nodded. "Can I have some of that popcorn?"

"Sure." Toby handed him the bag and he took another bite of his hot dog.

Bidge looked up at them in the stands and scowled, as if she could hear them conceding Panther defeat.

The rest of the first quarter was just as ugly. Bidge just couldn't get a shot off, so the Panthers altered their offense to avoid outside shots and to feed the ball to the forwards camped out on the baseline. This helped the situation a lot, and the Panthers started to close the gap in points against the Mustangs. On defense, since Bidge was physically unable to stop Amanda, they had to switch from man-to-man to a zone defense, double-teaming Amanda whenever possible. At the end of the first half the score was 37-25, with the Mustangs in a solid lead. Amanda had already scored ten points, well on her way to sixteen.

"So what's going on out there, Donnelly?" Coach Carver was clearly upset.

"They're just too big, Coach," Bidge replied. "But I think we're doing better now."

"Don't get too confident. They're not running up the score on us *right now*, but you can bet that their coach is telling them how to shore up their defense on the baseline. You've got to figure out a way to stop Pummelshrimp and make up those twelve points."

Bidge nodded, but she still had no idea what she could do to stop Amanda.

The second half started. The Mustangs got the ball, passing it to Amanda to bring it down court. Bidge bounced backwards in front of her, on the balls of her feet. She was still tense and wound-up inside. It had been an embarrassing game for her so far, unworthy of her status as star player and team captain.

Okay, Bidge, she said to herself. *You gotta relax and get in the zone.* She steadied herself and tried to shut out all the noise of the game and the crowd by focusing on the sound of her own breathing. Feeling somewhat calmer now, she thought, *All right, Amanda Pummelshrimp, what's your next move?*

"Passing right." Bidge heard Amanda say, but strangely, her lips never moved. Amanda then faked left, but not taking the bait, Bidge lunged to *her* left, which of course was Amanda's right, just in time to intercept the pass intended for Katie Watkins, their star forward who had just come up from the baseline. Bidge sprinted past the stunned Amanda on a fast break to her own goal, where she put in an easy layup.

Bidge was even more stunned than Amanda. Why would Amanda tell Bidge she was passing to the right? And why weren't Amanda's lips moving when she said it?

It was the Mustangs' ball. As usual, Amanda was bringing the ball down the court. Bidge was covering her, still trying her best to relax. Amanda looked at Bidge with contempt and again without moving her lips, said, "This little pipsqueak is going down."

To which Bidge replied out loud, "Who you calling pipsqueak? *You're* the one going down!"

Amanda's face went pale. "You *heard* that?" The baffled look on her face seemed to indicate surprise that she had apparently spoken out loud.

Bidge used Amanda's momentary confusion to once again steal the ball and go in for an easy layup at the Panther goal.

The crowd went wild.

Amanda held up her hands in a "T" shape to the referee, who blew his whistle and shouted, "Time out...Mustangs."

Bidge jogged back to the sideline where Coach Carver and the rest of the team were gathering. She was met with smiles and several high-fives.

"Now that's the kind of playing I expect from you, Donnelly!" Coach Carver was visibly stoked. The score was now 37-29, with the Panthers now down by eight points.

"I feel good Coach," Bidge replied. "I think I'm starting to read Amanda a little better now." Bidge didn't fully realize at the time how true that was. She was reading Amanda *perfectly*.

On the Mustang side, their coach's face was bright red from yelling at Amanda. "What are you trying to do, throw the game? You just gave up four points in twenty seconds."

"No coach, I'm just a little freaked out. I think Donnelly is reading my mind."

The coach stared at Amanda blankly. The other Lady Mustangs looked at each other and snickered. "Is that the best explanation you can come up with, Pummelshrimp?"

She looked down at the floorboards for a minute. "No coach. I'm probably just having a bad night."

"Do you want me to take you out of the game?"

"No! I'm okay. I'm not gonna let that little runt psych me out."

The buzzer rang and both teams went back onto the court. Amanda received the ball inbounds and dribbled forcefully down the center of the court. Bidge tried her best to defend, but Amanda took her deadly jump shot from the top of the key and sank it effortlessly, increasing their lead from eight to ten points.

But now that she was in the zone, Bidge didn't let this faze her. Instinctively, she knew what to do — disrupt Amanda's plans whenever possible. When the Mustangs were actually able to execute their plays, they were unstoppable. But Bidge had turned herself into a ball-stealing machine, creating numerous fast-break opportunities throughout the rest of the second half that eventually brought the score to an even 55-55 with thirty seconds left to play.

Bidge had been able to hold Amanda Pummelshrimp to only six points so far in the second half. Amanda was visibly agitated. Fortunately for the Panthers, her frustration had resulted in four personal fouls against Bidge. One more and Amanda would be out of the game.

Bidge had the ball and moved quickly toward the basket. Amanda was covering her tightly, but not too close, not wanting to get a fifth foul called. Bidge passed left to Jolene, who immediately bounced it back to Bidge, who then flicked it to Tammy on her right. Bidge pivoted around Amanda and headed toward the basket. Tammy bounce-passed the ball to Bidge, who was now only ten feet from the goal. She fake-pumped twice, into a fade-away jump shot. The fade-away was typically a low-percentage shot for Bidge, but it was the only one that she had been able to get past Amanda the whole game. Amanda jumped to block the shot, with her Amazon forearms angled toward the ball, which was still in Bidge's hands. Seizing this golden opportunity, Bidge drew the foul by slapping her own right arm against Amanda's left hand while releasing the shot, which flew away from the basket and fell harmlessly out of bounds.

The final buzzer sounded as the referee's whistle blew. His right arm went up and his left hand pointed to Amanda. She had fouled out with zero time left on the clock.

So now the game was effectively over, but Bidge had two free-throw opportunities from the foul line. The score was still 55-55, so she only needed one to win the game. Two misses would put the game into overtime.

Everyone in the gym went silent as Bidge approached the line. Bidge, consistent with her free-throw ritual, bounced the ball twice, spun it in her hands until the logo was face up, looked at the goal, bounced two more times, then took the shot. As soon she had performed first two bounces in preparation for the shot, the Mustang bleachers came alive with a deafening roar of yelling, screaming and foot-stomping — a desperate attempt to distract her.

And the distraction worked. Caught off-guard by the sudden noise — as well as Amanda's voice in her head saying, *"Miss it!"* — Bidge's first free throw bounced off the back right of the rim, sending it in a high arc off to the left. The referee retrieved the ball and handed back to Bidge for her second foul shot.

But Bidge was back in the zone now. She relaxed and shut out the noise of the crowd. Double bounce — spin — look — double bounce — look — shoot.

Swish.

Her second free throw sealed the victory for the Panthers, 56-55. Her ecstatic team rushed onto the court and swarmed around her, like bees on watermelon at a picnic.

The crowd eventually thinned out. Toby and Marc sat and waited on the bottom bleacher for Bidge to extract herself from her adoring Panther fans. As she walked over, Toby stood up and gave her one more high-five.

"That was amazing," Toby said. "I've never seen you play like that."

"I kept her to sixteen points."

"Just like you said you would."

"Just like I said I would." Bidge grinned.

"So, like, what happened in the second half? You were incredible with the ball stealing. It was like you were totally…"

"…reading her mind?" Bidge interrupted, finishing Toby's sentence as usual. "Yeah, I think I was just in the zone. It was a great night."

Marc's Dad and Trista walked over. "Awesome game, Bridget."

"Thanks Mr. Lopez. It was a team effort."

"Well, you should be proud of yourself." Mr. Lopez turned to Marc and Toby. "You boys ready to go?"

"Sure Dad," Marc replied. Marc and his dad headed toward the exit.

"I guess I'll see you Monday, then," Toby said awkwardly.

"Yup. I guess so," Bidge replied.

Toby started toward the exit, paused briefly, and then turned back around, walking over to give Bidge a hug, slimy as she was. She beamed and hugged back. After a brief moment, Toby released the hug, smiled, and took a small step backward thinking, *Gross. Now I'm totally going to have to wash this sweatshirt when I get home.*

Even though he hadn't said it out loud, Bidge hauled off and slugged him in the arm anyway, almost as if she knew what he was thinking.

CHAPTER 11

I Don't Belong Here

IT WAS EXCRUCIATING. ALTHOUGH Toby checked the stock ticker every afternoon at the Leonards' house, the next secret message didn't come until nearly three weeks later. He had been starting to wonder if M^2 had lost interest. Christmas vacation had come and gone. During the break, Toby had faithfully watched the ticker every day, since he was not in school and had plenty of time to waste in front of the television. But to his great disappointment, not a single new message had been sent...until today.

BDC 6.2K@37.51 ▼1.26 OSI 8.7K@39.41 ▲0.01
OMI 5.6K@31.47 ▲0.01 KRG 3.1K@18.26 ▲0.33
XNR 3.8K@4.27 ▲0.09 AFL 7.7K@46.44 UNCH
SFE 0.5K@2.31 ▲0.17 PGN 3.9K@49.26 ▼0.48
AFL 1.7K@46.46 UNCH B 6.0K@21.34 ▲0.17 GIL
6.7K@46.31 ▲0.31 NCT 6.0K@31.26 ▲0.56 ZQK
3.7K@15.41 ▲0.28 SCO 4.8K@2.40 ▲0.02 DNR
1.7K@26.31 ▲1.05

"APPLY TO CHOATE"

Toby almost gagged on his cookie. "Choate" was the elite private boarding school located on the other side of town. It was considered one of the top ten private high schools in the country. It was a school for kids who were rich, famous or really smart. Maybe all three. After all, it was the high school that John F. Kennedy graduated from.

Toby wasn't any of those things. He wasn't rich or famous by any stretch of the imagination, nor did he consider himself particularly smart. His grades weren't anything to write home about, even if he had actually had a real home to write home to, so to speak.

Worst of all, the Choaties were known as a bunch of rich spoiled brats who thought they were better than everyone else. As such, it was the duty of any self-respecting Townie to cut the Choaties down a notch whenever possible. To actually *apply* to Choate would be like admitting that being a Choatie was better than being a Townie. Why else would someone want to switch teams and go to the dark side?

Toby moped around for several days. He didn't want to apply to Choate. He didn't see the point, anyway. It cost something like forty thousand dollars a year to go to school there. Even if he could get accepted, he couldn't afford to go, so why bother? Plus, he didn't belong there. He wouldn't fit in at all. There must be some mistake. There *had* to be a mistake. So Toby ignored the message.

There was no mistake. One week later Toby received another message from M^2:

**BIG 7.4K@22.36 ▼0.08 QTM 1.5K@2.27 ▼0.01
ORI 3.7K@23.29 ▲0.23 MTX 9.5K@59.37 ▼0.97
ZZ 2.6K@14.26 ▼0.25 AEM 8.2K@38.29 UNCH
SSL 0.0K@35.27 ▲1.67 NBR 8.2K@28.40 ▲1.73
ALE 7.9K@46.46 UNCH BSC 4.7K@162.26 ▲0.05
IRS 5.6K@17.28 ▼0.43 PEC 1.1K@16.31 ▼0.22**

"APPLY TO CHOATE NOW"

"Well, that sounded a little less friendly. Oh well, I guess it won't hurt to apply since I won't get in anyway." Toby still didn't know who M^2 was, and why he was sending instructions, but anybody who could control the stock ticker must be important enough to deserve some respect. Besides, if M^2 *really* knew his parents, he shouldn't risk ticking him off.

Toby looked at Choate's admissions information online. He had already missed the January 10th application deadline by a few days, but that was for eighth graders. Choate was a high school, grades nine through twelve. Toby was only in seventh grade, so he couldn't apply yet anyway.

"This is good," thought Toby. "I missed this year's deadline so I have a whole year to get everything together." Everything was shaping up nicely. Toby downloaded the application and started looking at it. Most of the application was pretty straightforward, but there were a few things that were going to be a hassle, like recommendation letters.

"No big deal," he muttered. "Over the next year I can work on buttering up a couple teachers so that they'll write good ones." He was relieved that he wouldn't have to ask for recommendations anytime soon. He *really* didn't want anyone to know that he was applying to Choate, especially his friends. Could he trust his teachers to keep their mouths shut? How would they react to Toby applying? He didn't have the best grades, so they would probably think that the application was a waste of time. This whole situation was embarrassing.

The other big hurdle on the application was the SSAT — Secondary School Admission Test — the test that kids who want to go to private high school have to take. The online guide said that the test would take two hours to complete, and that it was like the SAT, with three main sections — writing, verbal, and quantitative.

Toby discovered that the next available test date was on February 7th at McGuire Gym, on the Choate campus. He only had a couple days left to register without late fees. Even without the additional late fee, the cost of the test was $105. It was possible in the case of financial hardship to get the fee waived by making a request to the school that you were applying to. Toby always qualified for those things since he was a foster child, but he rarely actually asked for the discounts. It was too embarrassing. To him, it would be like standing up and yelling, "Look at me, I'm poor!"

So Toby went down to the supermarket and bought a VISA gift card for $150 cash with his dog-walking money. That would be enough to cover both the hundred-dollar SSAT fee, as well as the Choate application fee. It was a lot of money, but it was less embarrassing than asking for charity. With the gift card, he could register for the SSAT online. The test was in less than four weeks.

▲ ▲ ▲

February seventh rolled around sooner than he expected, and Toby hadn't studied or prepared for the SSAT in any significant way. A month earlier, when he signed up and paid the fee to take the test, he seriously contemplated spending some time studying. As the days and weeks passed by, though, it became clear that preparing for the SSAT was pretty much at the bottom of his priority list. In truth, he was half hoping that he would do really poorly on the test. Maybe then M2 would drop the whole Choate thing and his life would go back to normal.

The alarm on Toby's watch went off at exactly six that morning. He had set it the night before to make sure he'd have enough time to take a shower, eat breakfast and get over to Choate where the test was to be given. Check-in time at the testing center was at 8:15, and it would take him a long time to walk to the bus, ride the bus across town, then walk the remaining distance to the gym where the test was.

Of course, it would have been much simpler to just ask FM10 for a ride, but Toby didn't want to do that. The whole Choate situation was still a secret, so asking for a ride was out of the question. He had to get himself there and back on his own.

The bus stop was two blocks from his house and the bus was scheduled to stop there at 7:20 on Saturday mornings. Toby left the house at exactly 7:12 a.m., since he knew that it took him exactly six minutes to walk there and he didn't want to stand in the cold for more than two minutes.

As he rounded the last corner, the bus stop was visible a hundred yards ahead. His bus, apparently two and a half minutes early, was just pulling up to the stop.

Toby felt his stomach in his throat. "Hey!" he yelled as he started sprinting for the bus stop. "Wait up!"

It only took Toby twenty seconds to cover the distance and the bus hadn't moved yet. He was sure that he would make it. He was still a few houses away and had started to slow down, thinking that the driver was waiting for him.

But the driver hadn't heard him, owing to the roar of the diesel engines. The bus pulled out and headed briskly down the street to the next stop, three blocks away. "Hey…" Toby yelled again, a little softer now, his right arm still waving, yet he now realized that the bus would not be stopping for him.

But there was still hope.

Toby looked down the street to the next stop. There were three people waiting for the bus down there, two women and a small child. Since there were riders waiting, the bus would have to stop there, and he could hope that the little kid might take a little longer to board the bus. So Toby started sprinting again. The bus had already opened up a lead of an entire block, which meant that it was going to be close. He settled into a good rhythm, pumping his legs as fast as he possibly could on the icy sidewalk, his calculator and number 2 pencils bouncing inside his coat pocket.

The bus stopped up ahead, letting an elderly lady off. One of the women waiting at the stop helped her step down and then over to the sidewalk. Meanwhile, the woman with the child stepped onto the bus, disappearing from Toby's view. He was still a hundred yards away and sprinting as hard as he could. He tried to yell to the other woman to tell the driver to wait, but since he was now gasping for breath, he couldn't manage to make a sound loud enough for her to hear.

The second woman disappeared inside the bus and Toby was still fifty yards away. Toby could see the door close on the bus. He waved frantically as he saw the left blinker turn on, signaling to traffic that the bus would be pulling out into the street.

Rat Snacks, thought Toby. There was no way he'd make it to the test in time now.

The bus driver looked in his side mirror and finally saw Toby. Surprised and embarrassed, he pulled back over to the curb and opened the door. "Good morning, Toby," the bus driver said with an apologetic tone, "I didn't see you there. C'mon in." It was Earl the Bus Driver.

Earl had been Toby's school bus driver since first grade. He was a tall, good-natured older man with thick gray hair that was cut short and always neatly in place. He always wore a jumpsuit, similar to something that a mechanic would have to wear as a uniform. Toby figured that since there was no name patch on the jumpsuit saying "Earl," then it must not be a uniform, but just his odd personal taste in clothing. Most of the time the jumpsuit was tan-colored, but Toby occasionally saw him wearing a gray or a blue one. Undoubtedly these were the times when Earl was feeling particularly daring in a fashion sense.

Even though Toby had moved around a lot to different neighborhoods and bus routes over the years, Earl had always somehow ended up as his driver, so they were on a first name basis. Earl was always friendly and always seemed to care how Toby was doing. This year, however, Toby lived within walking distance from school, so he hadn't seen Earl in a while. Clearly he was working for CTTransit now.

"Thanks," Toby gasped as he dropped four quarters into the money slot and slumped into the blue plastic seat two rows back.

Earl pulled back out into the street and continued along the bus route. "Long time no see, Mr. Gold," Earl said jovially. "What brings you to my bus this early on a Saturday morning?"

"I'm taking a test."

"Criminy, that doesn't sound like much fun," replied Earl. "What's it for?"

"Just a school thing." Toby really didn't want to talk about it.

Earl could sense this and just said, "Well, good luck. I'm sure you'll do great," and promptly dropped the subject.

Toby avoided Earl for the rest of the ride, occupying his time by pulling out his calculator and memorizing ten digits of pi.

The bus route did not actually go onto the Choate campus. The closest it came was a stop in front of the Silver Pond Apartments on Center, so Toby got off there. As he walked past Earl, he politely said, "Thank you."

"You're welcome, Toby. Good to see you again."

After Earl pulled away, Toby crossed the street and walked the remaining half-mile to McGuire Gym. It was still only 8:00 am, so he was fifteen minutes early for check-in. The proctor checked his documents and sent him into the gym to the next to last table. There was only one other kid there ahead of him. It was a blond fat kid with big round glasses.

The rest of the test-takers slowly filed in. There weren't that many, so every kid got his or her own table. As Toby looked around, most of them seemed to be about his age or a little older, but they were all dressed better. That's what he assumed anyway, based on seeing some of their coats and shirt logos, which indicated expensive brands. That year, like previous years, Toby's clothes came mostly from Goodwill. He didn't normally notice those things, but did today because he was already feeling out of place.

I don't belong here, he thought. *I might as well have a big sign on me that says 'Townie.'* He was certain that everyone was judging him. If they had been in cars rather than in a gym, he was sure they would have rolled down their windows to insult him. Car window insults were the traditional and cherished form of communication in Wallingford between Townies and Choaties.

Toby finished the test a few minutes early. The last section was math, so he breezed through it quickly. The verbal sections had been much tougher. He turned in the test to the proctor and headed back to the bus stop. "Well, that was fun," he said out loud as he left the gym and headed back across campus, with no one but himself to enjoy the sarcasm.

It had snowed twice in the past week, and there were still nearly six inches of snow on the ground. Toby was only wearing tennis shoes, not boots, so he kept to the sidewalks on his way back through the campus. It was Saturday and the students didn't have classes, but there was still plenty of activity. Several times, Toby cringed as he passed groups of Choaties talking and laughing as they walked down the wide snow-lined pathways. He half expected them to recognize him as a Townie intruder and inflict some sort of ritualistic punishment upon him. No one did. The girls mostly ignored him, and the guys either did the same, or just gave him the standard "what's up" nod that is universal among teenage boys.

Toby managed to escape from campus back to Center Street unmolested by Choaties and only had to wait five minutes for the bus to come. The driver opened the door. It was Earl again.

"Hello again," Earl said cheerfully. "How did the test go?"

"Okay, I guess." Toby averted his eyes and stepped onto the bus, hoping to pay his fare and slip past Earl without any more fuss. This time, he went directly to the back of the bus in order to be out of range of any more conversation.

Toby made it home just in time for lunch. "Where have you been this morning?" FM10 asked cheerfully as Toby came in the door.

"Just doing some school stuff," Toby replied. His ears felt a little red, but that could have just been from the cold since he wasn't *really* lying. He took off his thrift store coat and looked at it disapprovingly for a second before hanging it on a hook next to the door.

▲ ▲ ▲

It was a Monday afternoon, a week after Valentine's Day. It had been exactly two weeks and two days since Toby had taken the admissions test. He had just come home from walking the dogs and was sitting on the couch in the family room, watching the ticker, thinking about interest rates and finishing off the box of chocolates that Bidge had given him on the fourteenth. At the time, he was a little embarrassed that he had only given her a card, the kind of Valentine's card that comes shrink-wrapped in a box of forty-eight. But hey, why waste good chocolate. He was polishing off the last piece when the following message appeared on the ticker:

RNTA 2.1K@25.45 ▲0.88 BMS 8.5K@34.27 ▼0.62
ZLC 5.7K@28.51 ▼0.24 AHO 2.5K@10.26 UNCH
ZAP 1.4K@6.40 ▼0.06 DCX 7.9K@62.41 ▲0.62
RAH 0.0K@50.26 ▲0.10

"SAY YES"

"Say yes to what?" Toby wondered. Then the phone rang. Toby jumped, spilling the empty chocolate wrappers on the floor.

"H-h-hello?" Toby hesitated, still freaked out at the timing. Maybe M² had given up on the TV messages and was calling to finally have a real conversation.

"May I speak with Toby Gold, please?"

"This is Toby."

"Hi Toby, this is Mr. Windsor, the Director of Admission at Choate. How are you today?"

"I'm fine thanks."

"Toby, I'd like to set up a time to stop by to talk to you and your parents about your SSAT scores. They're a bit unusual."

"Who? My parents, or my scores?" Toby couldn't resist that one. There was only an awkward silence on the phone, so Toby quickly continued, "I don't have any parents, Mr. Windsor, just foster parents — and the SSAT scores haven't even come back yet."

Mr. Windsor hadn't laughed at Toby's joke attempt, so he either didn't get it, or chose to ignore it. "You and your foster parents, then. Yes, I guess you haven't seen your scores yet. They get sent to us electronically the same time that they are mailed to the students, so sometimes we get them a couple days earlier."

"How did I do?" Toby asked nervously.

"Unusual. That's as specific as I'm allowed to get right now. Can I speak to your foster mom or dad?"

"Nobody's here but me right now, but my foster mom usually gets home in about an hour. Can I have her call you back?"

Mr. Windsor agreed, so Toby wrote down his number and promised to have FM10 call him back as soon as she came home.

▲ ▲ ▲

"I don't understand. Why is Choate calling you? I didn't even know you had applied there," FM10 said when she got home and Toby told her about the phone call.

"I *didn't* apply," Toby said, "I'm still a year too young. Choate starts taking students as ninth graders. So far, all I've done is taken the admissions test."

"So you have no idea why he wants to talk to us?"

"Nope. He wouldn't tell me. But since he's the admissions guy, I assume it must be something about me going there to school."

"Toby, come sit down. We need to talk," FM10 said, pointing to the sofa. They sat down a couple feet from each other and she continued, "Listen, I'm not sure exactly what's going on here, but there's a few things you need to understand, because I don't want you to get your hopes up."

"Okay."

"You're a great kid, Toby, and we've loved having you live with us this past year, but you need to realize that there's no way we could send you to Choate even if you got in. It costs a fortune to go there. We couldn't even afford to send our own kids to a school like that."

"Oh, I know that," Toby replied. "I never really expected to get in anyway."

FM10 looked relieved. "I just didn't want you to be mad at us, or too disappointed. We really do care about you, Toby. Besides, you just don't belong there."

"What's that supposed to mean? Why don't I belong there?" Toby's face flushed. "Because I'm a *foster* kid?"

"Oh, dear. I'm sorry if that came out wrong. I didn't mean anything bad by that," FM10 said. "It's just that…did you know that I used to work at Choate?"

"Really?"

"It was nothing important. I just worked in the kitchen at one of the dining halls. It was several years ago." FM10 briefly glanced down at her feet, shod in modest, comfortable brown shoes, then looked up at Toby again. "It wasn't the best experience for me."

"What happened?" Toby leaned forward, hoping for a juicy story.

"Oh, nothing really. The school staff was very pleasant. I mean, it was hard work, but no harder than any of my other jobs. But the kids there…"

"What? What did they do?"

"Now that I'm saying this out loud it sounds rather silly. They didn't do anything, really. I mean, yes, a few of them were rude to me, but that wasn't very common. There were also a bunch of very polite kids who always said hello to me, and smiled and said thank you and stuff." FM10 smiled as she thought about that group of kids. Then the smile disappeared and her face darkened a little. "But the rude ones *and* the friendly ones were the exception. Most of the kids were just strangely in-between. They were the ones that completely ignored me, like I didn't even exist.

Toby didn't say anything. He just nodded. He was trying to remember if he ever said hello to the lunch ladies at his own school. He made a mental note to start being friendlier to them.

FM10 continued, "I mean, it's like I wasn't even there — like they couldn't even see me. Eventually, I had to quit because I couldn't handle being invisible like that. It made me feel like I was nothing."

"Bummer," was all Toby could think of to say. He liked being socially invisible, so he didn't quite understand what the problem was.

"But you, Toby, are a really good kid. You're a real person, like us. I just can't imagine that you would fit in at a school like that."

"No worries. Besides, I can't stand the Choaties, either. Who wants to hang out with a bunch of snobs all day? Can't hurt to hear what the guy has to say, though. Right?"

FM10 smiled again and nodded. When Mr. Windsor called, she explained the financial situation, but he insisted on coming to meet Toby anyway. They agreed on 7:00 pm the next night, so that FM10 and FD10 could both be there. Knowing how much his foster dad hated Choaties, Toby couldn't wait to see what happened when he and Mr. Windsor were in the same room together.

CHAPTER 12

His Royal Highness, Mr. Windsor

FMIO TORE BACK AND forth across the living room in a
blurred frenzy, armed only with a cleaning rag and a rapidly depleting can of Pledge. She had arrived home early
that afternoon to start cleaning the house in preparation for Mr.
Windsor's visit. Toby tried to help, but it was really stressing him
out to be around her when she was in a cleaning frenzy like that.

"He's the admission director at a high school, not the Prince
of Wales. You don't need to go to all this trouble," Toby pointed
out.

"I know," she replied. "I just don't want the house to be messy
when a visitor comes." They were a working class family and
didn't ever throw fancy parties or entertain much. Their house was
not impressive by any objective standard, so the idea of someone
rich and important coming to visit was overwhelming to her. The
way her eyes glistened as she feverishly cleaned told Toby that she
was barely holding it together inside.

Toby, on the other hand, didn't care one way or the other. He
didn't really want to go to Choate, and even if he did, he couldn't
afford it.

"Is that what you're wearing?" FM10 asked, looking disapprovingly at Toby's t-shirt and jeans.

Toby grimaced. He had always been annoyed when asked that question, since clearly if someone is wearing something, then that's exactly what they're wearing. It's somewhat like asking, "Are those your arms?" or "Do you exist?" The question implies the answer.

"Um, yeah…"

"At least go put on a shirt with a collar."

Apparently shirts with collars were more impressive to the upper classes. Toby smiled to himself as he imagined Mr. Windsor storming angrily out of their house, appalled by all the rampant collarlessness.

"Sure." Toby knew that his poor foster mom was on the edge of hysteria, so he decided to cooperate without any further fuss. He went to his room and put on a polo shirt.

Mr. Windsor arrived a few minutes after seven. They were all sitting in the living room waiting silently, the only sound in the room being the ticking of the wall clock. FD10 was wearing a tie, but not voluntarily. He was visibly uncomfortable and the top button of his shirt looked like it might pop at any moment. When the doorbell rang, FM10 sprang to her feet and bounced toward the door. "I'll get it!"

Toby and FD10 both smiled and briefly glanced at each other, amused at her nervous energy. But neither of them, out of personal safety concerns, made any comments about it.

She opened the door and Toby heard her say, "You must be Mr. Windsor. Please come in, *your majesty.*"

Well, she didn't actually say the part about "your majesty," but Toby thought it was clearly implied by her tone of voice.

"Thank you," replied Mr. Windsor, sounding much like a normal human being. Toby was expecting him to sound snobbier, although he wasn't quite sure how someone would say "thank you" in a snobby way. Probably with an English accent of some sort — holding a cup of tea with pinky extended.

Mr. Windsor followed FM10 into the living room. He shook FD10's hand and then walked over to Toby.

"And you must be Toby. It's a pleasure to finally meet you." Mr. Windsor offered his outstretched hand, which Toby shook as firmly as he could.

"Nice to meet you, too," replied Toby.

Mr. Windsor looked at Toby's collared shirt approvingly.

"Please, won't you sit down?" asked FM10, gesturing toward the comfy chair normally reserved for her husband. Toby saw a brief scowl pass over FD10's face. Normally, no one but him was allowed to sit in that chair when he was in the house.

"Thank you," Mr. Windsor said as he sat down. "I won't be taking much of your time. I appreciate you meeting with me on such short notice."

Mr. Windsor opened his briefcase and pulled out some papers. "The reason that I'm making this personal visit is because Toby had some extraordinary results on his SSAT. As you can see, his writing and verbal scores are fairly typical for a seventh grader. His math score, however, is another story." He pulled out a sheet of paper and handed it to Toby. "He scored a perfect 800 on the math section."

Toby stared at the score sheet in disbelief. He loved math, but this didn't seem possible.

"But I'm getting a B in my math class at school. Just a regular B, not even a B+. How can this be right?"

Mr. Windsor paused for a moment. Since Toby hadn't actually sent in his application yet, Mr. Windsor hadn't seen his grades. "How do you normally do on the exams in your math class?"

"Hey, everyone!" Eddie interrupted, walking into the room, as usual, like he owned the place. "What's going on?"

Toby and FM10 looked at each other. Toby stared into her eyes with a desperate look that said *please don't tell,* ever so slightly shaking his head from side to side.

"Hello, Eddy," FM10 said. "We're just talking about Toby's grades. Could you wait in your room until we're done?"

"No problem," replied Eddie. He started walking toward the hallway, stopped and turned around with his big friendly smile. "Toby, sorry you're having trouble in school. If you ever need any help with any of your classes, I'm here for you, buddy."

Toby rolled his eyes. He couldn't believe that FD10 and FM10 actually believed this act from Eddie. "Thanks Eddie, I'll let you know." Eddie turned and headed down the hall to his room. Toby looked at his foster parents, who were watching Eddie walk away, their faces glowing with pride at what a great son they had.

Toby turned to Mr. Windsor again. "I'm sorry. What was your question again?"

"Your math tests at school. How do you do, usually?"

"I ace the tests," responded Toby. "I just lose points on the homework and class participation."

"That's fairly common among gifted kids who aren't being challenged. I think that we can help with that, though. Toby, how would you like to come to school at Choate next year?"

"But I'm only in seventh grade," Toby responded, "Choate's a high school, right?"

"Yes, Toby, that's correct. It would mean that you would skip the eighth grade and start high school with us in the fall. In math, you are already more advanced than most freshmen in high school. In the other subjects, we may have to provide some extra help in order to get you up to the same level as the other ninth graders, but I'm certain that you can do it."

"Hold on a minute." FD10 had been sitting there listening this whole time without saying anything. The tightness of his top shirt button apparently made it a little difficult to speak. "Mr. Windsor, we really appreciate your time coming here and all, but I just don't think this is going to be possible. We don't have a lot of money to spend on private school tuition, and besides, we're only Toby's foster parents. This isn't his permanent home." FD10 looked over at Toby apologetically.

"No need to worry about that, Mr. Jones," Mr. Windsor said. "Most people around here don't realize that over 70% of our students receive some form of financial aid from the school. Choate is not just a school for rich kids. Usually, local students from here in Wallingford can live at home, so they only qualify for a discount in tuition, not room and board. Since Toby is an orphan, he's in a unique situation that, I must admit, we haven't encountered before. My gut instinct is that he would benefit from living in the dorms on campus, since he may have to spend extra time with tutors his first year. That only means that we would have to get more creative with the financial aid package so that it included food and housing."

"Um, can I say something?" Toby interrupted.

"Of course," said Mr. Windsor.

"Nobody has asked me whether or not I want to go to school at Choate."

Mr. Windsor looked surprised. "Since you took the test and requested the scores be sent to us, the admissions committee just assumed…"

"I was thinking that it would be fun to try to get in, but I didn't think I really had a chance. And I never even considered that it would be for this coming year. I thought I had another whole year to think about it."

"I completely understand, Toby. This must all be happening very quickly." Mr. Windsor pulled a folder out of his briefcase and handed it to Toby. "Here is some material for you to read about our school and our programs. I truly believe that you'd be happy and successful with us at Choate. We can help you achieve your highest potential. We have a very tight-knit community. It's almost like a family, except it's filled with other extraordinary kids like you."

"Can I think about it?"

"Of course you can," Mr. Windsor continued. "But since the official application deadline for next year has already past, we'll need to hear from you soon. At the end of the month, we start sending out acceptance letters, so we can only hold a spot open for you until then. We will still need a completed application package from you, though. So if I don't receive your application by the 28th, we'll assume that you're not coming. Does that sound fair?"

"More than fair," said Toby, relieved that he didn't have to give an answer on the spot. "Thank you for understanding."

"If you have any questions, don't hesitate to call me. My mobile phone number is on the card stapled to the brochure in your folder. You can call me day or night." Mr. Windsor smiled, shook everyone's hands, and took his leave.

Toby and his foster parents just sat there for what seemed to be an awkward eternity without saying a word.

FM10 finally broke the silence. "It seems like a great opportunity."

"But why would Toby want to live with a bunch of stuck-up little rich brats?" FD10's comment was blunt, but it accurately summarized exactly what Toby was thinking.

Toby was certain that this would be exactly Bidge and Marc's reaction, too. Choaties and Townies had been natural enemies since the dawn of time, like dogs and cats, Celtics and Lakers, or the French and the non-French. Choaties were creatures that you were supposed to yell insults at, or maybe even throw stuff at, if the opportunity presented itself. Friendship between a Choatie and a Townie was completely out of the question.

This was the core of Toby's hesitation. For most kids who go to boarding school, the toughest part of the decision would be leaving their family. Toby clearly didn't have that problem. Except for Eddie, his current foster family was pleasant enough, but he hadn't yet become particularly close to them. So the idea of going to live at a boarding school wasn't scary at all — no scarier than changing foster homes every year.

To Bidge and Marc, though, this would seem like a complete betrayal of their friendship.

"I have a lot to think about. I'm going to my room." Toby got up and walked down the hallway to his room. He closed the door, and then fell onto his bed face down, and pulled his pillow over his head.

▲ ▲ ▲

Bidge sat with her team at lunch the next day. On game days, the basketball team always wore their team warm-up jackets and sat together at lunch. It was supposed to build team spirit or something. Marc was sitting with his computer geek buddies, so Toby joined them. Fortunately, Marc was so busy bragging about a new motherboard to his other friends that he never noticed that Toby was being extra quiet.

If Bidge had been there, she would have noticed right away that he was hiding something and would have mercilessly badgered him until he gave up his secret. If that didn't work she would have resorted to physical violence. Marc wasn't quite as perceptive, and Toby was grateful for that. He felt a little guilty not confiding his problem to his two best friends. They would have been upset had they known he was making such a huge decision without asking their opinion. Since he already knew what their opinion would be, what was the point of asking?

Toby had never felt more alone in his life. For an orphan, that was saying a lot.

That afternoon, he received another ticker message from M^2 — and he would continue to receive the identical message for the next five days:

TXI 7.9K@64.45 ▼0.32 ZNT 5.6K@47.27 ▲0.49 X 1.7K@71.51 ▲1.83 AVX 7.6K@14.26 UNCH ZMH 0.1K@77.40 ▼1.28 FNM 4.4K@59.41 ▼0.47 TU 5.4K@44.26 ▼0.32

"SAY YES"

"Yeah, yeah. I already know how YOU feel about it, ticker dude."

Deep down, Toby already knew how he felt about it, too. It was a great opportunity they were offering him, and he would be a complete idiot if he turned it down. If having a future meant having to hold his nose and becoming a Choatie, then so be it. His friends would eventually understand — hopefully. When he got home from the Leonards' he pulled out the folder that Mr. Windsor had given him and went to work completing the application.

▲ ▲ ▲

"You're doing WHAT?" Bidge yelled it loudly enough that most of the lunchroom turned around to see what exactly Toby was doing that provoked such a response. He was just sitting there, not doing anything particularly exciting, so after a few seconds they all turned back around and resumed their own conversations.

"Would you mind keeping your voice down a little?" Toby was already embarrassed enough about the situation. He didn't need the whole school to be involved. Plus, the only way to avoid getting beaten up every day would be to keep the whole future-Choatie thing a secret.

"This is a joke right?" Bidge asked.

"No. You think I'd joke about becoming one of *them*?"

"I don't get it. I thought we were friends."

"We are. It's not about you, Bidge. This is about me. I'm a freaking orphan. I have no future. I don't have anyone who will help me get into college and then pay for it. This is an amazing opportunity for me to do something great for once." Toby lowered his voice. "If I graduate from Choate, it pretty much guarantees that I'll get into a top college, maybe even with a scholarship. The top five colleges for Choate grads are Georgetown, Yale, Brown, UPenn, Cornell, and Tufts. All the other Ivy League schools are also on the list. If I stay here, though, I'll just end up at UConn, or maybe even community college with everyone else, plus a boatload of student loan debt."

"What's wrong with UConn?" Bidge asked. "My parents went there, you know."

"I know. Look, there's nothing wrong with UConn. It's a great university with an awesome basketball team. Before this week, I barely even had a chance of going to UConn. I'm just saying that now I feel like maybe I can do something really great with my life. It might be a lot easier to do that starting from a place like Yale than from a state school."

"What about Marc and me? Doesn't our friendship mean anything to you?"

106

"Jeez, Bidge. Yes, of course it does. That's why I was really hoping that you would be happy for me."

"I don't know. If you go, you'll be a Choatie. The smell will be unbearable." Bidge let herself smile a little.

"I'm going to go. I've already decided. I know deep down that if I pass this up I'll always regret it. But you gotta believe that I'll never *really* be a Choatie. My Townie blood runs strong and pure." Toby sat up a little straighter and looked off into the distance majestically, like he was posing for a campaign poster.

"We'll miss you, dude," Marc said flatly. He hadn't said much so far. Toby could tell he was angry. Marc's dad was a public school teacher, and he had been raised with a strong loathing of the very existence of private schools.

"It's not like I'm dying. I'll still be around. Choate's just on the other side of town. Besides, we still have the whole rest of this school year together."

▲ ▲ ▲

It took Toby several more days to get his Choate application completed. The essay questions were the biggest pain, not only because they required writing, which he hated, but they also required soul searching, which made him cringe. In nearly every sense, Toby had no idea who he was, or who he even wanted to be. One essay question asked what someone would find if they Googled his name in twenty years. That was a tough question to answer for someone who'd lived in ten foster homes and didn't even know who his next family would be, or where he would be living the next year. Toby had trained himself not to think too much of the future or have too much hope. That way he avoided disappointment.

Since he had already been told he was accepted, Toby didn't put as much thought and time into writing the essays as he probably should have. He didn't have a real answer to the google question, so he just said that in twenty years he would either be a U.S. Senator or would be fighting crime after surviving a bite from a radioactive spider. Preferably both. He submitted the completed application a full week before the deadline that Mr. Windsor had imposed.

As it turned out, he probably should have taken the essays more seriously. Mr. Windsor called him a few days later.

"Toby, I can't tell you how pleased we were about your decision to become part of the Choate family. You won't regret it."

"I'm really excited about it," Toby replied. It was true. Once he made up his mind, he felt really good about the decision and knew he had made the right choice.

"There are, however, a few issues with your application."

Toby's heart sank a little.

Mr. Windsor continued, "Even though you are clearly ready to advance to 9th grade in math as indicated by your test scores, your grades in your other subjects are not up to our normal standards. Your essays on the application were particularly weak, even by 7th grade standards."

Toby swallowed hard. He had finished those essays in about fifteen minutes, figuring that they didn't matter.

"I understand. So should I try applying again next year?"

"Oh, no, that's not what I meant at all. We still want you to come. It's just that we'll need to make additional arrangements so that you'll be ready to join the freshman class in the fall. I've taken the liberty of admitting you to the Young Writers Workshop this summer. Our experience indicates that this workshop will successfully raise your English skills up to Choate standards.

We also need you to attend the Science Workshop to make sure you're ready for third-form Physics in the fall.

Summer school. Great, thought Toby. At least they were still letting him come to Choate, despite his super-lame application. "Sounds great, Mr. Windsor. Thanks again for the opportunity."

"You can plan on moving into the dorms in early July, a few days before classes start. Once the weather gets a little warmer this spring, I'll arrange for you to visit the campus and get a feel for your new home."

Home. Toby had never had a permanent home before. He had always hoped that someday he would be adopted, so it had never crossed his mind that 'home' would turn out to be a snobby boarding school. Still, the idea of living in just one place for the next four years gave him a good feeling inside.

XTO 2.0K@44.30 ▲2.40 PII 9.7K@47.31 ▼0.43 TIA 4.1K@25.45 ▲0.19 ACS 6.7K@49.46 UNCH BEC 5.0K@60.35 ▲0.60 GIS 3.2K@57.40 ▲0.17 NLS 7.4K@14.51 ▲0.05 RHD 0.1K@63.26 ▲1.02 FCL 7.0K@30.27 ▼1.42 AZZ 3.8K@51.49 UNCH XNR 0.4K@4.27 ▼0.09 HDL 7.1K@6.35 ▲0.05 RSG 2.5K@41.46 ▲0.33 DB 6.8K@135.45 ▲2.10 MWY 1.8K@6.26 ▼0.24 ZAP 9.6K@6.26 ▼0.06

"YOU CHOSE WISELY"

Toby raised his eyebrows at the message, still filled with doubt. This whole experience still felt completely out of control, like riding his bike down a steep gravel road toward a cliff. *Whatever,* Toby thought. *There are probably worse things than being a Choatie.* But at that moment he couldn't think of any.

CHAPTER 13

The Stench of Victory

B Y PINKY-SWEARING BIDGE AND Marc to total and complete secrecy, Toby succeeded in keeping his newfound choatiness a secret from the school for the rest of the year. For the Choate application he had only needed one teacher recommendation, from whom Toby had extracted a solemn oath of confidentiality. Mrs. Stephens, Toby's social worker, wrote the other recommendation. She was absolutely thrilled about the whole thing. Confidentiality was part of her job, so Toby's secret was safe with her.

Bidge and Marc knew, of course, but Toby could trust them not to squeal.

FM10 and FD10 also knew. Toby made them promise not to tell Eddie, who had a particularly strong dislike for Choaties. Eddie wouldn't dare do anything directly, but he might tell his buddies, who might show less self-restraint.

"But Eddie will be so proud of you," said FM10. "Are you sure you don't want to tell him?"

"I know he will," Toby fibbed. "It's not Eddie that I'm concerned about, it's his football buddies. They hate Choaties and if Eddie ever *accidently* told them, they would make my life miserable. It's safer if we just wait until school is out before telling anyone."

"All right, we won't say anything. But I know that Eddie's feelings will be hurt when he finds out you've been keeping this from him."

Yeah, he'll be heartbroken, Toby thought sarcastically before replying aloud, "Maybe, but I think he'll understand once he knows my reasons."

▲ ▲ ▲

The spring semester went excruciatingly slowly for Toby, mostly because he lost his motivation to do schoolwork. He was already accepted at Choate, so his current grades really didn't matter for anything. He knew deep down that he should always try his best, but despite his efforts to be a decent student, he just couldn't concentrate. It was by sheer luck that he avoided getting any C's, but his simultaneous avoidance of any A's had nothing to do with luck at all.

In late April, when the weather was warmer and the leaves were on the trees, Toby was invited over to Choate for his official campus tour. He was excited about it because the only other time he had seen any substantial part of the campus was when he took the SSAT back in February. The 450-acre campus was much prettier now that it was green with life, looking more like a park than a school. Toby was both impressed and intimidated by it. Everything was so beautiful and well maintained.

"Toby, I'd like you to meet Jennifer Strauss," Mr. Windsor said. A girl had just walked up to them in front of the admissions office. She was about the same height as Toby with long curly black hair pulled back in a severe ponytail. Her white skin held the faint trace of freckles just below her large brown eyes. It was an unseasonably warm day for April in Connecticut, so Jennifer was dressed for summer, wearing a skirt that went to her knees, sandals, and a designer t-shirt. "Jennifer is one of our brightest third-form students. She'll be attending summer session this year, so we've asked her to be your tutor. She'll help you get up to speed with what you need to know for this fall."

Whoa, thought Toby. *I'm starting to like this better all the time.* "Nice to meet you," was all Toby was able to choke out as he shook Jennifer's outstretched hand. To him, Jennifer's facial features made her look like a real life version of an anime character, with her porcelain skin, tiny nose and mouth, and strikingly large brown eyes — all coming together in an impossibly cute package. Toby half expected her to pull out a magic sword and start fighting brightly colored monsters at any moment.

She didn't.

"Welcome to Choate, Toby," Jennifer said as she flashed a warm smile. Toby was mildly surprised that her words and lips appeared to be fully synchronized. So much for the anime character theory.

"Jennifer will be taking you on your campus tour today. We find that other students provide the best answers to questions about real life around here. I'll meet you two back here at admissions later this afternoon. Take your time seeing the school." Mr. Windsor turned and headed back inside the building.

"Would you like to see where you'll be living?" Jennifer asked.

"Sure, Jennifer, I've actually been really curious about that."

"Call me Jen. Only the teachers call me Jennifer."

"Got it. Can I call you Jenny?"

"No," she replied curtly, sounding annoyed.

Great, thought Toby, *I can't talk to a high school girl for even two minutes without making her hate me.*

The first stop on the tour was Memorial Hall, which is the ninth grade boy's dormitory. "Don't ever call it Memorial Hall, though. Everyone just calls it Mem. The resident director and his family live in this apartment on the ground floor. He'll be your Physics teacher in the fall. You'll really like him, and his wife is totally sweet, too."

"This is nice." There was a lounge area on the ground floor filled with comfortable furniture.

"Let's go look at one of the rooms. I'm sure someone will be up there to show you theirs." Jen led Toby up the stairs and they walked down the hallway until they found a door where they could hear music.

"Sounds like someone's home in this one." Jen knocked on the door.

"Whattaya want?" A voice yelled from inside, clearly annoyed at the interruption.

"New Student Tour," replied Jen. "I've got coed visiting."

"Coed visiting?" Toby whispered.

"Yeah. Coed visiting means that I have special permission to be in a boys dorm."

"Just a sec," a voice said from inside the closed door. Jen and Toby could hear frantic cleaning noises coming from inside.

The door opened. It was a kid roughly Toby's size with messy blond hair and glasses. He was wearing soccer shorts and a Choate T-shirt. He saw that it was Jennifer and leaned against his doorway, trying unsuccessfully to look cool. He ignored Toby at first and just spoke to Jen. "Well, hello there, gorgeous."

Jen rolled her eyes and ignored his comment. "Hey, Dill," Jen said casually. "This is Toby. He'll be starting this summer."

"Welcome to our humble home. The name's Dillon." He made a sweeping gesture with his right arm indicating that Jen and Toby were permitted to enter. "So, where ya from, Toby?" Dillon asked once they were inside.

"Umm…Wallingford," Toby replied somewhat sheepishly.

"No way! A native of *Wallyworld*. Outstanding!" Dillon said, slapping Toby on the back. "I'm from The City myself." Having grown up in Connecticut, Toby knew that 'The City' meant New York City — and most likely the island of Manhattan.

Toby looked around. It was a long, narrow room, about ten feet wide and twenty feet deep. It was smallish, yet comfortable. The room was, in fact, quite similar in size to Toby's current bedroom, except two people lived in it instead of just one. The closet was located on the right side, just inside the doorway. Continuing along that wall were two upper bunk beds, each with a built-in desk underneath. The opposite wall on the left side was plain white painted cinderblock. The only natural light source was a window on the narrow wall at the other end of the room.

"Nice to meet you, Toby. Impressive, huh?" Dillon said, looking around the room. "Get used to it. This is where all the third formers spend their first year."

"Third formers?" Toby had heard Mr. Windsor use the term earlier, and still didn't know what it meant.

"Third Form is ninth grade," Jen said. "It's prep school lingo. Third form means ninth grade, fourth form is tenth grade, and so on. So a third-former is a freshman."

"But why third?" Toby asked. "Why not ninth form for ninth grade, or first form for the first year of high school?"

"Because that would make sense," Dillon said with a grin. "And we can't have that. It's critically important that Choate alums be able to have conversations among themselves that no one else can understand. So you'll spend four years here getting immersed in traditions and vocabulary that can only be deciphered by other Choaties. Think of it as a secret code."

"I'm okay with secret codes," Toby said. *Especially when they come to me mysteriously from the TV.*

"Cool. Then you'll fit in fine here at Choate. We're all about secret passwords and handshakes and stuff. That's how we rule the world, you know." Dillon tried to keep a straight face.

Toby wasn't sure how to respond to that.

"He's kidding," Jen said, coming to Toby's rescue. "They don't let us start ruling the world until we're seniors." She flashed a brilliant smile that made Toby go a little gooey inside. Jen had given the impression of being the serious type up until then, so the lightened mood was a relief.

"Sixth formers, don't you mean?" Toby was doing his best to learn the new lingo.

Dillon laughed. "He's pretty quick…"

"Let's get going, Toby. There's still a lot left to see." Jen was getting serious again.

"Stop by anytime, Jen. This is the first time I've ever had a girl in my room. I kinda like it."

"In your dreams, Dill," Jen said, "My parents would kill me if I ever broke coed. Besides, your room smells like a gym locker. I'll have to take a shower later to get the stink off me." Toby and Jen walked out the door and started down the hall.

"It's the Stench of Victory. Wear it with pride!" Dillon yelled after them, poking his head out the door. He then sniffed his armpit triumphantly, and with a look of satisfaction retreated back into his room.

Jen and Toby walked out of Mem House and over to a large building across the street and a few minutes away by foot.

"Let me show you the SAC. You'll be spending a lot of time there instead of studying, if you're like the rest of the boys, that is."

"SAC?"

"Student Activities Center. It's where everyone hangs out when they don't have anything better to do."

Toby thought it was the most awesome thing he had ever seen. There were pool tables, food and video games — everything a boy could want. "I like that it's so close to Mem." They finished their tour of the SAC by going into the Tuck Shop for an ice cream.

"Somebody obviously wasn't thinking straight the day they decided to put the arcade games within a hundred yards of the freshman boys' dorm," Jen said with an annoyed scowl. "It's way too much of a temptation for the poor little tykes."

Toby wasn't sure he liked Jen referring to boys roughly his age as "little tykes." She was probably just kidding, but with her it was hard to tell, since she said everything with a totally straight face.

Jen showed him the other major points of interest, including the sports facilities, the arts center and a couple of classrooms.

"Where are all the desks?" Toby asked, noticing how few there were in each classroom. He was used to having thirty kids in his classes at Dag.

"That's all of them," said Jen. "The classes here are really small. You'll probably never have more than fifteen kids in a class, and it's usually less. That's the best part of being here. The teachers are really good and the classes are small enough that class time is more of a conversation than a lecture. You'll really get to know your teachers well, and they actually care about us."

"Cool." Toby wasn't saying much, but inside he was starting to get really excited about school for the first time in his life.

Jen glanced at her watch. "Let's head back to Mr. Windsor's office. He's expecting us back there before they close for the day."

They walked the short distance across campus back to Archbold Hall. Mr. Windsor's office door was open, but a distinguished-looking gentleman was already inside talking to him, so Jen just knocked on the door frame to get their attention.

"Good, you're back! So how was the tour, Toby?"

"It was awesome. I can't wait to start."

The distinguished-looking gentleman stepped forward, extending his hand in greeting. "So this is the Mr. Gold we've heard so much about?"

Mr. Windsor responded, "Yes it is." He turned toward Toby. "Toby, this is Mr. Shaheen, the headmaster here at Choate."

"Nice to meet you." Toby was somewhat surprised at Mr. Shaheen's appearance, since the only headmaster Toby had ever seen before was in the movies, and that was Albus Dumbledore. Mr. Shaheen looked *nothing* like Dumbledore. Instead of a flowing white beard, a robe and a wand, Mr. Shaheen had short hair, a navy blazer, and a briefcase. It was *very* disappointing.

"We're excited that you're coming. Everybody on the admissions committee agrees that you'll be a wonderful addition to our student body."

"Thanks Mr. Shaheen. I can't wait to start."

Mr. Windsor then turned toward Jen, "Thank you, Jennifer, for showing Toby around today."

"Anytime, Mr. Windsor. It was fun. If you don't need me for anything else, I need to go change for tennis practice." Jen started walking toward the door. Before exiting, she turned and said, "It was nice meeting you, Toby, I'll see you this summer."

"See you, Jen. Thanks for the tour," Toby said.

Jen walked out the door, but Toby didn't stop watching her soon enough to escape Mr. Windsor's notice.

"She's very pretty, isn't she?" Mr. Windsor said with a fatherly grin.

Toby snapped out of his trance. "Oh, uh, yeah, I guess. I hadn't really noticed." Toby felt his face turn bright crimson.

Mr. Windsor put his hand on Toby's shoulder and steered him toward the hallway. "Come with me, Toby, there's someone else you need to meet." They walked out of the office and up the stairs to the second floor.

"Although your tuition is fully paid through your academic scholarship, there is still the matter of the cost of your room and meals. The school will also pay those costs, but that kind of assistance requires that you work part-time on campus. Does that sound okay with you, Toby?"

"Of course, Mr. Windsor." Toby had no problem with that arrangement at all. He had always been a hard worker.

"Most students receiving financial aid work in the kitchens or for groundskeeping."

Groundskeeping sounded fun to Toby.

"We have something unique in mind for you, though. We have received a special request for your services from a member of our Board of Trustees."

"Board of Trustees?" Toby had never heard that term before, but it sounded important. "Is that anything like a board of directors?" Toby knew from the financial news and from reading *The Wall Street Journal* that the stockholders elected a board of directors of a corporation. The directors were then responsible for hiring and firing the company president.

"Yes, quite like a board of directors, in fact. Very good, Toby. A company has a board of directors, but a school generally has a board of trustees. They make the really big decisions, as well

118

as hire and fire the top administrators of the school. One of our trustees has specifically requested that you work directly for him."

"Why me?" Toby was confused. He was a nobody. Why would someone important like a big shot private school trustee want a 13-year-old orphan *nobody* to work directly for him?

"You'll have to ask him that yourself. Here we are." They had just arrived at a dark wooden door at the end of the hallway. Mr. Windsor knocked. A deep familiar voice from inside responded, "Come in."

Mr. Windsor opened the door and motioned for Toby to enter. The office had a single small window to the left and the remaining walls were covered with dark wooden bookcases that seemed to absorb most of the light filtering in through the sheer curtains on the window. Thus although it was the middle of the afternoon on a sunny day, the office was bathed in a faint silvery light similar to moonlight, interrupted only by the glow of a metallic lamp on the oversized mahogany desk. "Toby, I'd like you to meet Jack Leonard."

The deep voice from behind the desk said, "Oh, Toby and I are already well acquainted. He walks my dogs six days a week and I suspect that he eats all my cookies, too!"

"Oh! Hi, Mr. Leonard." Toby was glad to see a familiar face, but still surprised that the familiar face was in such an unexpected location.

"Thank you, Mr. Windsor, I'll take it from here," said Mr. Leonard. Mr. Windsor took the cue and excused himself.

"Have a seat, Toby." Mr. Leonard pointed to one of the leather chairs in front of his desk. "How was your tour today?"

"It was great," said Toby, who still had a perplexed look on his face. "But I'm confused. I thought you worked in New York City. I didn't expect to see you here in Wallingford during the day."

119

"Yes, you're right. I work on Wall Street as an asset manager. I help wealthy people and institutions manage their investments. I've managed Choate's endowment for a few years now and apparently I've done such a good job that they put me on the Board of Trustees.

"Endowment?"

"Yes, endowment refers to the all the financial investments of the school — its wealth. Choate's endowment is now over two hundred million dollars."

Toby's eyes grew impossibly wide.

Mr. Leonard continued, "You see, private schools have two main sources of money that they use to pay their expenses each year. One source is tuition from the students, but that makes up only about half of what we need. The other main source of funds is investment income from the endowment."

"You mean like interest?"

"Investment income includes interest, yes, but that's not everything. It also includes things like dividends, capital gains, rent, and royalties. Choate's endowment earns all of these things, which help pay the teachers' salaries and maintain the campus."

"And provide scholarships to Townie orphans?"

"Officially, I am not familiar with that term, but yes," replied Mr. Leonard. "Which brings us to why you're sitting here today. Toby, you've impressed me as a hard-working kid who has a good instinct for business and investing. I'd like you to work for me here in the trustees' office."

"Absolutely! What do you need me to do?" Toby could hardly contain himself he was so excited. He tried to look calm and business-like, but did not succeed.

"For the time being, you just need to learn the details about how I manage the endowment. The school owns a wide variety of investments beyond the typical portfolio of stocks and bonds.

120

Your first task is to get a feel for Choate's investment portfolio. If there's something you don't understand, look it up. If you still can't figure it out, call me at my New York office."

Toby nodded. This was all happening pretty fast. "When do you want me to start?"

"You don't have to start work until you begin living on campus this summer. This job is intended as the fulfillment of your work-study duties in return for your room and board scholarship. At that point, you will be expected to come here for at least one hour every weekday after classes."

"Can I start sooner?"

"That's the spirit!" Mr. Leonard replied. "To be honest, I would have been a little disappointed in you if you hadn't asked that. Your self-motivation and ambition are exactly why I picked you for this job. You can start anytime you want."

"Choate is pretty far from my house, so I won't be able to come here every day. Would a couple days a week be okay?"

"That would be just fine. You can use this office, since I usually spend my weekdays in the city."

Toby took another quick look around the finely appointed office. *Sweet. This is definitely better than walking dogs*, he thought.

"You see that filing cabinet over there in the corner?"

Toby nodded.

"That's where you'll start. It's filled with account statements, trade confirmations and meeting minutes of the finance committee of the Board of Trustees. Once you familiarize yourself with the contents of that filing cabinet, you'll have the basic knowledge you need to understand what we do here. Start with the annual reports in the top drawer and work your way down."

"Got it."

"But stay out of the bottom drawer. Nothing in there is relevant to your job here." The friendly tone of voice had disappeared for a moment, making his last statement seem more like a warning than an instruction.

"Bottom drawer's off limits. Got it," Toby replied matter-of-factly.

"Here's a key to my office." Mr. Leonard's friendly tone returned as quickly as it had vanished. He handed Toby a silver key that looked like a typical house key. "If you have any questions, my mobile phone number is on the desk. That should be a last resort, though. I am a busy man and you are a bright kid, so I'd prefer that you make a serious effort to figure out the answers to questions yourself first."

"Don't bug Mr. Leonard. Got it." Toby smiled.

"I can see that we're going to have a very good working relationship." Mr. Leonard looked at his watch. "Wow, look at the time. I need to get going to my next meeting."

"Do you mind if I stay here for a little while and get started? I'll have trouble sleeping tonight if I don't."

"Knock yourself out, Toby. And welcome aboard. I'm sure I'll see you soon." With that, Mr. Leonard grabbed his coat and briefcase and headed for the door.

"Umm…Mr. Leonard? I have one more question…"

Leonard stopped mid-stride and turned toward Toby, looking slightly miffed that his smooth exit had been interrupted. "Yes, Toby?"

"Well, I was just wondering if you still want me to walk your dogs, or if this is a special promotion that means that I'm only supposed to do *this* job now."

Mr. Leonard brought his thumb and forefinger to his chin and thought hard for a second. "I hadn't really thought about that, Toby. But Max and Ginnie really love seeing you every day. Do you *want* to keep walking the dogs?"

"Oh, yes! Absolutely!"

"Then I guess you have two jobs now." Mr. Leonard flashed a big smile, and with long strides was down the hall, down the stairs, and out the door into the parking lot in no time at all. Toby watched out the window as Mr. Leonard pulled out of the parking lot in his silver Porsche 356, the unrequited love of Toby's life.

Man, that's one sweet car, thought Toby, a tiny drop of drool appearing in the corner of his mouth as the classic speedster elegantly made its way down Christian Street. As soon as it disappeared from view, Toby turned around and headed over to the filing cabinet to get started.

CHAPTER 14

Net Worth

Anxious to get started with his new job, Toby walked over to the filing cabinet, pausing briefly to glance at the unlabeled bottom drawer. He couldn't help but wonder what was in there that he wasn't supposed to see. *Maybe just a quick peek*, he thought, reaching for the bottom handle. Just as he began to open the file drawer a crack, he was startled by a noise near the doorway. Toby jumped up and spun around, keeping his back to the cabinet. "I was just..."

But there was no one there. The noise had come from his backpack toppling off the chair to the floor by the door. Toby let out a relieved sigh. Having learned his lesson, he turned back around toward the filing cabinet and opened the *top* drawer. The first folder was labeled *Annual Reports*. His hands still shaking, Toby grabbed the most recent file and sat down at Mr. Leonard's huge mahogany desk. The desktop was completely clean, except for the desk lamp, a phone, and a small white statue of the head and shoulders of some ancient Roman-looking guy with one of those crowns of leaves on his head. Toby turned off the lamp by pulling the little brass chain, and then pulled it again to turn it back on. He picked up the statue to take a closer look. The inscription said *Julius Nepos*. Toby shrugged. He had never heard of Julius Nepos. He set the statue back down and positioned it so that his new pal Julius would be sure to get a good look at the annual reports folder as Toby was reviewing it. It seemed like the polite thing to do.

The dark leather chair had wheels so it could roll back and forth as well as spin around. Unable to resist, Toby slipped off his tennis shoes and propelled himself into an impressive spin, holding his knees tightly against his chest. As he extended his legs back out, the spin slowed until he came to a complete stop. Thinking that this was extremely cool, Toby tried it again, but even faster. What he didn't realize, however, was that he had inadvertently pushed himself nearly a foot closer to the desk while getting up to speed. This time, as he extended his legs to slow down, his left foot made contact with the little statue of Julius Nepos, knocking it off the desk and onto the floor with a resounding thud.

"Rat Snacks!" Toby said out loud. He jumped out of the leather chair, on all fours, down to the spot where Julius lay motionless on his side. Toby checked the statue for injuries and discovered to his dismay that one of the leaves on the laurel crown had broken off. Toby picked up the statue and the broken leaf and set them back on the desk. Just as he started rummaging through the top desk drawer looking for glue, the phone rang. Toby stopped and stared at the phone for a second. The little screen on the phone said *Incoming Call: Judith Krebbs*.

Uh oh, thought Toby. Filled with the dread of bustedness, he answered the phone. "H-hello?"

"Hi, this is Mrs. Krebbs downstairs. Is everything okay up there? I thought I heard a noise."

"Everything's fine." Toby's ears turned a little pink.

"All righty then," Mrs. Krebbs said cheerfully. "Let me know if you need anything."

Toby thought for a second and then asked, "I don't suppose you have any glue, do you?"

"Maybe," Mrs. Krebbs replied suspiciously. "Why do you ask?"

Toby immediately regretted asking that question. "Oh, no reason in particular. Never mind. Thanks for checking in," Toby said nervously, then quickly hung up the phone. He made a mental note to remember to bring glue the next time. He put the broken leaf in the very back of the top desk drawer for safekeeping.

Getting back to the business at hand, he opened the folder on the desk and started reading a document called *The Annual Financial Report to the Board of Trustees of Choate Rosemary Hall.* It contained a balance sheet, income statement and statement of cash flows, just like company annual reports did. Most public companies provided their annual reports online, so Toby had previously read several of them and so he had a general idea of the kind of information that was inside.

The first time that Toby heard the term *cash flow* he was much younger and became very excited because he thought that it might refer to a river of money that he could dip into with a bucket and become instantly rich. He figured that all he needed was a map to where one of these magical cash flows was located — perhaps in Florida. His disappointment, understandably, was great when he learned that cash flows were something much simpler. You have a positive cash flow if you make more than you spend, and you have a negative cash flow if you spend more than you make.

Since Toby would be working for the guy managing Choate's investment assets, he wasn't as concerned with the cash flow statement, but rather needed to focus on the balance sheet, where the assets belonged. This was because the balance sheet is like a financial picture, a snapshot of the finances frozen at a specific point in time. It describes instantly how rich or how poor the person or organization is at that particular moment. There are three basic pieces of information on a balance sheet: Assets, Liabilities, and Net Worth. Net Worth is another way of saying *How Rich*. Being a millionaire means that your total net worth is at least one million dollars. It is calculated using this simple formula:

Net Worth = Assets – Liabilities

Assets are all the things the company owns at the time the picture is taken. They include cash, stocks, bonds, real estate, bank accounts, equipment, vehicles, baseball cards, and whatever else has value. Liabilities, on the other hand, are all the debts the company owes. For example loans, or any other thing that is borrowed, would show up as a liability on the balance sheet. So as long as liabilities are smaller than assets, net worth is positive, and that's good. On the other hand, having liabilities greater than total assets is bad.

Toby opened the annual report to the Balance Sheet page and set it down on the desk directly in front of the statue of Julius Nepos, who was looking even grumpier now that his laurel had been damaged. Toby felt bad about that, so he was making a special effort to be polite and include the statue in his research efforts. Toby saw that Choate's balance sheet for the year looked pretty good:

On the left side of the balance sheet, under the assets column, were *Cash, Accounts Receivable, Real Property* and the *Endowment*. The endowment was the investment money that Mr. Leonard managed. It was more than $241 million dollars.

"That's a lot of drachmas," Toby said lightly to Julius, using the word for Greek money because he couldn't think of the word for ancient Roman money. The statue did not respond, but continued to look somewhat annoyed. Toby made a mental note to look up the word for Roman money when he got home.

The previous category on the balance sheet was *Real Property*. Toby pulled out the folder with that name and discovered that real property consisted of the physical assets that the school owned, such as the campus and buildings. There were detailed listings of each facility, with a documented estimate of its value. *Accounts Receivable* were the money that is owed to the school by other persons and businesses, which the school expects to receive soon, like tuition payments.

Balance Sheet

Assets		Liabilities	
Cash	$350,000	Accounts Payable	$45,000
Accounts Receivable	650,000	Short-Term Loan	430,000
Real Property	45,000,000	Total Liabilities	475,000
Long-Term Investments	241,200,000		
(endowment)		Net Assets (or Net Worth)	285,725,000
Total Assets	**$287,200,000**	**Total Liabilities & Net Worth**	**$287,200,000**

On the liability side, *Loans* refer to money borrowed from banks or individuals for things such as construction projects. *Accounts Payable* refer to money owed by the school to other businesses that would be paid very soon. By subtracting the liabilities from the assets, Toby verified the value of the net worth on the balance sheet. It's just the difference between the two. The word used to describe the difference between assets and liabilities is completely different depending on who the balance sheet is for. Up until that moment, Toby had only seen balance sheets for people and for companies. For a person, it's called *net worth*. For a corporation, it's called *shareholder's equity*.

"I guess schools call it *net assets*," Toby said out loud to Julius, who continued his stubborn silence. "That's a new one." He gave a shrug and let the size of the numbers on the paper sink into his mind fully. It was impressive. "Whoa. Choate is worth almost three hundred million dollars." Toby could barely comprehend that much money. He quickly built a balance sheet for his own finances in his head. "Let's see, for assets, all I have is my dog-walking money, my bike, and my clothes. I've saved $443 so far. My bike might be worth fifty bucks. I could probably sell all my clothes for $180. So my total assets are $443+50 +180 = $673. My only liability is the five dollars I owe Bidge from last week. So my net worth is $673 − 5 = $668."

It wasn't three hundred million, but it was a good start. $668 is a much better net worth than zero. There are even some people that have a *negative* net worth, which means that they owe more than the value of what they have. Toby instinctively knew that was wrong. It seemed obvious that he should never owe more than he owned, and that over time, his net worth should be going up, not down.

Toby next looked at the income statement and noticed that the endowment had been growing quite well over the past several years. The growth came from two sources: donations from alumni and investment income from the endowment itself. Apparently, Mr. Leonard had indeed been doing an exceedingly good job managing the endowment. Just in the past year, the endowment had earned nearly thirty-one million dollars in investment income.

"That's over fourteen percent!" Toby had watched enough financial news to know that a fourteen percent return for an investment portfolio was pretty good. "No wonder they put him on the Board of Trustees. He's darn good at this." Julius did not disagree with this Toby's assessment of Mr. Leonard's skills, but continued to sit smugly on the desk looking on in statuesque silence.

It was starting to get late, so Toby replaced all the materials into folder and the folder into the filing cabinet. He slid the statue of Julius Nepos back into its original position on the desk. "See you soon dude," Toby said to the statue. "I'll fix your crown the next time I come back." Julius just stared back in his usual aloof way.

Toby gave Julius a polite salute, picked up his backpack and left the room. He closed the office door behind him, carefully locked it, and headed down the stairs to the front door. The gray-haired lady with horn-rimmed glasses at the front desk looked up and said, "See you soon, Toby."

Toby hadn't met her before. It felt a little creepy that she knew his name, but she seemed normal enough. Fortunately there was a nameplate on her desk. *Judith Krebbs.* He recognized the name as the same lady who had called him when he broke the statue. She looked more pleasant in person than she had sounded over the telephone. "See you later, Mrs. Krebbs. I'll be back sometime next week."

"Mr. Leonard gave you a key, right?" Mrs. Krebbs asked.

"Sure did." Toby proudly held up his key.

"Good. That key works in the front door as well as Mr. Leonard's office. Whenever I'm here, the front door will be unlocked, but if I'm at lunch or something, just use your key."

"Got it. Thanks!" With that, Toby glided out the front door and took a moment to flop down on the lush green grass beneath the flagpole that flew the United States, Connecticut and Choate flags, in that order. With hands outstretched to his sides, he gently ran his fingertips through the grass as he gazed up past the flags into the late afternoon sky. The sun, already low on the horizon, brilliantly caught the gold letters of the Choate flag, gleaming warmly as if by their own light source. He could have stayed there that way for hours, but it would be dark soon, so Toby got on his bike and headed away from what would soon be his new home.

He still wondered, though, what was in that bottom drawer in Mr. Leonard's office.

CHAPTER 15

The Bird

TOBY KNEW BETTER THAN to call Marc to tell him about the day's exciting events at Choate. As the son of a public school teacher, Marc was openly hostile to the mere mention of private schools. Bidge, on the other hand, still wasn't thrilled about the whole idea, but at least she pretended to be supportive. That was really all Toby could reasonably expect.

Toby tried calling Bidge when he arrived home, but her older brother Joey answered the phone and told him she was at the library working on a project for school. Joey emphasized more than once that he was really hungry, so if Toby found her, please send her home to make dinner.

Since she wasn't available, he spent the rest of the evening researching balance sheets and income statements on the Internet. Some creative googling also revealed that the most popular ancient Roman coin was the silver denarius, and that the last Roman emperor to appear on a denarius happened to be Julius Nepos around the year 480 A.D.

"Well, that's pretty cool," Toby said. "My statue buddy Julius was on the last Roman coins. No wonder he looked annoyed when I mentioned drachmas."

▲ ▲ ▲

The next morning, Toby awoke with sample balance sheets stuck to his face. Apparently he had fallen asleep reading them. He still hadn't been able to share his Choatie experiences with anyone and there was no way he could wait until lunchtime, so after breakfast he rode his bike over to Bidge's house to walk to school together.

She was mostly silent as they walked while Toby jabbered on and on about Jennifer's guided tour of the dorms, the class-rooms, and ice cream at the Tuck Shop. He also told her about his "dream job" in the Trustees' office. He was excited about all of it, yet it became increasingly clear that Bidge was still not on board with the whole Choate thing. She just politely smiled and said, "That's nice."

Toby frowned. "I know you don't want me to go to Choate," he replied. "But since it's *going* to happen, don't you think we should just make the best…"

"I don't want to walk this way. Let's turn here," Bidge inter-rupted.

In his excitement, Toby had forgotten himself and was mind-lessly taking the direct path from Bidge's house to school. Bidge never walked that way because it took her past the intersection of Elm and Maple, the exact spot where her dad and older sister Lauren died in a car accident two years earlier. Bidge had also been in the car, but survived with only a few minor bruises. There were still two little white crosses that other parishioners had placed there after the funeral. Bidge had never seen the crosses, though, because she had never gone back to that corner.

Despite Toby's discomfort at his forgetfulness, Bidge contin-ued the conversation as if nothing had happened. "All I know is that my best friend is leaving. How do you expect me to feel about that?"

"I'm not really leaving. I'll still be right here in Wallingford. Don't be stupid."

The punch to his arm was fast and powerful, like a backfist in an old kung fu movie. It was much more painful than usual. Clearly she had been working out this season.

"So now I'm stupid?" Bidge exclaimed. "I guess my little brain is just no match for the awesome mental powers of a freaking Choatie!"

"You know that's not what I meant."

"Isn't it? You've been acting weird ever since this whole Choate thing started." Bidge paused when she saw something small and gray moving on the grass underneath a tree between the sidewalk and the road. "Hey, look at that!"

It was a baby bird, a robin, covered with the scraggly silver-gray fluff that robins have before they grow their feathers. It had to be less than a week old. Toby frantically looked up into the tree and spotted the nest, about fifteen feet up.

"He must have fallen out," Toby said.

"Or maybe *she* was pushed out," Bidge replied, "sometimes the birds will do that if there's something wrong with the baby."

Toby angrily spun around toward Bidge. "Don't say that!" His eyes were filled with panic and rage, but almost immediately melted into a look of deep sadness and pleading. "What should we do? We have to do *something*."

Bidge understood. "Here, give me a boost up to the first branch." Bidge had always had superior climbing skills, which had won her the nickname "Tarzan" for a while in the first grade. The nickname was accompanied by frequent offers of bananas, which although intended as teasing, was actually fine with her since she liked bananas.

Toby meshed his fingers together and lifted Bidge's left foot up so that she could reach the first branch. She then deftly swung herself up so that she was crouching on the first branch while holding onto the second branch with her right hand. She then held down her left hand and said, "Okay, hand me the bird."

He took a notebook out of his backpack and removed a piece of paper. He put the paper on the ground next to the bird and using the notebook, gingerly rolled the bird onto the paper to avoid passing any human scent. It seemed so fragile and helpless. He picked the paper up by its four corners, reached up and handed it gently to Bidge. "Be careful with *him*."

"No worries." Bidge then climbed up the remaining two branches and slid the bird back in its nest with two other identical-looking babies. She then swung back down and dismounted from the lowest branch, sticking a perfect landing on the grass next to Toby. "Mission accomplished."

Toby was quiet and still shaken by the experience as they walked the rest of the remaining short distance to school. He really had a thing about abandoned baby animals. He was relieved that Tarzan had been right there on the scene to provide the victim with ground-to-nest delivery. And Tarzan seemed happy to have been of service.

▲ ▲ ▲

Toby and Marc sat at the same table that day at lunch, but Bidge sat with her basketball team instead. The season had just ended, but sometimes the team still sat together in the cafeteria.

"I think Bidge is mad at me."

"Duh," replied Marc. "I'm mad at you, too, Choatie-boy. The only reason I'm sitting here with you is because my only other

friends are the computer club guys, and I don't want them to tarnish my lunchtime image of coolness."

Marc picked his nose with his pinky finger as he said that last part. Toby assumed that it was just for ironic effect, but decided not to comment — in case it wasn't.

As he recounted his previous day's experience at Choate, Toby was grateful that at least *Marc* could appreciate his description of the campus tour. He was especially interested in the awesome computer lab. Toby also told him about the new job with Mr. Leonard and how successfully Leonard had managed Choate's endowment. Toby was gratified that Marc also did not know what an endowment was, and needed it to be explained.

"It's like a person's retirement savings account, but instead of a person, it's a non-profit charity or a school," Toby explained.

"Why would a school need to retire?"

"Well, it wouldn't I guess." Toby looked up at the ceiling, searching in his mind for the right words to explain it. Finding them, his gaze came back down and refocused on Marc. "Why does your dad have a retirement account?"

"So that when he gets old enough, he won't have to work anymore."

"How old?"

"I dunno, like 65 or something."

"So what happens if he turns 65 and still doesn't have enough money saved?"

"He'd have to keep working, I guess."

"Right. What if he has enough money to retire at age 55 instead of 65?"

"Then I guess he could retire early."

"Exactly. So he can retire as soon as his *endowment* is large enough for him to live on the investment income. It's not really about age, it's about freedom, dude. That means not having to trust or depend on anyone else. It's the same thing with schools."

"You lost me there at that last part."

"Private schools save up an endowment over the years. A lot of it comes from donations from former students who strike it rich. The goal is to accumulate an endowment so large that the interest and dividends from it are enough to run the school. Then the school is financially independent and doesn't have to necessarily worry about the number of students that attend and how much tuition they pay."

"Got it. So how much did you say they were earning on their investments each year?"

"Fourteen percent," Toby replied.

"Fourteen percent per year?" Marc repeated curiously, "I don't know a whole lot about investing, but it seems like my dad is really happy when his retirement account grows by just nine or ten percent. Mr. Leonard must be really good. I wonder how he does it."

Marc was right. Fourteen percent growth, year after year was astoundingly good. Toby had casually wondered about this himself, but now with Marc also finding it strange, Toby's curiosity had become overwhelming.

"Hmm. That's actually a really good question. I don't know how he does it, but since I have access to all the records, it shouldn't be too difficult to figure out what he's doing."

"When you discover his secret to success, let me know so I can tell my dad."

Mr. Leonard was clearly a world-class investment manager. Toby was anxious to get back to the office as soon as possible to start learning his secrets to success. Toby donned a crooked smile as he considered whether Mr. Leonard might keep his investment secrets in that bottom drawer of the filing cabinet. *Maybe that's why he doesn't want me looking in there...*

CHAPTER 16

No One Helps Me Around Here

As Bidge walked home that afternoon, she passed that same tree with the robin's nest. Looking down on the ground, she noticed that the baby bird was right there in the same spot again. This time, though, it was dead.

Bidge stopped and just stared at the small gray motionless lump for a few seconds. Then she looked up at the nest and watched the mother and father robin feeding worms to the two eager babies that remained, like nothing had happened. Anger toward the mother and father robins welled up inside her and threatened to boil over, like a pot of macaroni on a stove that's turned up too high. How could they treat death so casually? She thought they should at least be acting depressed or something.

Bidge looked away and gathered her thoughts for a moment. Then she looked down again at the dead bird. She knew she had to be strong and responsible, like everyone expected her to be. She stooped down and matter-of-factly picked up the dead bird and carried it home. The bird was so small that she could tenderly carry it unseen in her left fist, not quite closed. It felt gross, like a hairy baggie full of jelly, all soft and squishy, except for the beak. After taking care of three unsupervised brothers for so long, it took a lot for Bidge to get grossed out. When Bidge arrived home, she dropped her backpack and the two plastic grocery bags on the front steps and went around the house, grabbing a small shovel out of the shed on the way. She walked up to the old Norway Maple tree in the backyard and looked up into its massive and twisted branches. That tree was always first to get its leaves every year. Though Spring was still only a few weeks old, the maple tree was already covered in large green leaves, but its oak tree neighbors had barely started budding.

Bidge sank her shovel into the soil and pulled up a large clump of sod along with three or four inches of the topsoil underneath. She dropped the bird unceremoniously into the hole, stared frowningly at it for a few seconds, and then filled the hole back up, carefully replacing the grassy sod on the top. She could barely tell where the hole had been. *There's no reason Toby needs to know about this.*

And she never told him.

She put away the shovel, and returned to the front steps where she had left her bags. "Mom! I'm home!" Bidge yelled as she came in the back door of the Donnelly home. She yelled that every day when she got home, but if an answer came, she never heard it. Her mom had become a permanent fixture in the family room, just sitting in her dead husband's comfortable reclining chair watching television. She'd been doing that for two years now, ever since the accident.

Bidge set the two plastic bags of groceries on the counter. She stopped at the store every day to buy milk and whatever else she needed to make the meals. Before putting the groceries away, she went to the sink and washed her hands with anti-bacterial soap for exactly fifteen seconds.

"What's for dinner?" Joey was the youngest of her three big brothers. He was a year older than Bidge, but seemed a year younger.

"Lasagna," Bidge replied. She looked around the kitchen disapprovingly. "This place is a total disaster. You guys never pick up after yourselves. Can you help me clean up the kitchen for a minute?"

"Can't. Still doing my homework." Joey grabbed a slice of bread and disappeared down the hall into his room.

"No one helps me around here," Bidge mumbled as she put the frozen lasagna in the oven and started cleaning the kitchen. Within ten minutes it was spotless and completely disinfected. Bidge's mom used to keep the house clean, but that was before the car accident that changed everything.

It was a snowy night two years ago, when they were on their way home from a dance recital. Lauren, Bidge's older sister, as usual, was the star of the show. She was naturally graceful and beautiful like her mom had been in earlier years, before having five kids and then ceasing all physical activity. Her mom and brothers had left a few minutes earlier in the other car. Bidge waited in the lobby with her dad for Lauren to finish changing into her street clothes. Bidge and Lauren could not have been more different. Bidge was daddy's girl. She was tough, athletic and full of energy, just like him. Lauren, on the other hand, had inherited from her mother all the genes for beauty, grace, and talent. But *everyone* loved Lauren, especially Bidge.

She could never quite remember clearly what happened next. She was riding home with her Dad and Lauren. One second they were alive and chatting about the performance. The next second, they were gone. The roads were slick that night and a truck slid past the stop sign and smashed into the driver's side of their car. Her dad was in the driver's seat and Lauren was on that same side of the car, but in the back seat. Bidge was also in the back seat, but on the other side, relatively safe from the impact.

Ever since that terrible night, Bidge had never seen her mom smile. They never talked about it. Bidge was pretty sure that her mom was still mad at her for being the one that survived. In that one fateful second, Bidge lost her dad, her sister, and for the most part, even her mom. But she was daddy's tough little girl, so she stepped up and took care of the family the best she knew how. Being busy helped her heart to heal. But her mother had a hole in her soul that even daytime television couldn't fill. The hole seemed to keep getting bigger.

Bidge didn't know else what to do about it, so she cleaned the house.

CHAPTER 17

The Unexpected Statement of Karl Marx

IT WAS ANOTHER UNSEASONABLY warm afternoon in late spring and Toby deeply inhaled the smell of freshly cut grass as he rode his bike onto the Choate campus. The rich green of the great lawn was dotted with the occasional golden dandelion, which while being a great annoyance to the groundskeeping staff, nevertheless succeeded in giving the place a warm, homey feel. Three days passed since Toby had been to the office. He was eager for the chance to get back in there to continue his study of the Choate financials.

Toby chained his bike to the handicapped parking sign and went inside. Mrs. Krebbs was at her desk in the lobby, looking like she had never moved from that spot in four days. He could have sworn she was wearing that same dress the last time. Toby wondered if maybe she lived in a box right there behind the desk.

"Hello there, Toby! It's good to see you again."

"Hi, Mrs. Krebbs. How are you today?"

"Just fine, thanks for asking. Don't work too hard up there, now." Mrs. Krebbs turned her attention back to the crossword puzzle on her desk.

Toby bounded up the stairs and unlocked Mr. Leonard's office. It was exactly as Toby had left it four days earlier. If Mr. Leonard had been here during that time, then he hadn't left any sign of it. Toby walked over to the desk and picked up the statue of Julius Nepos. To Toby's surprise, the laurel crown was perfect, with absolutely no sign of the broken leaf. Mrs. Krebbs must have repaired it herself. He was quite impressed that she had even been able to find the broken leaf. He thought he had hidden it well. He set the statue down carefully in its rightful place and walked over to the filing cabinet.

Resisting the temptation to look in the bottom drawer, Toby opened the top drawer instead and returned to the annual reports folder. He pulled it out and took it over to the desk, where he sat down and clicked on the silver lamp so he could see a little better. Toby flipped through the reports a year at a time. It was pretty boring stuff, since all the other years were mostly the same as the most recent year, which he had reviewed last time. The numbers were slightly different, but not much. The values of the assets had been steadily increasing. Other than that, each report was nearly identical to all the others.

"No secrets to success here," Toby mused.

He replaced the annual reports folder and grabbed the next folder, marked *Real Estate*. This file had lists of Choate's real estate holdings that, besides the campus itself, included both commercial and residential investment properties. There were statements from the property managers detailing the rental income and expenses. Most of the properties were in the Wallingford area, but a few were elsewhere, such as a commercial property in New York City that had a sickeningly high value but apparently no rental income. For the most part, however, the real estate portion of Choate's investment portfolio was solid, reliable and boring. The asset values had climbed slowly but steadily over the past several years, and the rental income likewise.

He found the next folder much more interesting. It was marked *Securities*. Toby had learned from years of reading *The Wall Street Journal* that securities were easily traded stocks and bonds. The Choate investment portfolio had both. Lots of them. The school had over one hundred million dollars in stocks and somewhat less in bonds.

"Holy cow." Toby was having a hard time getting used to numbers that large.

The stocks were all sitting in an account at a Wall Street brokerage firm. Toby recognized the name of the firm as the same one Mr. Leonard worked for downtown, *Legio Investments*. Toby moved down to the second drawer in the filing cabinet where all the statements resided. He thumbed through the tabs until he found the folder for Legio, then pulled it out and sat down at the desk.

There was a statement from Legio Investments for each month for the last several years. Each statement documented the starting and ending balance for that month, as well as any stock trades and dividends paid during that month.

Toby knew that a portfolio of blue chip stocks like that should grow at a steady, but modest rate. Seven percent would be respectable. Mr. Leonard, however, was doing much better than that, so there had to be a good reason. Or a bad reason. Either way, Toby was determined to find out.

"Lookee here," Toby said. Each month there had been a couple of stock trades that accounted for the exceptional performance. In the previous month's statement, which was for March, there were two trades on the 17th of the month. In the morning, all of Choate's 23,000 shares of one particular blue-chip stock were sold. They were repurchased later that same day at a price that was $1.15 per share lower.

"Wow. That was a lucky move," Toby said, still talking to himself, "23,000 times $1.15 equals $26,450. Not a bad profit for one day!" As he looked through the other statements, there were at least one or two similar trades each month. There were a few times when Mr. Leonard had apparently guessed wrong and there was a small loss, but the vast majority of these same-day trades were significantly profitable.

Toby was impressed. Mr. Leonard seemed to have an uncanny ability to know when to buy and sell. "Maybe he's like me, but can predict movements of individual stocks, not just the market as a whole." Toby liked the idea that someone else possessed a similar ability. The idea made him feel a little less lonely.

He looked at his watch. It was getting late, so he gathered up the statements to put them back in the Legio file. As he did so, he noticed that the statement from February had an extra page stuck to the back that clearly didn't belong in that file. It was a statement from CheapTrade, an online discount brokerage. The name on the account was:

Karl Marx
P. O. Box 18180505
Wallingford, CT 86492

Toby laughed out loud. "This guy has the same name as the father of socialism. That's gotta totally suck for him." Toby also noticed that in the upper right hand corner was written in pencil *Porsche 356.*

The brokerage account had a little more than one hundred thousand dollars in cash, but no stocks. Toby saw that on the

147

afternoon of February 10th, Marx purchased the exact same stock as Leonard had done for Choate, and at approximately the same time. He sold it early the next day for a small profit.

"That can't be a coincidence," thought Toby. He wondered if this Marx guy was giving stock tips to Leonard, or maybe vice-versa. He made a mental note to ask Mr. Leonard about it next time he saw him. He put the CheapTrade statement back in its original place in the pile of Legio statements, then put the folder back in the filing cabinet.

It was already 6:00 p.m. and, feeling tired and hungry, Toby headed home for the evening. Mrs. Krebbs had already left for the day, proving that she didn't live there in a box. Toby was relieved. He didn't feel like talking to anyone, so he was glad that the other employees apparently left work promptly at five. He rode home on his bike with a furrowed brow, distracted by the day's events. He had gone there today specifically seeking answers to Leonard's success, but left with even more questions than he started with.

▲ ▲ ▲

Toby told Marc about Karl Marx.

"Man, that guy must get a lot of teasing," Marc said, "I think I would change my name if I were him."

"Yeah, me too. I wonder if his parents were communists or something. A guy can only take so much teasing about something like that."

Toby and Marc looked in the online white pages to see where he lived, and maybe make a prank call if they got up enough courage. There was no Karl Marx listed anywhere around Wallingford.

"Maybe he's unlisted, because of dorks like us," Marc suggested. That sounded reasonable so they called 411. There was no listing anywhere in Connecticut or New York for Karl Marx.

Marc tried every directory he could find online and encountered dead-ends at every turn. As the challenge continued to grow, he became increasingly determined. "Toby, what was that post office box number, again?"

"What do you mean 'again'? I don't recall actually giving it to you."

"Whatever. Do you remember it or not?" Marc already knew the answer to this question, of course. He knew quite well that Toby never, ever forgot a number. Ever. He still knew the combination to every bike lock he had ever owned.

"99840."

Marc wrote the number on his hand with a pen. "All righty then. You just leave it to me and I'll find our mystery man Marx."

Toby squinted his eyes into narrow slits. "What are you going to do, exactly?" Marc had a prior history of questionable computer-related activities.

"Never you mind about that. It's probably better if you don't know, anyway. Plausible deniability and all." Marc motioned toward the door, indicating that Toby was dismissed. "I'll let you know if I find anything."

Once Marc was on a quest, there was no stopping him. And now since Mr. Marx clearly did not want to be found, Marc was compelled to find him *at all costs*. So with nothing left to do, Toby went home.

It took fewer than ten minutes to walk home from Marc's house. Toby walked in the back door and yelled, "I'm home!"

"Oh, there you are, Toby," FM10 replied, walking into the kitchen from the living room. "I was just looking for you. Marc called just now and he sounded quite anxious to talk to you."

So soon? That didn't take long. "Okey dokey." Toby picked up the phone and called Marc.

"Hello?"

"Hey, Marcos, what's up?"

"You can quit the innocent act anytime now." Marc sounded mad.

"What are you talking about?"

"You know what I'm talking about. It's bad enough that you played your little practical joke on me, but you crossed the line with this one. I could have been in serious trouble over this. You can be such a real jerk sometimes."

It was true that Toby did, in fact, enjoy being a jerk sometimes, but he still had no clue what Marc was talking about. "Dude, I'm still lost here. What did I do?"

"I checked out the post office box number you gave me to find out who it's rented to."

"How'd you do *that?*"

"Never mind about that. The important thing is that it wasn't rented by anyone named Karl Marx."

"Who then?"

"It was rented by Tobias Gold."

Toby was silent for several seconds while he processed this information. All he could say was, "Are you serious?" Maybe Marc was the one playing the practical joke.

"Sit tight, I'm coming over." Marc hung up the phone.

Toby didn't know what to think. Somebody had rented a post office box in his name. A long dead communist philosopher had received at least one stock brokerage statement at that address. What was he *supposed* to think in a situation like this?

Once Marc arrived at Toby's house, they spent several minutes convincing each other that they weren't playing a practical joke. Once beyond that, Toby and Marc concluded that Mr. Leonard was somehow involved in something questionable. The brokerage statement was in his files. The statement even had "Porsche 356" written on it, which was the kind of car that Mr. Leonard drove.

"But why? Why would he use your name like that?"

"I don't know, but we're definitely going to find out." Toby was relieved that he hadn't asked Mr. Leonard yet about the stray Karl Marx statement he found in the Legio file, as he had been planning to do.

Toby went back to the trustee's office the next afternoon, right after walking the dogs. He first checked the Legio file. "Good, the Marx statement is still there," he said to himself. He quickly committed the account number to memory and then put the file back. For the next two hours, Toby scanned through the entire remainder of the filing cabinet, looking for any mention of himself or Marx. Nothing.

But there was still the bottom drawer.

Tentatively, he reached down and pulled the handle, slowly opening the bottom drawer. To his surprise, he found it completely empty, except for a single piece of note paper.

Dear Toby,

If you are reading this note, it means that you are not as trustworthy as I had hoped.

Sincerely,

Jack Leonard

Admittedly, Toby felt badly about it. But not nearly as bad as he would have felt a few days ago before his opinion of Mr. Leonard had soured. He called Marc at home from the phone on Mr. Leonard's desk. "Okay, there's nothing else here about me or Marx. What now?"

Marc replied, "He must have left that brokerage statement in there by accident. Where else do you think he might keep stuff like that?"

"My only guess would be his other two offices, the one in New York or the one at his house."

"We need to see those files," Marc said.

"Well, I don't know where his New York office is, but his home office is no problem. I have the access code. I'll check it out tomorrow when I go over there to walk the dogs."

CHAPTER 18

Hitler's Dog

Toby covered his face with his forearms in a futile attempt to protect himself from the merciless lashings being delivered in rapid succession from the two fur-covered whips. These two particular furry whips, however, each happened to be attached to a golden retriever's butt. As always, Max and Ginnie were beside themselves with joy to see Toby. Whereas most dogs just wag their tails, Max and Ginnie wagged their entire bodies. It was impressive that they could do that and not fall over. Max shimmied his way to Toby and dropped a slimy tennis ball at his feet. But Toby looked at the dogs a little differently now. If their owner was evil, were the dogs evil, too?

"Nah." Toby dismissed that thought almost as soon as it came. Golden retrievers were genetically incapable of evil. Toby then gave them both a big hug. They liked that. Then again, they were golden retrievers, so they liked everything.

"Okay, guys, I'll take you outside in a little while. There's something I need to do first."

Toby went into Mr. Leonard's study and sat down in the big leather chair behind the desk. The computer was already turned on, so he quickly checked his email. No messages. The desk had a large file drawer on each side. His heart was racing and his hands were shaking as he opened the one on the left. Toby wasn't accustomed to being sneaky, even under extreme circumstances. He was incurably honest. Even the bottom drawer incident had left him thoroughly shaken and feeling very guilty.

All the files in the left drawer were for personal bank statements, utility bills, mortgage, car loans, and other stuff like that. "I guess even evil people need to pay their bills," Toby mused. He conjured up an image in his head of Adolf Hitler, at his desk paying his utility bills with his dog Blondi at his feet. According to history, Hitler's dog Blondi was a German shepherd. Toby figured that if she had been a golden retriever like Ginnie, maybe Hitler would have turned out less evil. Not that German shepherds were inherently evil — Toby was certain that there must be lots of friendly ones out there. But in the back of his mind he also knew that there must be a good reason why he had never seen a golden retriever as a police dog.

He closed that drawer, swiveled his chair clockwise, and opened the drawer on the right.

His eyes were immediately drawn to a big fat file folder in the middle marked *Stock Accounts*. Toby pulled it out and plopped it down on the desk.

"Bingo."

The folder was filled with brokerage account statements. Each of them had only been open for a few months. They were in alphabetical order starting with David Hume and ending with Adam Smith. Karl Marx was about two-thirds of the way through, but he was missing one of his statements. Toby knew where that one was.

"I've heard some of these names before," Toby said out loud. He couldn't remember where, so he scooted over in front of Mr. Leonard's computer and did an online search for the first few names on the list.

"They're *all* famous dead economists!" Toby exclaimed. Max lifted his head and looked at Toby. "What do you think it means, Max?"

Max tilted his head to the side and went back to chewing on the tennis ball pinned between his paws.

There were a total of twenty-four bogus brokerage accounts, each of them with approximately $100,000 in cash... no stocks, no bonds. All of them had the mailing address of P.O. Box 99840 — the mailbox in Wallingford rented in Toby's name.

Toby put the statements back in the file folder and replaced the folder in the cabinet. He pulled out the next folder, which was labeled "TG."

The pit of his stomach sank as he realized that "TG" stood for Toby Gold. The file was all about him. Hospital records, report cards, social worker reports were all in there, some dated as recently as two weeks ago. Toby also found his passport in there, which was particularly surprising because Toby didn't even own a passport. He had never been outside the tri-state area, let alone outside the country. The picture in the passport was definitely Toby. It looked a lot like his school picture from last year, but with a different background — plain white instead of that splotchy gray background that the school normally used for those types of pictures.

Even though he had planned to leave everything as he had found it, Toby was so bothered that someone else had a passport made in his name that he took it out of the file and put it in his pocket. *Toby Gold is the only person that should have a Toby Gold passport*, he thought defiantly.

Toby's hands were shaking now. He couldn't help it. The last item in the file was another online stock brokerage statement. The name on this one was none other than 'Tobias Gold' and the address was that very same post office box. Toby looked at the statement balance. Unlike the other accounts, this one had a balance of $250,000.

"$250,000! I'm rich!" Toby said sarcastically — and out loud. Max looked up again and wagged his tail. Under normal circumstances, a sudden discovery of a quarter-million dollars in an account in his own name would have been a happy event for Toby. Under these circumstances, however, it just made him feel like throwing up. For Toby, Mr. Leonard was the first grown-up that had ever believed in him or given him a chance. He wanted there to be a good explanation for all this.

Toby felt confused and powerless, and he didn't like that. Confused and powerless had been the story of his life. Five minutes ago, he had a good job and a bright future for the first time in his life. Now, once again, he was back to confused and powerless. *Great.*

As he placed the statement back in the file, he noticed that *Porsche 356* had been written in the upper right hand corner of this statement, just as it had been on the Karl Marx statement. He paused for a second, thinking that was a strange coincidence, then closed the folder and put it back in the drawer. He quickly checked his email on Leonard's computer. Marc had promised to email him if he found out anything else about the post office box. No messages.

"C'mon Max, let's find Ginnie and go for a walk."

Max jumped up and ran to the front door, where Ginnie was asleep on the rug. Jostled from her peaceful nap, Ginnie also sprang to her feet, ready for the highlight of their day. Toby hooked the dogs up to their leashes and headed out the door as quickly as possible, startling several crows that had been foraging on the front lawn. The Leonard house was giving him the creeps, and he just wanted to get out of there. Seeing the birds, Max and Ginnie immediately gave chase, which came to an abrupt conclusion less than a second later when their retractable leashes reached the end of the spools.

Toby took the dogs on a longer walk than usual that day, which was perfectly fine with Max and Ginnie. Toby's mind was racing, trying to put all the pieces together. He did his best thinking while walking.

Why are all the accounts under fake names? Why do they all have the same address, registered to me? Why does Mr. Leonard have a brokerage account and a passport in my name?

None of it made sense.

When Toby arrived back at the Leonard house with the dogs, he had no more idea of what was going on than when he started. He entered his code on the door and walked in with Max and Ginnie.

"Hello Toby." Toby just about jumped out of his skin. It was Mr. Leonard.

"Geez, you scared me. I didn't know anyone was home."

"I just got here a few minutes ago. Toby, have you been in my study?"

Toby froze. *He knows.* At that point, Toby probably should have just said something like, *Yeah, I was checking my email before I took the dogs out.* That would have been the smart thing to do. Instead Toby lied, something he never did intentionally.

"No, sir. Why do you ask?" Toby was a really bad liar and could never get away with it. Today was no exception. He immediately felt awful about lying to Mr. Leonard — even though his reasons were good.

Mr. Leonard looked at Toby for a moment without saying anything. "I couldn't help noticing the chair is in a different position than when I left this morning. No big deal. It was probably just my wife."

Now Mr. Leonard was the one who was lying. It was written all over his face.

"Well, I better be going," Toby said. He was relieved that his lame lie apparently had gone undetected.

"Good to see you again, Toby," Mr. Leonard replied. "I'm sure I'll be seeing you again very soon."

Toby wasn't sure he liked the tone in Mr. Leonard's voice when he said that.

▲ ▲ ▲

Toby went directly to Marc's house. He had a lot of new information, but so far had not been able to make any sense of it. Clearly Mr. Leonard was up to something bad, but he could not figure out what it was.

"There's a whole file folder full of stock brokerage statements for fictional investors. They're all being sent to my post office box. Plus there's a big fat account in my name, and a passport." Toby pulled out the passport and showed it to Marc.

Marc took Toby's passport and flipped through it. "Looks real enough to me, but let's compare it with mine." Marc disappeared back to his room for a minute, and then came back with his own. "This is my passport. I used it last summer when my family went to El Salvador to visit my cousins. Let's compare."

Toby and Marc examined each page of both passports, one at a time, to see if they could detect any obvious differences. After a few minutes, Toby declared, "I'm no expert, but they look the same to me."

Marc nodded. "Agreed. Yours is either real, or an extremely good fake."

"Yeah, but the question is, why does he have a passport for *me*?"

Marc held a passport in each hand and looked up at Toby. "I don't know, but it can't be anything good."

"There's probably a perfectly reasonable explanation, and we're making a big deal out of nothing. Maybe he's just planning on taking me on a trip and he wanted it to be a surprise."

Marc rolled his eyes and set the passports aside. "What about the brokerage statements? Did you get copies?"

"No, I didn't think about that. There was a copy machine sitting right there, too."

"Do you remember any of the account numbers?" Marc asked.

Toby was a little annoyed that Marc would automatically assume that he would be able to casually recall a ten-digit account number that he had only seen once. Even more annoying was the fact that Marc was right. "I remember the first one. It was for David Hume." Toby rattled off the account number while Marc wrote it down in his notebook. "I'm not sure what good that does us, though. We don't have the password."

"One step at a time, my friend." Marc pulled up the brokerage site on his computer and punched in the account number. "Okay, Mr. Leonard's got dozens of these accounts, right?"

"Right."

"And you didn't find a big list of passwords anywhere, right?"

"Right." Toby didn't see where Marc was going with this.

"So it would be reasonable to assume that Leonard is using the same password for all these accounts — probably something easy to remember. What's his wife's name?"

"Ummm...Mrs. Leonard."

Marc gave him a dirty look.

"Well, I don't know her first name. She never told me."

"How about kids. What are their names?"

"I don't think that they have kids."

Marc was getting frustrated at the lack of progress. "You walk their dogs, right? What are the dogs' names?"

"Max and Ginnie."

"Okay, 'Max' is too short to be a password. Let's try 'Ginnie'." Marc typed in the word 'Ginnie' and hit the *Enter* key. *Invalid Username/Password* was the response. Marc sighed.

"What now?" Toby asked.

"I doubt we're going to be able to guess the password before the site locks us out. In most systems, you usually only get three tries before the account gets flagged that someone might be trying to break in. Most of these financial institutions have pretty good security and require a strong password — one that has both letters and numbers." Marc sat back in his chair and folded his arms.

"Letters and numbers," Toby mused. He was racking his brain trying to think of a combination of letters and numbers that might be significant to Mr. Leonard. He sat down on Marc's bed and put his face down into his hands. The possibilities were endless, so the chances of guessing right, and within three tries, were pretty much zero.

Marc and Toby sat that way, in silence, for what seemed like several minutes.

Gradually, a smile crept across his face. Toby started laughing.

Marc stared at him. "I'm glad you're enjoying this, old sport, because I'm certainly not."

"I've got something for you to try," Toby said, "how about *Porsche356.*"

"Not to sound like an idiot or anything, but since we only have two more tries left, could you remind me how to spell that?" Marc wasn't into cars like Toby was.

"P-o-r-s-c-h-e-3-5-6"

"Glad I asked. I would have left out the 'c.'" Marc typed it all in, paused for a moment, and pressed the *Enter* key.

The computer thought about it for several seconds, then returned with the message, *Welcome back, David.*

"YES!" Toby and Marc yelled simultaneously, and then gave each other a congratulatory high-five.

"Okay, we're in. So now what?" asked Toby.

"I dunno," Marc replied, "you're the financial wizard here. What do *you* think we should do?"

"Move over, I'll drive."

Marc vacated the seat in front of the computer and Toby sat down and started clicking through the account setup screens. "It looks like this is set up as a margin account, not a cash account," Toby said.

Marc stood there with a blank expression.

Toby perceived Marc's lack of familiarity with stock trading lingo. "A cash trading account is one where you can only buy stock up to the value of the money you deposit in the account. A margin account lets you buy more stock than that by letting you borrow extra money for that purpose."

"Why would anyone borrow money to buy stock?"

"It only makes sense if you absolutely know for a fact that you're right about the stock you're buying — so it's very risky. If you buy stock on margin and then the stock goes up, you can sell the stock at a profit, pay back the loan, and then keep the extra profit. On the other hand, if the stock goes down after you buy it, then you might be forced to sell and be stuck for a huge loss after paying back the loan. So buying stock on margin will make both your gains and your losses much bigger than normal."

"So, your buddy David Hume likes taking risks," Marc said.

"He's not my buddy. He's been dead for over two hundred years."

Marc smiled. "I just figured since you're getting his mail, you must be friends."

"Very funny."

"Too bad you didn't get the other account numbers. Are you sure you can't remember any of the others? I'd sure like to test my theory that Mr. Leonard is using the same password for all of them."

"I think I might be able to remember the number on the account that was in *my* name. I didn't actually pay attention to the account number, but I did look at the page for a good minute or so."

Toby sat back in the chair and closed his eyes. He tried to picture the brokerage statement in his mind. He could see the dollar amounts in his head quite clearly, but the account number was hazy, up in the right hand corner. "Marc, grab a pencil and paper and write this down. I'm going to say the number three different times, so write it down three times. Don't read it back to me or say the numbers. Just listen and write."

Marc was about to ask why they had to do it three times, but instead decided to just shut up and write the numbers.

Toby's eyes were still closed. The first time, he said each of the ten digits slowly, with a longer pause between digits six and seven. The second and third time he said the numbers much faster. After the third time, he opened his eyes and turned to Marc.

"So how did I do?"

Marc replied, "Well, the first and the third time, you gave exactly the same numbers. The second time was slightly different. You switched the third and fourth digits with each other."

"Let's assume that the first and third ones are right, then. Let me see that paper."

Marc handed Toby the paper. He navigated to the login screen and typed in the account number and used "Porsche356" as the password again.

Welcome back, Tobias.

Toby cringed. He hated the name Tobias, which is why he always went by Toby. The thing that stunk most was that even though he didn't know what his real name was, he was 100% certain that it *wasn't* Tobias. This meant that he had to suffer with that name for no good reason. The county had initially assumed his name was Tobias since it was written on a piece of paper in the green handbag in which he had been found on the train that night. It eventually turned out that the handbag had been stolen from a luggage shop at Penn Station, and that Tobias was just the name of the handbag quality inspector. By the time they figured that out, of course, the name "Baby Tobias" had already stuck. So far, Toby had come up with over three hundred first names that he preferred. He kept a list in the back of his journal. The names "Steve" and "Ben" were number one and two on his list.

In five more years he would be an adult, and he would get a judge to legally change his name to something more normal.

This brokerage account was set up the same way as the one for David Hume. It was authorized for margin trading, as well as electronically authorized wire transfers in and out of the account. Money could be transferred instantly in and out of the account with a click of the mouse and the password.

"That's a lot of money." Marc was looking over his shoulder.

"Uh huh." Toby agreed. "Do you think I should change the password on my account?"

"But the account isn't really yours."

Marc was right. It was in Toby's name, but the money wasn't really Toby's. He didn't know who it really belonged to.

"Besides," continued Marc, "if we change the password, then Mr. Leonard will know we've been in there. And it wouldn't do any good to change it anyway, since he could just call the brokerage and have the password reset to something else. We'd be locked out then. It's better to stay under the radar for the time being."

As usual, Marc was right. They left all the passwords as Porsche356.

"We need to get the rest of those account numbers. The next time I'm alone at the Leonards' house I'll make copies." Although that sounded like a simple task, it turned out to be easier said than done.

▲　▲　▲

According to plan, the next day after school Toby rode his bike straight to the Leonards' house. He let himself in as usual, but was surprised to find Mrs. Leonard home, in the kitchen. She was dressed in jeans and a T-shirt and was wrapping a dinner plate and carefully placing it into a packing box.

"Oh. Hi, Mrs. Leonard," Toby said abruptly. "I didn't expect to see you here so early."

Mrs. Leonard turned toward Toby. Her eyes were red and puffy like she had been crying recently. "Hello, Toby. The dogs are out back." She grabbed another plate from the open cabinet and started wrapping it.

"Is something wrong? What's with all the boxes?"

164

"No, Toby, nothing's wrong." Her shaky voice contradicted her words. "We're having some major renovations done on the house, so we have to move out for a while."

"For how long?

"At least three months," Mrs. Leonard replied, staring at her shoes.

"Are you staying somewhere here in Wallingford?"

"No, we're renting a place closer to the city. We're going there to decide between two houses tomorrow afternoon. We'll have our stuff moved there this weekend."

"I guess you won't need my dog-walking services anymore." Toby said sadly. He would miss Max and Ginnie. He had never had a dog before, and he had started to think of them as his own.

"I'm afraid not," Mrs. Leonard said. Then she hastily added, "Not until we come back, anyway."

Toby got the distinct impression, however, that they weren't coming back.

Mrs. Leonard walked over to where her purse was sitting on the kitchen desk. "Tell you what, since this is all so sudden, I'll go ahead and pay you for the rest of the month, but after today there's no need to come back."

"Thanks, but I can still come back the rest of this week and walk the dogs until you actually leave."

"No!" Mrs. Leonard snapped, then immediately softened her expression. She placed her hands on Toby's shoulders. "It's better if you don't come back. Trust me."

"Have I done something wrong, Mrs. Leonard?"

Her eyes moistened again, like she was about to cry. "No, Toby, you've been absolutely perfect. You've done nothing wrong. It's just dangerous for you here…"

Toby looked startled.

"...you know, with all the boxes and furniture stacked up and all," Mrs. Leonard hastily added. "It's just better that you're not walking around here alone during the move."

"I understand."

Toby understood more than Mrs. Leonard knew. It was clear that something bad was happening, and Mrs. Leonard was trying to warn him to stay away.

Toby tried to act natural, but wasn't quite sure how to do that. "Thanks for everything. I'll take the dogs out for their walk now." He gave Mrs. Leonard a hug. It just seemed like the right thing to do. She held him tight for a second, then let go and went back to packing.

Toby went out to the garage to get the leashes. The next to last bay was already stacked high with packing boxes, so that the Porsche was barely visible behind it. With the leashes in hand, he went out the side door to the garage to get Max and Ginnie from the backyard.

The dogs immediately tackled him, showing their joy with much less restraint than they normally did inside the house. Their licking was as relentless as it was slobbery.

Laughing and thoroughly slimed, Toby got up and tossed them the tennis ball a few times in the backyard before starting their last walk together. A murder of crows watched the backyard activities from the maple tree high above, well out of reach of the bird-loving retrievers.

Mrs. Leonard secretly watched the playful scene from the kitchen window, sobbing as if she were watching a funeral.

CHAPTER 19

The Meeting

SINCE MRS. LEONARD HAD been unexpectedly at home, Toby didn't stay to watch the end-of-day stock ticker there. As he was walking home along Center Street, a dark green pickup truck pulled up beside him and screeched to a stop. The man inside reached over and popped open the passenger side door. It was Earl, the bus driver.

"Hi, Toby. You need to get in, right now. I can't explain it to you here, but it's very important that you come with me."

Toby took two steps backwards. He knew he wasn't supposed to get into a stranger's car, but he couldn't decide whether Earl counted as a stranger or not. Since he didn't know Earl's last name, he decided to play it safe. "I-I think I should ask my foster parents first," Toby stammered.

Earl used his most reassuring tone of voice. "I understand your concern Toby. I really do. But there's no time to ask permission. You have to trust me."

But Toby didn't. He took another step backward, looking around for the best escape route.

Earl had clearly lost the argument. He sighed and moved his arm slightly toward Toby and closed his fist as though grabbing

something. Toby felt something invisible grab his belt buckle —
even though Earl was still at least ten feet away from him. Toby,
confused, looked up at Earl and said, "Hey!"

Earl yanked his fist back toward himself. Toby's feet slid along
the ground toward the truck and then he popped up into the
passenger seat. The door of the truck slammed shut and locked,
seemingly under its own power. Earl put the truck in gear and
sped away.

Toby sat in silence for a few seconds before he found the
courage to speak. "H-How did you *do* that?" he asked. "I wasn't
anywhere near you, but you pulled me into the truck."

"Criminy," Earl lamented. "That wasn't supposed to happen.
But you looked like you were about to bolt, and I couldn't let you
do that. It would have ruined everything."

"Are you going to kill me?" Toby asked, barely whispering.

"Kill you!" Earl laughed. "I'm the last person on earth that
would hurt you in any way, you little potlicker! Who do you
think has been protecting you these past twelve years?"

"Huh?" Toby was completely confused. "But you're just my
bus driver."

"And today I'm your personal chauffeur," Earl replied with a
chuckle, but then got a very serious look on his face. "Your life is
in danger, and there's someone who needs to talk to you. My job
today is just to take you to a meeting."

"But who *are* you, really?"

Earl scratched his chin. "Let's just say that your granddad and
I are old friends. He sent me to Wallingford a long time ago to
look after you."

"You know my *grandfather*!" Toby exclaimed. "Who is he?
Who are my parents? WHO AM I? Why haven't you ever said
anything all these years?"

"Whoa there, young fella," Earl replied. "Let's just say that your family has *very* powerful enemies. Keeping you in the dark about your identity was the only way to keep you alive. And it worked. They've pretty much left you alone all these years...until now."

Toby had so many questions that he couldn't decide which to ask first. But he wouldn't get the chance. Earl's truck skidded to a stop in front of Wallingford Station.

"Am I taking a train ride somewhere?" Toby asked.

"Nope," Earl replied. "This is where your meeting will be. Just head on up to the platform and have a seat on the benches. A woman will get off the next train and approach you. You can trust her."

Toby stepped out of the truck. "Are you going to wait for me here?"

"Sorry, Toby," Earl replied. "I've taken a big chance approaching you directly like this, so I can't risk hanging around. Good luck!" Earl put the truck in gear and took off down the street.

Toby looked at his watch. It was 5:25. He walked around the outside of the train station and over to the bench directly under the sign that said *Wallingford R3*. He sat down and rested his head against the red brick station wall and waited.

At 5:29, the piercing horn of the Vermonter announced its imminent arrival at the station on its way from New York City to Vermont. Toby leaned forward and looked down the tracks. He could see the bright headlight of the train coming, slowing down as it approached the station. When the train stopped, thirty or so passengers got off. Most were dressed in suits carrying briefcases, doubtlessly returning from their jobs in the City.

As the crowd thinned, a tall blond muscular man and stylish middle-aged woman in a long hooded overcoat and high heels got off the train. They walked together toward Toby, but after they

169

had covered approximately half the distance, the man glanced at the woman and nodded, then veered off to the left toward the station exit. Already jumpy, this exchange made Toby even more nervous. *Where was the man going? Was this a trap?* The woman continued forward and walked over to where Toby was sitting. Her glasses were tinted, so Toby couldn't see her eyes clearly. She pulled back the hood of her coat from off her head, revealing her long, dark brown curly hair, which was casually pulled back into a pony tail.

"Hello, Toby. I'm Angela." She smiled warmly and held out her hand.

Toby stood up and shook her hand. "Nice to meet you Angela." It was all he could think of to say at the moment, but afterwards he wished it could have been something more cool and clandestine, like *Gold…Toby Gold.*

"And it's wonderful to finally meet you, too. Please sit down, Toby. We only have a few minutes."

Toby sat back down on the bench, and Angela sat down next to him. Something about her looks and demeanor reminded him of Mrs. Leonard, but only vaguely. Angela was much taller and prettier.

"We're taking a huge risk meeting like this, but these are extraordinary circumstances."

"Who are you?" Toby asked.

"It's best that you just call me Angela."

"Is that your real name?"

"No."

"Fair enough, I guess, since Toby's not *my* real name, either."

"I am aware of that."

"So you know who I really am?"

"Yes, Toby, I do. But unfortunately I can't provide that information to you."

Toby's face fell with disappointment. "I realize that probably wasn't the answer you were looking for," Angela added. There was a sympathetic tone to Angela's voice, but Toby was angry anyway.

"Why not?" Toby haltingly asked. He was nearly in tears. All his life he'd been trying to figure this out. Now, in the last ten minutes he's met two different people who knew the truth but neither of them would tell him. It wasn't fair.

"All in due time, Toby. Soon enough you will know everything. Giving you those answers right now would put you in even more danger than you're already in. And please try to keep your voice down." Angela looked around. Toby's outburst had caused a couple of commuters to briefly look in their direction.

Toby lowered his voice. "I'm really in danger? That wasn't just Earl being melodramatic?"

"Grave danger. Jack Leonard is part of a very bad organization called *Legio Argentum*. It is a group that has existed since 475 A.D., the final years of the Roman Empire. It was founded by the emperor Julius Nepos and a small group of his most trusted army generals. The Roman Empire was crumbling around them, but they devised a plan to keep as much power as possible. Since that time, Legio Argentum has been dedicated to conquering the world and dividing up the spoils among its leadership."

"Ledge-ee-o ar-jen-tum," Toby mused, pronouncing the words slowly to be sure he got it right. "Is that Latin or something?"

"Precisely," Angela replied. "It means Silver Legion. They are a very old and *very* dangerous secret society…"

"Wait a sec," interrupted Toby. "I've seen the name *Legio* before. Legio Investments is the name of the company Mr. Leonard works for."

"Yes, that is one of their front companies."

"Why would a bunch of guys who are trying to take over the world have a Wall Street investment company?"

"You've hit the nail right on the head, Toby. After the fall of the Roman Empire, it became clear to Legio Argentum that military conquest was not the best way to achieve world domination. Military victories are inherently fragile and always temporary. Financial conquest, however, is much stronger and longer lasting."

"That makes sense, I guess."

"Their primary approach has always been to take control of financial markets and institutions. You'd be shocked at how far their influence reaches. Our organization was founded over two centuries ago for the express purpose of fighting Legio. We use our gifts to promote free and democratic markets and, by doing so, prevent much of the world economy from falling in the hands of Legio."

"What do you mean by *gifts*, exactly?" Toby asked. "I remember you telling me in one of your messages to 'use my gift wisely.' What did you mean by that?"

Angela took a deep breath and was silent for a moment. She had to be careful about what she revealed next. "Toby, I'm sorry to say that those messages did not come from us. They were sent by Legio, who either is trying to recruit you to their side or trying to force us to reveal ourselves. Possibly both."

"Recruit me? What would they want with a thirteen year old nobody?"

"Toby, the world is not as it seems. By now you've realized that you have an ability that is far beyond what other people can do."

"You mean about understanding financial data?"

"That's only scratching the surface of what you can do, which is why Legio is so interested in you. It is also why you are now in great peril. Your abilities would be of great use to them in achieving their goals. Most likely, Jack Leonard's primary mission is to recruit you. If he cannot do that, he will *kill* you to prevent you from ever working with us — and against them."

"Kill me? But why me?" Toby had never considered that his life might be in danger. He still wasn't exactly sure what he wanted to be when he grew up, but he was certain that he did, in fact, want to eventually grow up. There's nothing more career-limiting than a coffin.

"Right now you are still a child, but a very special one. You are becoming more and more powerful every day, and therefore more of a threat to Legio. Most people require extensive training to develop their gift into a power, but you have done surprisingly well on your own, with no training. You have no idea how rare that is. This is why they are mobilizing against you now. They only suspect what we already *know*. You are what we call a *vessel*."

"A vessel? Like a ship?"

"No, a vessel like a container," Angela replied. "A container specifically designed to hold special abilities or gifts. You see, every single person in this world is born with at least one special gift. Only one in ten ever discovers his or her gift and develops it into a talent. Even those that do barely scratch the surface of what their talent can really do. Only one in a thousand ever spends any significant time developing their talent. Only one in a million does with his talent what you've done already, Toby. You've already tapped into the part of your talent that most people would consider superhuman. A fully developed talent becomes a power, and you have the potential to become exceptionally powerful one day. "

"So I'm one-in-a-million?" Toby responded glibly.

"More like one-in-a-billion, actually."

"But you just said…"

"You didn't let me finish. People with your gift for numbers and financial data are called cyphers. Your kind is potentially *very* powerful and thus *very* dangerous. Given the obvious importance of world financial markets, it has long been clear that *money is the most dangerous magic.*"

"Wow," Toby mumbled, "I never thought of it that way."

"Few do," Angela replied. "Have you ever heard of the economist Adam Smith? He was a cypher like you — and was one of the founders of our organization."

"Adam Smith, the guy with the powdered wig? The father of modern economics? He was your founder?" Toby asked. Adam Smith was one of the dead economists that Toby and Marc had looked up online.

"One of the founders, yes," Angela replied. "The other one was Benjamin Franklin."

"Ben Franklin?" Toby was incredulous. "THE Ben Franklin? The guy on the hundred dollar bill that flew kites in thunder storms?"

"Out of respect, we refer to him as Benjamin, not Ben."

"Okay. *Benjamin*, then," Toby corrected himself. "What was *his* power?"

"He had more than one," answered Angela. "But he was primarily what we call a *spark*."

"A spark?"

"Yes, it's quite a rare and dramatic ability. Sparks have the ability to generate and manipulate electrical currents. It's why he was able to fly a kite in a lightning storm without being fried to a crisp."

"Cool." Toby was duly impressed. "But Benjamin Franklin was an American. Adam Smith was English or Scottish or something. How did they even know each other?"

"They met in 1767," Angela replied. "They had both been invited to Paris to be inducted into Legio Argentum. It was considered quite an honor to be asked to be a member, since its ranks included the most powerful and influential men in Europe."

Toby was crestfallen. "But they're the *enemy*. Why would they join the enemy?"

"They didn't know the true nature of Legio. Smith and Franklin met during the induction ceremony. But the more they learned about Legio, the less they liked it. Its principals were completely contrary to their ideas of freedom. The rest of the story is complicated, but it ends with Smith and Franklin leaving Legio Argentum and founding a new secret society dedicated to Legio's downfall and to the protection of financial liberty."

"Wow. I'd really like to hear the rest of that story."

"Someday," Angela replied wistfully.

Suddenly Toby remembered something. "You know, Adam Smith's name was on one of the bogus brokerage statements that I found at Jack Leonard's house."

"Really?" Angela apparently hadn't known that. Her expression gradually melted into a crooked smile and she continued, "It actually doesn't surprise me that much, now that I think about it. It's just Jack Leonard's warped sense of humor to use the names of our revered founders as part of his scheme against us."

"So Adam Smith was a cypher like me." Toby was starting to feel proud of his talent.

"Yes, there are actually many people born with the cypher gift. But the 'one-in-a-hundred' kind of cypher never really develops it — and ends up as an accountant. If you were just a fully developed cypher, then you'd be one-in-a-million. Being a vessel, however, you are *much* rarer."

"I don't get it. If people are born with just *one* talent, how can I be both a cypher *and* a vessel?

"That's just it. Being a cypher is your natural gift. But you were also born as a vessel, which is not in itself a power, but rather it is the ability to learn the powers of other people. Vessels are one-in-a-billion, Toby, so you are a *very* special young man — and that's why Legio wants you."

"So when you said that being a spark was Franklin's *primary* gift, does that mean…"

"Very good, Toby." Angela was impressed at how quickly Toby was catching on. "Yes, like you, Benjamin Franklin was a vessel. Before his death, he had accumulated many powers. So, like you, he was viewed as a very rare threat to Legio Argentum."

Toby thought for a moment. "But currently there are like six billion people on the planet. So that means that besides me there are only…"

"…potentially five other vessels, yes, more or less. That's just an estimate, of course. We only know of two others at the moment. One of them is the head of Legio, but he is very old and is growing weak with age. The other vessel is part of our organization."

"You haven't mentioned the name of your organization, by the way."

"There's a very good reason for that, Toby. It would be dangerous for our name to be in your mind. Leonard would sense it and would know that we've been in contact with you. The only reason you are still alive is because he still holds out hope that you can be recruited."

"How could he possibly know what's in my mind?"

"Leonard is a *telepath*."

"A mind-reader?"

"More than that, I'm afraid. There are three advanced levels to all of the mental talents. As I mentioned, most people live their entire lives without even reaching the first level, which is called discernment. Discernment is the powerful, yet passive, use of the talent. For a telepath, this means having the ability to read the thoughts of others."

"Sounds like Bidge."

"Do you mean your redheaded girlfriend, Bridget?"

"She's not my girlfriend!" Toby protested. "But sometimes I swear she's reading my mind. She finishes my sentences and hits me whenever I think anything rude about her."

"That sounds about right. She probably *is* a telepath. Lots of people are, since it's the most common of all the mental talents. But the vast majority of telepaths will never actually be able to intentionally read another person's mind. They're just labeled as very 'perceptive' or simply 'good at reading others.' Most of them eventually end up with jobs in sales."

"So Bidge is a telepath then." Toby thought this was pretty cool. "I guess I'll just have to be more careful what I think about when I'm with her."

"Yes, in fact, from now on you need to try to keep better control of your thoughts at all times. You never know who's eavesdropping in your head."

Toby didn't like the sound of that. Was someone listening to his thoughts right now? "Okay, so you were explaining to me about the first ability level…"

"That's right. So, for a cypher like you, level one means seeing the patterns in financial data. For an omniglot, on the other hand, it means understanding what anyone says in any language."

Omniglot. That gift sounded pretty cool. "What's the second level?"

"The second level is defense. For a telepath, it means blocking someone else from reading your mind. The third level is projection. Again, using the telepathy example, this means that the telepath can actively change another person's thoughts, or even make them forget things.

Toby remained silent, lost in thought. Angela continued, "I'm using the telepathy example because this is your biggest vulnerability right now. As a vessel, you are more difficult to read than most, but still not impossible. With the proper training, however, you would be able to block even the most powerful telepath."

"Then why don't you train me?"

"If you would like to begin your training now, then that is a choice that is open to you."

Toby paused, lifting one eyebrow. "I'm sensing that there's a 'but' attached to that offer."

"Indeed there is," Angela replied. "The training center is in a very safe and very remote location. Once you begin, there is no going back. No one can know where you are. For all intents and purposes, you will have dropped off the face of the earth."

"That's a big but."

Just then a yellow taxi pulled up to the front of the station. The light on the top indicated that it was off duty so no customers would try to get in. Toby noticed that the same tall blond man that had arrived with Angela was sitting in the backseat.

"Who's the mean-looking blond guy in the taxi?" Toby asked.

"That's my bodyguard, Gunter."

"German?"

"No, Swiss."

"He looks dangerous," Toby commented.

Angela nodded. "You have no idea."

"Is he always with you?"

"Yes," Angela replied. "He is now, anyway. He left me alone briefly twelve years ago with disastrous results. He hasn't let me out of his sight since."

Angela reached over and placed her hands gently and affectionately on Toby's shoulders. "So you can get in that taxi right now with me and start your new life. I can promise excitement and a tremendously meaningful existence. You will no longer be Toby Gold, and your life here in Wallingford will be over."

A new life fighting evil sounded awfully exciting to a thirteen-year-old orphan boy. "What about my friends? Can I say good-bye?"

"Absolutely not. But your friends *do* present another potential problem."

"What's that?"

"Jack Leonard knows who Bridget and Marc are and how close you are to them. If you suddenly disappear, he'll know that my organization is the reason. He's likely to use your friends to try get to you."

Toby paled. "He wouldn't actually hurt them, would he?"

"I don't know the answer to that, Toby. But I know for a fact that Jack Leonard has killed before."

Toby felt a chill. Under these circumstances there was only one decision he could live with. "In that case I think I need to stay here and finish this. I can't let anything happen to Bidge and Marc."

"That's an honorable decision, Toby. I have to admit, though, that I'd feel a lot better if you were under our full protection."

Full protection sounded good to Toby, too. Even more tempting was the idea of finding out everything about who he was and what had happened to his parents. "So do you have any advice for going up against Leonard?"

"Keep your thoughts uninteresting and try not to look in his eyes."

"Does that work?"

"Not entirely, but it makes it a little harder for him," Angela replied.

"Well that's something, I guess," Toby said snidely.

Angela looked at her watch. "I've already stayed here too long. Gunter can't project his protective field around me from this distance for more than five minutes at a time. Good luck, Toby. Please remember that you have a lot of friends that care about you and are rooting for you."

"So how can I reach you if I have more questions?" Toby asked hopefully.

"You can't. Until you learn to block a telepath, it is far too dangerous to us for you to have a way to contact us."

"Bummer."

"Don't worry too much. We're keeping a close watch on the situation and Earl will contact you if necessary."

Toby paused and shifted his weight. "Speaking of Earl, how did he do that thing where pulled me into his truck without even touching me?

Angela smiled broadly. "Come join us and I'll be happy to show you."

"Nice try." Toby laughed.

"Yes, I thought so, too." Angela gave Toby a tender hug and walked briskly to the waiting taxicab around the front of the station. She opened the yellow rear door and slid in, closing it behind her.

Toby watched the taxi drive away into the distance, then started walking home. He was annoyed that Angela hadn't at least offered him a ride home. The long walk gave him a chance to plan out his next move, though. He still needed to figure out exactly what Mr. Leonard was doing with those bogus accounts. To do that, Toby definitely would have to get another peek at Mr. Leonard's personal file cabinet.

▲ ▲ ▲

In the back of the taxi, Angela removed her sunglasses, revealing thin black makeup streaks where the tears had run down her cheeks. Her eyes were bright blue, the color of the sky at midday, with some flecks of gold color surrounding her right pupil in a thin amber band.

"Are you okay?" Gunter asked, handing her a handkerchief.

"No, not really. He wouldn't come with us."

"You shouldn't have been the one to come here. *He* should have sent someone else," Gunter lamented.

Angela sighed. "No, it had to be me. If anyone could have talked him into it, it was me. I'm just afraid that we won't be able to protect him out here like this."

"We could always just abduct him, " Gunter said lightly. "Just say the word and I'll go bag him right now. It'll only take a second. Easy-peasy." Gunter pretended to reach for the door latch in order to get out and do the kidnapping.

Angela grabbed his arm. "No, Gunter. It's very tempting, but he really has to decide this on his own. He'll come around eventually." She smiled to herself because Gunter sounded really silly whenever he said things like *easy-peasy* with his thick Swiss-German accent.

CHAPTER 20

Mind Games

TOBY REPLAYED THE MEETING at the train station over and over again in his mind all night long. He may have fallen asleep once or twice, but if so he couldn't remember. To him, it felt like he had been up all night.

When morning came, he had already been staring unblinkingly at his alarm clock for several minutes before it went off. He was exhausted, both mentally and physically, and not looking forward to a full day of school. Toby left his house a little earlier than normal so that he could catch Bidge and walk with her. He was intensely curious to figure out about the whole telepathy thing. He walked up the two concrete steps to her front door and knocked twice. Bidge's mom didn't like visitors to use the doorbell.

The door opened and it was one of Bidge's brothers — Joey, the one just a year older.

"Is Bridget here?" Toby asked.

"Yeah, I think she's still in the bathroom getting ready. C'mon in."

Toby walked in and set his backpack down on the floor. He could see the boys' bedroom at an angle from the foyer. As usual, it looked like it had been trashed by a band of silverback gorillas. It typically smelled that way, too.

The kitchen, on the other hand, was completely spotless. The kitchen was Bidge's domain and anyone leaving a mess there would have to face her wrath. Her bedroom, the kitchen and the bathroom were Bidge's only islands of orderliness within the sea of chaos that was the rest of the Donnelly house.

Bidge walked into the foyer from the hallway. "Oh, hi Toby! I didn't know you were coming this morning." Bidge looked happy to see him as usual. She grabbed her backpack and called loudly in the direction of the family room, "Have a good day, mom! I'm leaving for school!" Toby thought he heard a mumbled response from the family room, but couldn't quite make it out.

Bidge and Toby walked out the front door, down the steps and out to the sidewalk. Turning right, they headed to school. Bidge couldn't help noticing the dark circles under Toby's eyes.

"You look terrible," Bidge said.

"Thanks. I didn't get much sleep last night."

"Soooo…to what do I owe the honor of your company this morning?" Bidge said cautiously. Toby thought she sounded a bit sarcastic, but with Bidge it was hard to tell for sure.

"I wanted to talk to you alone for a while."

"About what?" Bidge asked hopefully.

"About you reading people's minds."

"Excuse me?" Bidge's expression immediately changed from hope to disappointment and annoyance. "Are you serious?"

"Yeah. Actually, I am. I've been thinking a lot about the game against Moran. I was watching you pretty closely, and it really seemed like you knew in advance what that girl was going to do. It was kind of eerie."

"So you think I'm a mind-reader?" Bidge asked dismissively.

"I think that maybe you *could* be one," Toby replied. "I heard that a lot of people have the ability to do it, but never develop it. Maybe it's one of those things locked away in the part of our brains that we don't use. Do you mind trying an experiment?"

"Whatever." Bidge thought the whole thing was pretty silly.

Toby stopped and turned to face Bidge, who took the cue and stopped too. He waited a few seconds for a big yellow noisy school bus to go by. They were only a few blocks from the school now, so buses were passing frequently. He looked Bidge straight in the eyes and said, "I'm thinking of a number between one and ten. Can you tell me what it is?"

"I don't know. Seven?" Bidge said casually.

"No, it was three."

"See? I knew this was silly."

"But you weren't even trying." Toby scowled and grew quiet for a moment while he mentally searched for an answer to why this wasn't working. He tried to remember what he felt like when he zoned out watching the stock ticker. It was like floating — a completely relaxed body and very slow breathing.

"Okay, let's try this again," Toby continued. "Close your eyes and try to relax. Breathe really slowly."

"Got it," Bidge said, rolling her eyes before closing them.

"It'll probably work better if you drop the attitude," Toby observed.

"Sorry." Bidge did her best to wipe the smirk off her face. With her eyes closed she did her best to relax and breathe slowly.

"Now open your eyes."

Bidge opened her eyes.

"I'm thinking of another number now," Toby said calmly.

Bidge relaxed and kept looking in his eyes. "One?"

Toby smiled broadly. "Yup."

"No way!"

"Way."

"Are you just yanking my chain? How do I know you weren't thinking of another number and aren't just pranking me?" Bidge asked incredulously.

Toby thought for a second. He set down his backpack on the sidewalk and pulled out a notepad and a pencil. "Okay, Bidge. This time I'm thinking of another number and writing it down." He held the paper so that Bidge couldn't see.

"Nine," she said after a brief moment.

Toby turned the notepad around so that she could see it. It had a big number nine on it. Toby smiled. Bidge just looked scared.

"Let's try it one more time, but without looking at my eyes." He wanted to test Angela's theory. Toby turned his head to the side and thought of another number.

"Five...no wait. Four."

"It was five," Toby said.

"It wasn't nearly as clear that time."

Toby smugly put his notepad away and slung his backpack over his shoulder again. "Bidge, we should probably keep this thing a secret for the time being."

She became paler than normal as a look of panic spread across her face. "What's going on here, Toby? Am I actually reading your mind? How is that possible?"

Toby paused momentarily while he decided how much he could — or should — tell her. Then he took a deep breath and began, "I learned some pretty interesting things recently. One of them is that every person on earth is born with an amazing gift. Apparently, your gift is telepathy."

"But that doesn't make sense," Bidge protested. "If that were true, wouldn't *everyone* we know have some sort of random superpower? I've never seen anything like this. Well, anything like this that wasn't just a trick."

"Just because everyone is born with a gift doesn't mean that they ever discover what it is, or learn how to develop it into something powerful."

"So how did you figure out that I had this telepathy thingy?"

"I didn't know for sure. I just suspected. It's how you predicted those girl's moves in the basketball game. It's probably also the reason why you're always finishing…"

"…your sentences?" Bidge smiled, chuckling at how amazingly funny she was.

"Um…yeah." Toby looked annoyed. Clearly they had two different opinions about her level of comedy genius. "But I needed to test you to know for sure."

"But I still don't get how you know this stuff. Do you have one of these gifts?"

"Everybody does. Mine is just a little more developed than most."

"So do you read minds, too?"

Toby paused again. He wasn't sure if he was supposed to reveal his gift to others. But this was *Bidge* he was talking to, and since he already knew *her* gift, it only seemed fair that she should know his. "No, my gift is that I'm really good with money and numbers and stuff."

"Pffft. I could have told you *that*." Bidge rolled her eyes. Clearly she was unimpressed with Toby's gift. It didn't seem nearly as cool as mind reading.

"Well, I think that most people's gifts aren't a big secret. It's just the stuff that they naturally do best. The only difference

186

between them and us is that we've developed them to the next level."

"Yeah, about that. If people generally don't know how to take their gifts to the *next level*, as you say, how did I happen to do it by accident?"

"I'm not totally sure," Toby mused. "At the basketball game, you were totally playing like a sloth the first half."

Bidge glared at Toby, slowly and deliberately clenching her fingers into a fist. Sensing danger, Toby quickly continued. "Wait. Hear me out. In the second half, all of the sudden you were totally in the zone, predicting that girl's moves every time. Do you remember what you did differently?"

Bidge thought hard for a few seconds. "I don't know really. I was totally stressed. Nothing was working for me, and the coach was mad. I couldn't focus, so I tried doing those breathing exercises you showed me a couple years ago. Remember?"

"You mean the yoga breathing?" A light went on in Toby's mind. His eighth foster parents, back in the fifth grade, had been very *alternative*. They were vegans, Buddhists, and dedicated practitioners of an extreme form of south Asian yoga. They unsuccessfully tried to teach it to Toby. The only things that stuck with him were the breathing exercises. It was supposed to be a way of clearing the mind. He found it somewhat relaxing, so he taught it to Bidge since she seemed stressed out most of the time.

"Yeah," Bidge replied. "It was the same thing a minute ago when you told me to close my eyes and relax. I did it the same way you taught me back in fifth grade. I just clear my mind, breathe slowly, and concentrate on the sound of my own breathing. It actually works pretty well."

"So when you did that during the game, you started knowing what your opponent was thinking?"

"Now that you mention it, yeah, I guess so."

"Cool." Toby replied. It was all starting to make more sense to him. The patterns that he saw in the market data were only visible to him when his mind was clear and relaxed.

Then he remembered the point he was originally trying to make. "So Bidge, are we agreed that we won't talk about this stuff to anyone else?"

"*Duh*. You think I want people to know I'm a freak? My lips are sealed." She made a zipper motion across her lips.

As they walked the remaining short distance to school, they continued their little mind game.

"Seven?" Bidge asked.

"Yup."

"Two?"

"Yup."

"Two again."

"Yup." Toby paused for a moment, then smiled impishly.

"*Mango?*" Bidge scowled and punched Toby on the arm. "Hey, that's a fruit, not a number. No fair changing the game!"

They both laughed as they walked up the steps into the school. As usual, Toby was sporting a freshly bruised arm. He grew quiet as he rubbed the aching spot with his other hand. He desperately wanted to tell Bidge what was going on. Of all people, she understood him best. But the idea of putting her in danger made him feel queezy inside.

Despite his silence, Bidge could sense that something was wrong. "Something's up. Spill it, Toby."

"It's nothing," Toby replied, mustering a casual smile. "I'll see you at lunch." Toby abruptly turned and headed down the hall toward his locker.

CHAPTER 21

Stop Calling Me That

ONTRARY TO MRS. LEONARD's direct orders, Toby went
back to their house that afternoon after school to make
copies of the remaining bogus brokerage statements. He
knew they would be out of town looking at houses, so this might
be his last chance.

Max and Ginnie, of course, were quivering with glee when
he came in. "Not today, guys. I just stopped by to grab something, so I can't take you out." Toby was sincerely sorry. He would
have much preferred taking the dogs for a walk over rummaging
through Mr. Leonard's files, scared to death of getting caught. He
went straight to the study, sat down at the desk, and opened the
right-hand file drawer.

It was empty. Toby felt his stomach tighten into a ball as
a sense of panic overwhelmed him. "Rat Snacks!" He quickly
looked around the office and realized that it had been packed up
already. The books were gone from the shelves, but the computer
was still there, and the printer/fax/copier was still on the credenza,
with its green light indicating it was ready for action.

He headed out to the garage. Max and Ginnie followed him,
thinking he was going out to get the leashes. Toby scanned the

piles of boxes in the second garage bay. Those were the piles added since he was there yesterday. He caught sight of some boxes labeled "Study." On top of those were two file boxes, the kind that you put hanging folders in and that have a little cardboard lid. He pulled the first one down and pulled off the lid.

"Just bills and stuff."

Toby pulled down the second one and pulled off the lid.

"Bingo." Inside the box were the contents of the right hand desk drawer.

Toby grabbed the file containing the brokerage statements and rushed inside to the study, where he put the stack of statements into the automatic feeder on the top of the copier and pressed the start button. It seemed like was taking forever. It was one of those slow home copiers, not one of the fast copy machines like they had in the front office at school. When the last statement was finished, Toby put the original statements back in the folder and stuffed the copies into his backpack. He ran back out to the garage and carefully put the folder back in the box where he found it, and then lifted the file boxes back into the spot in the stack where he found them.

"Well that wasn't so bad," he said smilingly to Max and Ginnie, who were standing next to the leashes hanging on the wall.

Just then the garage door opener in the first bay sprang into action and the door began to slowly open. Toby must have jumped two feet in the air. The sliver of afternoon sun squeezing under the garage door grew wider and wider as the door slowly opened. The Leonards were home already.

Toby panicked. He was standing on the far side of the pile of boxes in the second bay. He looked over at the door to the mudroom, which he had left open. *Rat Snacks!* He couldn't get across the first bay to close that door without the Leonards seeing him. Behind him, in the third bay, was the silver Porsche. Toby quickly ran around the Porsche and ducked down behind it as Mr. and Mrs. Leonard pulled their black BMW into the first bay.

Max and Ginnie ran to greet them as they exited the car. When Mrs. Leonard stooped down to give Ginnie a kiss on the nose, she was at eye level with Toby, who was peering out from under the front bumper of the Porsche in the next bay. They briefly made eye contact. Mrs. Leonard's face went pale with fear and she quickly stood up. Toby's heart was pounding with enough force that he was certain Mr. Leonard could probably hear it.

"What are you guys doing out here?" Mr. Leonard asked the dogs, who not surprisingly failed to offer any explanation for their presence. Ginnie licked his hand instead. He then noticed the open mudroom door. "How did that door get left open? The alarm won't engage if that door is left open."

Mrs. Leonard lied. "Oh, I'm sorry, I was in a hurry when we left and I guess I didn't check to see if it latched."

Mr. Leonard rolled his eyes. He had an obsession about security that his wife didn't quite share. They went inside with the dogs and shut the door behind them.

Toby quietly opened the side door of the garage, stepped outside, and then closed it just as quietly. He slung his backpack over his shoulder and pulled his bike out of the bushes where he had stashed it earlier. *Why had Mrs. Leonard covered for him?* He had ridden for nearly two blocks before he remembered to start breathing again.

▲　▲　▲

It was perfectly clear to Toby that time was running out. Whatever Mr. Leonard was planning was going to happen soon, or why else would he be packing up his house and moving? Toby still didn't have the faintest idea what exactly Mr. Leonard was scheming, but with each passing hour, the chances of stopping it were growing dimmer. Mr. Leonard was packing up the evidence and leaving town.

Toby headed straight to Mr. Leonard's office at Choate. There might still be something there that could solve the mystery. So he stood up on the pedals of his bike and pumped as hard as he could for the remaining mile and a half. When he got there, he just dumped the bike at the doorway and headed inside, passing Mrs. Krebbs at her desk.

"Hello, Toby," said Mrs. Krebbs pleasantly. "Beautiful spring day, don't you think?"

"Hi, Mrs. Krebbs." Toby tried to act cheerful, but inside he was wound up tight like a yo-yo, and just as dizzy, due to all the disconnected information and theories spinning through his head. He just smiled, but didn't pause as he walked by her desk toward the stairs. Mrs. Krebbs smiled back. As Toby started up the stairs, he saw her pick up the black telephone receiver and press the fifth speed-dial button.

Toby tried the office door, but it was locked. He pulled out his keychain and found the silver key that Mr. Leonard had given him. His hands were shaking so it took him four tries to get the key into the lock, but once he did, the bolt turned easily and he was in.

He dropped his backpack on the floor beside the coat rack and headed straight to the filing cabinet. He had already searched through the top two drawers, so only the bottom one remained. But he had already opened it the other day and it had been empty except for the note. Then he had an idea. He opened the bottom drawer again. It was completely empty — even the note was gone. He paused for a moment, staring at the empty drawer. Something seemed different from the other drawers. He reached down and lightly knocked on the bottom of the drawer — it had a distinctly hollow sound.

Well hello there, thought Toby. He gripped the drawer bottom by both edges and pulled it up, revealing a secret compartment underneath containing three file folders. The first one was labeled *Sell-offs*. Toby pulled the file out and took it over to the desk and sat down. He yanked the little silver chain on the lamp and it clicked on, casting its ghostly light across the surface of the desk.

Toby opened the folder. It contained charts that tracked the prices of various stocks. Each chart was for a different stock on a different day. The only similarity between them was that on each chart there was a huge drop in price for that particular day. Stapled to each chart were news stories about the company dated the same day. The headlines were things like *Analysts Predict Earnings Shortfall* or *Stock Price Falls on Merger Rumors*.

Toby thought he recognized the companies on the charts. He went back to the filing cabinet and removed the brokerage statement folder from the top drawer and flipped through the statements. Many of the stocks owned by Choate were included in the sell-off folder.

One statement caught his eye. It had a large stock trade listed, and the date looked familiar. He took the folder over to the desk and laid it out so that it was open to that statement. He then thumbed through the charts in the other folder until he found the one he was looking for.

The dates were the same. Leonard had done a large sale of that stock in the morning, and then the stock took a big plunge that very afternoon because of a merger rumor. There had been a ton of corporate mergers that year, which is when one company buys another company. Toby had seen new mergers announced in *The Wall Street Journal* on a seemingly daily basis the past several months. Typically, when a merger is announced, the stock price of the company being bought goes up, while the stock price of the company doing the buying goes down.

According to the statement, Mr. Leonard repurchased the same stock the very next morning. The merger rumor was determined to be false, and over the next two days, the stock price went back up to its original price.

"There's no way that's a coincidence," Toby said out loud.

"I agree. I don't really believe in coincidences, either."

For the second time in less than one hour, Toby nearly jumped out of his skin. He looked up from the paperwork to see Mr. Leonard standing in the doorway. He was smiling, but not in a friendly way. He stepped inside and closed the door, locking it with his key. Toby didn't think this was a good sign.

Toby tried to act casual. "Hi, Mr. Leonard. I was just reviewing the files like you suggested." Toby looked down at the open files spread out on the desk. "Oh, and sorry about the mess; I didn't realize that you needed the office today. It will only take me a minute to clean up and get out of here."

"No need to clean up, Toby. I'll only be here a minute."

They looked at each other for a few awkward seconds until Toby, remembering Angela's advice, broke eye contact and looked down at the papers again. Mr. Leonard had been staring at Toby's right eye.

Mr. Leonard continued staring at Toby in silence, as if he was still deciding what to say next. He shifted his weight from his right foot to his left and spoke.

"I think you have something that belongs to me."

Toby could think of three things in his possession that belonged to Mr. Leonard: the passport, the brokerage statement copies, and the dog-walking money that Mrs. Leonard had given him in advance. It was unlikely that Mr. Leonard was talking about the last one, so it must have been one of the first two.

"I'm not sure what you're talking about." Toby was telling the truth.

"You took a passport that was in my desk drawer. I'll need it back."

Oh that. "I don't have it on me." This statement was, of course, only *technically* true. The passport was in the front pocket of Toby's backpack, which was at that moment sitting on the floor under the coat rack, within kicking distance of Mr. Leonard's feet. "What were you doing with a passport for me, anyway?"

"It's complicated, and I'm not feeling particularly inclined to explain it to you at the moment."

"Well then I'm not particularly inclined to give it back to you, either."

Mr. Leonard laughed, but not in a good way. "Mr. Gold, you are not in any position to make demands, or to refuse mine. I am going to tell you exactly what you are going to do, and then you are going to do it, no questions asked."

"Why would I want to do that?"

"Because you have been a very naughty young man. I have evidence that you have been engaging in a substantial amount of illegal stock trading over the past month…"

Toby interrupted, his voice a little higher pitched than normal, "But I haven't done anything like that…"

"On the contrary, son, I have the brokerage statements to prove it. And I'm sure that you wouldn't want the authorities to find out about these crimes. You'd surely end up in juvenile detention for a long time, and I'm sure that Choate would no longer be interested in you becoming a student here."

Toby cringed, especially about that last part. "But I'd tell them the truth. I'd tell them that *you* did it."

Mr. Leonard smiled. "Who are they going to believe, son, you or me?"

I wish he'd stop calling me that. "So all you want is the passport?"

"Oh heavens, no," he laughed, "I have a very important job for you to do. If you do it right, you just might still have a future."

"What do want me to do?" Toby figured that it couldn't hurt to at least *appear* cooperative.

Mr. Leonard walked toward the desk and sat down in one of the leather club chairs in front of it. He motioned to the desk chair that Toby was standing in front of. "Have a seat, son."

Toby bristled again at that word, but didn't say anything as he plopped down in the chair.

"Because you've been poking around where you don't belong, we are going to have to advance the timetable for our little project."

"What little project?"

"No questions, please. All you need to know is your job. Fortunately, it should be quite easy for you. All you have to do is stay home from school tomorrow and watch TV."

"Excuse me?" Toby wasn't quite sure he had heard that right.

"I am well aware of your talent for predicting price movements in the stock market. All I need you to do is to sit home and watch the financial news. When you sense that the market is about to head downward, you just give me a call right here." Leonard pointed to the black phone on his desk.

"Here? Why not call you on your cell phone?"

Mr. Leonard appeared annoyed at the question. "Because I'll be here most of the day tomorrow and my cell phone doesn't get good reception in this office. I have a finance committee meeting first thing in the morning, and it could last all day. Just call me at this number. If I'm in a meeting, Mrs. Krebbs will pick up and pull me out of the meeting if it's you."

"Sounds easy enough," Toby said.

"Should be a piece of cake."

"And if I do this, you'll leave me alone?"

Mr. Leonard paused for a second and then said, "Of course. If that's what you really want. But what I actually said was that you would have a *future*. You are a young man of extraordinary talents. You just need someone to train you properly. Your future will be very bright and successful indeed if you join me and my friends." Mr. Leonard paused again to let this offer sink in. "Or you can go to jail. It's your choice, really."

Toby looked at the floor to avoid making eye contact. "Not much of a choice. I guess I'm in." Toby was lying, but he hoped Mr. Leonard couldn't tell.

CHAPTER 22

Manipulating the Market

S LEEPING HAD BECOME INCREASINGLY difficult for Toby over the past few days and his appetite had all but disappeared. It was all just too much for him to process, and it was rapidly grinding him down and wearing him out. As he rode his bike home today from Choate, all the pieces to the puzzle were swirling around in his foggy, sleep-deprived mind, looking for a place to fit. Now there were two additional pieces: first; the file that tracked stocks that dropped in price based on rumors, and second; Mr. Leonard's request to be told when the market was about to head downward.

Then the pieces started to fall into place in Toby's head.

"Market manipulation!" Toby said this out loud, but no one was around to hear him, not that it would have mattered.

Toby had read about market manipulation in the Wall Street Journal. Two stock traders in New York had recently gone to federal prison for doing it. The way it works is pretty simple. Stock prices went up and down based on the way investors envisioned the future of the company as compared with its present condition. If investors thought the company would become more profitable in the future, then the stock price would go up. If, on the

198

other hand, investors believed that the company was headed for trouble in the future, then the price went down. So at any given time, the current stock price of a company reflected the sum total of all the information and beliefs of the investors about the future of that company.

A dishonest person, therefore, could make an illegal profit by selling a stock when it was high, and then spreading a false negative rumor about the company. If investors believed it, then the price of the stock would temporarily drop, until the rumor was proven false. After the price dropped, the criminal would buy back the stock at a low price, making a huge profit when the stock price eventually returned to its correct level.

An institutional investor like Mr. Leonard, who controlled a large number of shares, could also manipulate stock prices simply by selling or buying a bunch of shares all at once. If there were more shares for sale than there were buyers, then the price will naturally go down in order to attract more buyers. Likewise, if there were more buyers than sellers, the price would go up in order to attract more sellers into the market.

As the pieces began to fall into place in Toby's mind, he realized that Mr. Leonard's scheme was to do both simultaneously. He was going to start rumors to affect investors' beliefs, and then make the problem worse by selling off Choate's stock at the same time. Toby got a sick feeling when he realized his own part in the plan. Mr. Leonard was planning to put his scheme in motion as soon as he received word from Toby that the market was about to head lower anyway. The downward effect on the market would be like giving a sledder a big push as he started down an icy hill.

The stock market could totally panic, and Choate would lose a fortune. Clearly, Mr. Leonard was planning to use the fake brokerage accounts to scoop up the stocks once they were cheap and then take a huge profit when they went back up. Even if someone pulled this off, though, there was no way they could actually get away with it. The government paid pretty close attention to these things. Professional investors went to jail all the time for shady trading. And now Toby had been set up to take the blame as blackmail if he didn't join Legio.

"I'm going to get blamed. I'll be either dead or in jail, and Mr. Leonard is going to be a very rich and very free man." Toby had to stop this from happening. He changed course on his bike and headed straight for Marc's house.

Toby was sweaty and out of breath when he rang the doorbell. Marc opened the door and looked him over.

"You look like heck warmed over."

"Thanks," Toby replied, as he brushed past Marc and strode uninvited into the house.

"So what's going on?"

"Call Bridge and have her come over right now. I'm going to need both of you tomorrow afternoon for a new mission. The stakes are much higher on this one, so we have a lot of planning to do."

Marc smiled, snapped to attention and saluted, "Yes, sir!" He spun on his heels and went to the kitchen to grab the phone.

Toby could hear one side of the phone conversation from the other room. After a few short words Marc came back in the room. "She's on her way."

CHAPTER 23

Toby Goes It Alone

WHEN TOBY DIDN'T SHOW up in the kitchen for breakfast the next morning, FM10 went to check on him. Her brow furrowed with worry, she briskly walked down the hallway and knocked on his door.

"Come in," came a muffled groan from within.

FM10 opened the door and walked into the room. Toby was on the bed, curled up like a guy who had just been kicked in the stomach for owing too much money to the mob. Like most kids, when Toby faked a tummy ache, he went a little overboard with the acting.

"Are you feeling okay?" FM10 sat down on the edge of the bed and felt his forehead.

Toby didn't want to lie to FM10, so he just grabbed his stomach and said, "I don't think I can go to school today," in the most pathetic voice he could muster.

"Do you want me to take you to the doctor?" she asked. "I've noticed that you haven't been eating much lately."

"NO! No…I'm sure I'll be okay. I probably just need some rest." Toby felt his ears starting to go beet red. He was certain that if she had taken his ear temperature right then, it would have shown a high-grade fever. Technically, he still hadn't told any lies, but he still felt guilty about deceiving FM10. She had always been kind to him.

"Alright, sweetie. I'll call the school and let them know."

Toby bristled and made a face whenever she called him "sweetie," but deep down he kind of liked it.

Toby forced a dismal half smile. "Thanks."

"You be sure to call me at work if you need anything."

"Okay." Toby then rolled back over on his side and gave one more little groan, for effect.

FM10 left the room, still looking quite concerned. Toby could hear her calling the school to report his absence. He then listened, one by one, as each of the inhabitants of the house left for the day. The last one to leave was always FM10 herself, because she didn't like to leave the house unless the kitchen was clean. She couldn't guarantee that result unless she left last.

Finally, Toby heard the back door shut, followed by the unique sound of FM10's car backing out of the driveway. There was something wrong with the power steering, so when she turned the wheel while backing up, the high-pitched choppy squeal of the steering mechanism sounded like an injured hyena was trapped under the hood.

Toby hopped out of bed, miraculously recovered from his stomach problems. He strapped on his watch, which he had synchronized with Marc and Bidge the night before. It was still more than an hour before the markets opened, so he took a shower, got dressed, and went to the kitchen to grab a bowl of cereal and read the *Journal.*

At 9:00 am, he went into the family room and turned on the financial news. It was still thirty minutes before the market opened. Stock futures were sharply higher in pre-market trading.

"Hmmm. Maybe there won't be any sharp drops today at all. That would certainly be a bummer for poor Mr. Leonard." Toby smiled.

As expected, the market opened higher — stocks were, on average, immediately trading at higher prices at the start of trading today than they were at the close of trading yesterday.

At 9:45 the phone rang.

"Hello?"

"I just wanted to see how you were feeling today." It was Mr. Leonard.

"Just a little under the weather. Blackmail has that effect on me. I'm staying home from school today to see if I can recover."

"Funny." It was clear that Mr. Leonard was not amused by Toby's attempt at humor. "Everything's in place. I'm just waiting for a signal from you."

"I understand. The market is feeling optimistic this morning, so I wouldn't hold my breath if I were you. You could be waiting quite a while for the mood to change. I'll call you when it does."

In reality, regardless of the mood of the market, Toby knew he wouldn't be making that phone call until Marc and Bidge were out of school. But Toby was beginning to have serious second thoughts about involving his two friends in this scheme. In the excitement of planning their new operation, Toby had lost sight of the whole reason that he did not get into that taxi with Angela and leave Wallingford forever. He needed to protect Bidge and Marc from Mr. Leonard.

But the bigger question was what he should do now. It would be infinitely easier if he didn't have any friends. He could just drop off the face of the earth, get trained in all the really cool superpowers, and then fight evil for the rest of his life. It was every kid's dream. On the other hand, though, there was no way Toby could turn his back on his best friends. And so there was no way he could risk exposing them in a direct confrontation with Mr. Leonard. If things went badly, Bidge and Marc could end up as bait to lure him back to work for Legio. If things went *really* badly, they could end up dead.

Ultimately, there were three choices: run, fight as a team, or fight alone. The first two options would both put Bidge and Marc at risk. The third option, fight alone, would only put himself at risk.

When he thought of it that way, there was really only one rational decision — Toby had to fight alone. He would go through with the plan that he had made with Bidge and Marc the night before. But now, he had to do it by himself. He could risk his own life, but not theirs.

▲ ▲ ▲

Bidge and Marc showed up together at Toby's house promptly at 2:45 pm, as planned.

"C'mon in."

"So are we ready to rock and roll?" Marc seemed energetic as they stepped into Toby's kitchen. He was probably faking.

Toby was not nearly as energetic. "Change in plans, guys. I'm doing this alone."

"What are you talking about?" Bidge fumed. "We went over Operation Pantalones II like a hundred times last night. How can you do it alone?"

"It's not that I don't want your help. It's just that I realized today that there is more risk than I had thought. I'm still going ahead with the plan, but I can't put you guys in danger, too."

"I don't care what the risks are. You're not doing this alone. We're all in this together, right Marc?" Bidge looked over at Marc so that he could chime in.

Marc looked at the floor, not sure what to say. If looks could have killed, Marc definitely would not have survived Bidge's glare at that moment.

She turned back to Toby and stuck her finger toward Toby's face. "You listen to me...I know you have this whole orphan-alone-against-the-world thing going on, but you can't shut me out at a time like this. That's not how friendship works."

"Look, it's my decision, not yours. I appreciate your concern, but this is something I have to do myself." He looked at his watch. It was nearly 3:00, only one hour until market close. "I really gotta go now." He started heading for the door.

"If you walk out that door without me, Toby, we're not friends anymore. I'm *serious*."

Toby turned and looked at Bidge. He felt as though she had just stuck a knife in his heart. "I'm really sorry, Bidge. I have to do this alone." With that, Toby ran out the kitchen door and hopped on his bike, leaving Bidge and Marc just staring after him with their jaws hanging open.

▲ ▲ ▲

Toby rode his bike straight to Mr. Leonard's house. He punched in the security code on the keypad, pressed his thumb against the scanner and let himself in the front door.

"Hello?" Toby called out. No one was home, and Max and Ginnie didn't meet him at the door as usual. Looking out the sliding glass door in the kitchen, he could see the dogs in the backyard chasing crows again. Toby went directly into Mr. Leonard's study. The room was different now, with all the books and knickknacks gone from the shelves. The furniture and the computer were still there, though — they would be the last things to go. Toby turned on the TV to watch the ticker. There was normally a lot of volatility in the last hour of trading. Toby was counting on this. As he watched the ticker, he turned on the computer, which had been moved off the desk onto the floor, but was still connected. The market seemed fairly stable, and the computer was taking its sweet time booting up, so he went to the garage to get things ready. In the last bay, Mr. Leonard's Porsche was gone. He must have taken it to Choate this morning.

Leaning against the wall across from where the car would have been was a shovel, with a roll of duct tape and a folded-up black garbage bag hanging on the handle. Toby felt a chill go down his spine as he wondered if those things were intended for him — to help dispose of his body. He shook it off and walked over to the side door of the garage and propped it open. He would need a quick escape path and might not have time to stop and open a locked door.

Toby went back into the house and sat down at the desk in the study. He checked the stock ticker on the TV. Still no sign of a big drop in the market. The computer had booted up, so Toby pulled up his email. There were no new messages, but he left the email page open anyway. He then opened up a new browser window and pulled up "his" brokerage account and logged in. There had been no activity since the last night. All the cash was still sitting there in the account, and Mr. Leonard had not done any purchases or sales of stock.

"Good." Toby sat back and thought for a few seconds. Making a command decision, he leaned forward and clicked the account settings link, then changed his password to "BidgeRules1." Now Mr. Leonard would at least be locked out of the one account that was actually in Toby's name. He just had to make sure he didn't think of the password when Mr. Leonard was around to read his mind. It's the hardest thing in the world to try *not* to

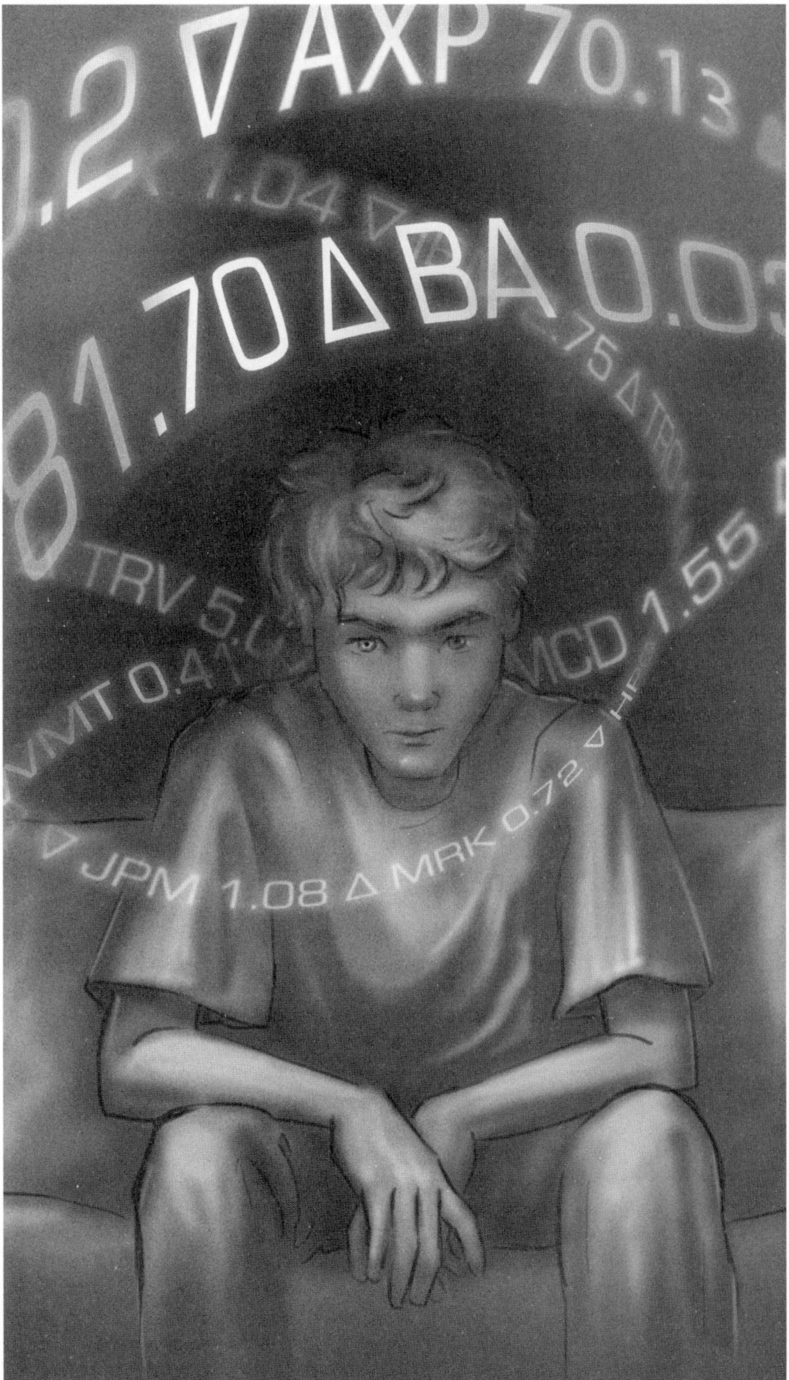
0.2 ▽ AXP 70.13
1.70 △ BA 0.0
TRV 5.0
MMIT 0.41
MCD 1.55
▽ JPM 1.08 △ MRK 0.72 △

think of something. Attempting to do so makes you think of it even more. Maybe if he recited a poem or song lyrics in his head he could keep himself from thinking anything inappropriate.

He turned his full attention to the television. It was 3:10. With any luck, Mr. Leonard hadn't started to freak out and tried to call Toby at home. Toby put that idea out of his mind and tried to relax and listen to the music of the market. The market was having a small rally. This meant that the mood was good, and overall prices were rising. Toby knew, though, that it wouldn't last. There had been no significant good news out there today, so it was just a rally based on mild positive emotion. And Toby could see that it was losing its steam quickly. He picked up the phone and called Mr. Leonard's office.

"Good afternoon, Jack Leonard's office." It was Mrs. Krebbs.

"Hi, Mrs. Krebbs. It's Toby. Can I speak to Mr. Leonard, please?"

"He's in a meeting right now with the Board of Trustees, but he told me to pull him out immediately if you called. Hold on a minute."

Mrs. Krebbs put Toby on hold. The on-hold music that was playing was a smarmy orchestral version of the 1980's song *Private Eyes*. Toby recognized it because FD4 had been a huge Hall and Oates fan. Their music was constantly playing in his car.

"Toby! I was starting to think that you weren't going to call. That would have been a mistake."

"Yeah, you made that pretty clear."

"So, do you have any good news for me?"

"Yup. The market is about to take a dive."

"I don't know. It looks more like a rally to me…" Mr. Leonard was skeptical.

"Yes, there's been a mild rally all afternoon, but it's losing its steam. It will start heading down any minute. Trust me."

"You're the expert, Toby. Hold on a sec while I get started with the trades."

▲ ▲ ▲

Mr. Leonard cradled the phone between his ear and shoulder so that he could use both hands on his laptop. Sure enough, within thirty seconds, the market started turning south. Mr. Leonard had crafted a very devious, but false, anonymous email message implicating several large companies in a corruption scheme. He addressed it to a handful of well-placed stock brokers who were part of the Wall Street rumor mill. A smile came across Mr. Leonard's face as clicked "send" on his email and started entering his "sell" orders on the computer. With each order, the market went into more of a tailspin.

Toby was still on the phone. Mr. Leonard then noticed the caller ID on the little screen on the black phone. Horrified, he realized that the call from Toby was coming from his own house!

"Son of a …"

Mr. Leonard silently placed the phone receiver down on the desk without hanging up. He entered his last two sell orders and logged off the computer. Opening his briefcase, he placed the papers from his desk into the inside lid pocket. He then removed a black nine-millimeter handgun from the briefcase and gently slid it into the pocket of his expensive Italian suit coat. He closed the briefcase, locked it, and slipped out the door and down the stairs.

On the TV set in the corner, the market continued to spiral downward.

Mrs. Krebbs looked up from her crossword puzzle. "Is the Board of Trustees meeting over already?"

"Not yet. I just realized I forgot something at home. I'll be back in a few minutes if anyone asks for me."

Mr. Leonard ran out the door and hopped into his Porsche. It was a warm sunny day, so he had left the top down. He pulled out of the parking lot and raced down Christian Street, much faster than the legal speed limit allowed. A speeding ticket was the least of his worries.

▲ ▲ ▲

Toby was still waiting on the other end of the phone. "Mr. Leonard? Hello?" When Mr. Leonard didn't respond, Toby knew that he had figured out where the call was coming from. He only had a few minutes before Mr. Leonard arrived, so he got into position. He took out of his pants pocket the small digital voice recorder that Marc had given him earlier and made sure that he knew where the red "record" button was. He put it into his right jacket pocket where he could easily reach in and turn it on.

Toby walked into the garage and down to where the pile of file boxes was. He took down the file box with all the brokerage statements and placed it in the middle of the garage floor. Pulling out a few of the files, he dumped the contents on the floor around the box. He needed to make it perfectly clear that he had discovered what was inside.

He then went back into the mudroom, closed the door to the garage, and hid in the pantry with the door shut. And waited.

He only had to wait a few minutes, but it seemed like forever. Time does weird things when you're sitting in a dark closet waiting for a guy to come kill you. Toby looked at his watch. It was 3:23. Only thirty-seven minutes until market close. Toby could still hear the TV from Mr. Leonard's study. The market had slid into a deep panic. Everyone wanted to sell and very few traders wanted to buy.

Then came the unmistakable squeal of the classic Porsche 356 turning into the driveway at high speed and coming to a sudden stop. Toby heard the front door open and Mr. Leonard walk quickly to his study. There was a pause, after which Toby heard a noise which sounded like it might have been an ammo clip being popped out of a handgun and then back in. Toby hoped it was just his imagination playing tricks on him.

"Toby?" Mr. Leonard yelled into the rest of the house. "Are you here, son?"

Toby *really* hated when he called him that. Toby reached into his jacket pocket and clicked the red button on the voice recorder. *It's showtime.*

▲ ▲ ▲

Toby opened the door to the pantry and rushed to the garage door, intentionally making plenty of noise. He opened the door to the garage and went inside, closing the door behind him. He could hear Mr. Leonard sprinting toward the source of the noise. It took him fewer than five seconds to reach the mudroom door to the garage. He flung it open, not even bothering to hide the weapon in his right hand. Toby had made it clear that he didn't intend on being recruited, so there was no longer any need for polite pretense.

Toby stood calmly in the middle of the garage floor, facing Mr. Leonard with as much courage as he could muster. He was holding something dark in both his left and right hands, which he immediately flicked toward Mr. Leonard using a smooth wrist and forearm motion.

A big glob of chocolate pudding hit Mr. Leonard squarely in each eye, temporarily blinding him. It was Toby's weapon of choice, and he had developed deadly aim. Mr. Leonard screamed and accidently fired a shot from his gun as he belatedly tried to block the incoming chocolaty projectiles with his arms. The bullet lodged harmlessly in the garage ceiling.

Toby took the opportunity to hide behind the metal trashcans along the wall. While Mr. Leonard was still scooping the pudding out of his eyes, Toby called out, "Mr. Leonard, I know what you're doing. Market manipulation is illegal. You'll never get away with it."

Jack Leonard stumbled down the two steps into the garage. He was holding the gun in his right hand and wiping the pudding out of his eyes with the left sleeve of his expensive Italian suit. The way he was stumbling aimlessly betrayed the fact that he still couldn't see where Toby was hiding. But he didn't really need to physically see Toby, whose thoughts would give away the details of his hiding place just as easily. Mr. Leonard stood motionless, with a look of concentration on his pudding-stained face.

Toby, in his mind, just recited, *"Mary had a little lamb. Its fleece was white as snow…"*

It was the classic blocking technique that Mr. Leonard himself probably had learned in Telepathy Defense 101. The mind can normally only think of one thing at a time, so the simplest way to defend a secret from a telepath is to consciously think of something else. But the fact that Toby was doing that did indeed reveal an import piece of information. It revealed that he knew about Mr. Leonard's ability and was therefore likely already to be working for the other side.

"Actually, son, I've already gotten away with it. I'm just here to tie up a few loose ends." He waved the gun back and forth in the air, clearly indicating that he still couldn't see where Toby was hiding.

"How did you open all those accounts in the name of dead economists?"

Mr. Leonard stopped briefly. "You know about those?" He shrugged and continued his semi-blind search. "It's actually not that hard. You just need a valid social security number to open the accounts. Eventually, they would have figured out that the names didn't match the numbers, but since the money will have been wired out of the accounts by then, it doesn't really matter that the authorities figure it out. Besides, as far as they're concerned, you did it, not me."

Toby was starting to get really ticked. "So how much will you make off this scam?"

"Enough. Depends on how much the market goes back up tomorrow. But in the end, it wasn't really about the money. That's just a side bonus."

"Why are you doing this, then?" Toby was attempting to draw out as much information as possible for the digital voice recorder in his pocket.

"Because when all this is over, you'll be dead, but everyone will think you're a crook and escaped to South America with the money. You will be remembered around here as a criminal."

"South America? Is that what the passport was for? You were going to fake like I had left the country?"

"You catch on quickly."

"But why me? Why do you hate me so much?"

"I don't hate you," Mr. Leonard laughed. "You actually seem like a pretty nice kid. I just hate everything your family represents. I would have preferred it if you had decided to join us."

"What do you mean? I don't even *have* a family."

"You still don't have any idea who you are, do you?"

Toby went cold. Until very recently, he had no idea. Now he had a vague idea of who he was, but still no detail. "No, I don't. Nobody does." Toby was trying desperately to keep himself from thinking about his meeting with Angela. *"...and everywhere that Mary went, the lamb was sure to go..."*

"Technically, that's not correct. I do. And because I know who you are, I also know what you can do."

"What do mean *what I can do*? You mean the stock market thing?"

Mr. Leonard laughed. "The *stock market thing*, as you call it, is just a parlor trick compared to your real talents. You see, son, everyone is born with at least one talent. But you are even more gifted than most. Your right eye makes that clear. That makes you extremely dangerous.

"I'm not dangerous. And what does my eye have to do with all this?"

Mr. Leonard had cleared enough pudding from his eyes that he could vaguely see Toby crouched behind the garbage cans. He raised his gun and slowly walked toward him. "You get it from your mother. Long story. Maybe I'll tell you the story some other time. Oh wait," Mr. Leonard continued sarcastically, "that won't be possible since you'll be buried under my flower beds in the backyard. Bummer."

"You *have* to tell me who I am!" Toby started to panic. When he planned his escape through the side door of the garage, he hadn't figured on Mr. Leonard having a gun. *Stupid!* He now couldn't see any possible way to make a break for the door without getting a bullet in the back.

"Sorry, not gonna happen, son. The only important thing is that as far as the world is concerned, you're just an evil orphan that stole a lot of money. No one will miss you when you're gone, because no one really cares about you."

Suddenly a familiar female voice came from behind the pile of boxes in the first garage bay, "One person cares." Bidge stepped out from behind the boxes with her video camera in her hand.

Mr. Leonard spun around to see her. Toby could see from the stunned look on his face that he hadn't been able to sense another person's thoughts in the room.

Bidge popped the memory disk out and held it up where Mr. Leonard could clearly see it in his still-vision-impaired state. She waved it in front of him, taunting him.

"Give me that!" Mr. Leonard screamed.

Then another voice came from the open side door of the garage, "Correction — two people care." It was Marc.

Toby wasn't sure if he was angry or happy that they had disobeyed his very clear instructions to stay home.

Bidge tossed the memory card high over Mr. Leonard's head into Marc's outstretched hand. If she had been on the basketball court, it would have been a three-pointer. In a flash, Marc disappeared out the door to his waiting bike and was gone.

"Stop!" Mr. Leonard commanded, attempting to project his mind forcefully into Marc's. Marc didn't obey. Mr. Leonard just stood there dumbfounded for a moment. Mr. Leonard, now realizing that he had to stop Marc the old-fashioned way, ran out the door and around the front of the garage to his car, which was parked in the driveway. He skidded around to the driver's side, placed his hand on the door, and catapulted himself over the door and into the driver's seat.

Splat. Mr. Leonard clearly hadn't noticed the big pile of pudding that Marc had put in the seat while waiting for Bidge to get the confession on videotape.

"Aaaaarrrr!!" Mr. Leonard's screamed with fury now that his coat, pants, and even his expensive leather upholstery were stained with chocolate. He jammed the car into reverse, spinning the tires loudly as he jolted out of the driveway after Marc.

Toby and Bidge ran out of the garage in time to see Marc way down the street, pumping his legs as hard as they would go, heading straight for Choate. According to plan, he cut through the yard between two houses so that Mr. Leonard couldn't easily follow, disappearing out of sight.

▲ ▲ ▲

Toby gave Bidge a long hug, then pulled back at arm's length and scowled. "I distinctly remember telling you guys *not* to come here today."

"I've never been very good at taking direction," Bidge observed. "It's been a common theme at all my parent-teacher conferences. Are you mad?"

"Are you nuts? You saved my freaking life. I didn't even consider that Mr. Leonard might have a gun. As far as I know, most Wall Street financial crimes don't usually involve weapons. If you guys hadn't shown up, I'd probably be dead by now."

"I'm really glad you're not," Bidge said, stating the obvious.

There was an uncomfortable silence for a few seconds, so Bidge punched him in the arm to end it.

"Ow!"

"That's for risking your life without us."

"Point taken. Next time I'll be sure to use you as a human shield against my adversaries." Toby grinned. "You got the real memory card?"

"Of course." She handed it to him.

"C'mon inside." They ran into Mr. Leonard's study and uploaded the video file onto his computer. Toby had prepared an email earlier, which was still open and ready to go. He dragged the video file onto the email message with the subject, "Choate Trustee Illegal Trading Evidence." Toby had pre-addressed the

216

message to all of the Board of Trustees, the Enforcement Division of the Securities and Exchange Commission, and to Mrs. Krebbs.

Toby clicked *Send* and then picked up the phone and dialed Mr. Leonard's office again.

"Good afternoon, Jack Leonard's office." Mrs. Krebbs had answered the phone.

"Hi, Mrs. Krebbs, this is Toby."

"Well, hello Toby. Mr. Leonard's not in right now."

"I know. I have something really important that you need to do right away."

"What is it?

"I just sent an email to you a few seconds ago. Has it arrived?"

Mrs. Krebbs pulled up her email account. "Nope. I don't see anything from you at all. Wait…there it is. It just came up."

Toby sighed with relief. "Okay, this is a life-or-death situation. I sent that same email to the Board of Trustees. It's about Mr. Leonard. Is the board still in their meeting?"

"Yes, they'll be there until after five. What's this about?" Mrs. Krebbs was starting to sound a little annoyed.

"I need you to interrupt their meeting and have them watch the video I sent. It's very important."

"I can't just go in there and make them do something," Mrs. Krebbs replied, her annoyance clearly present in her voice. "I like my job here, and that sounds like a sure way to lose it."

"Go ahead and watch the video yourself first, then. Just double-click on the file. You'll understand why the board needs to see it. Please hurry, we're on our way there right now." Toby hung up the phone and they sprinted out the front door to their bikes. It was 3:30 pm, only thirty minutes until the stock market closed.

CHAPTER 24

Red Means Bad

MARC WAS RUNNING OUT of steam. He hadn't been able to ride straight to Choate, since he had been forced to take evasive maneuvers to escape the Porsche. Mr. Leonard had almost caught him a couple of times. Marc finally got the lead he needed by riding right into the lower level of the Half Moon Café, on the hillside by the parking lot. He hopped off his bike and ran it up the stairs into the main cafeteria section of the restaurant. The manager yelled at him and threatened to call the cops. Involving the cops might actually have worked out okay, but it wasn't the plan. He saw Mr. Leonard circling around the building a few times waiting for him to come out. After a couple minutes, it become obvious that Marc wasn't coming out, so he parked the car and walked menacingly toward the entrance. As soon as Mr. Leonard stepped inside, Marc booked it out the door on the other side of the restaurant. This move gave Marc a thirty-second jump on Mr. Leonard, as well as a much-needed chance to catch his breath. It was times like these that Marc wished that he was in better shape. Fortunately, the Choate campus was just across the street.

Marc rode the last quarter mile over the grass to the administration building. By this point, Mr. Leonard had figured out where he was headed, so he took the long way around, down Christian Street, rather than try to go across the lawn in the Porsche. Marc stood up on his pedals and pumped like there was no tomorrow. Because if he didn't get to that building first, there might not *be* a tomorrow.

Marc jumped off his bike in front of the building just as Mr. Leonard tried taking the corner into the parking lot just a little too fast and spun out. Mr. Leonard sprang out of the car and ran toward Marc just as he ducked in the door.

Marc had never been there before, but Toby had described in detail the layout of the building. He ran for the stairs and headed for the second floor. He could hear Mr. Leonard's heavy footsteps on the stairs right behind him. Just as he reached the top of the stairs, Mr. Leonard in a lucky grab got a brief hold on Marc's left foot. Marc went down hard, face first into the carpet of the second floor hallway. Yanking his foot away, he kicked Mr. Leonard squarely in the face, sending him backwards down five steps onto the landing below. Mr. Leonard was still holding Marc's left shoe.

Marc just sat there for a second, impressed with his own fully awesome kung fu moves, when he realized that he should really still be running. Marc scrambled to his feet and sprinted toward the conference room at the end of the hallway.

Mr. Leonard was right behind him, catching up again quickly. "Give me that disk, you little punk!" He dove for Marc again, football style, this time catching him around both legs as they crashed through the door into the board of trustees meeting. They came to a stop huddled in a pile at the feet of Mrs. Krebbs, who was controlling the video projector on the conference table. On the video screen was the end of a very recognizable scene from just a few minutes earlier in Mr. Leonard's garage. From the computer speakers came the voice of Jack Leonard saying "Give me that!" and Marc interrupting with "Correction — two people care." The video ended with Mr. Leonard commencing the chase of Marc, which had just coincidentally ended right there on the floor of the conference room in a live-action finale.

The gray-haired man at the head of the conference table spoke first. It was Jerry Ott, the executive director. He looked unsmilingly at Mr. Leonard there on the floor still holding onto the legs of a thirteen-year-old boy. He noticed the pudding stains on the seat of Mr. Leonard's expensive Italian suite. "Hello, Jack. Is that poop on your pants?"

Mr. Leonard didn't bother to correct the mistake. "I can explain," he said, still trying to catch his breath.

"Excellent," replied Mr. Ott. "I've already called the police. You can explain it to *them*."

Mr. Leonard got a concentrated look on his face and made eye contact with Mr. Ott. "It's not what it looks like, Jerry, you've got it all wrong. *Toby Gold is the only criminal here.*"

Mr. Ott's angry expression only got angrier. "We're not idiots, Jack. We just saw the whole thing on video. You're not going to be able to talk your way out of this one."

Confused by his unsuccessful attempt to use mind-control, Mr. Leonard put two fingers against the side of his neck and looked at his watch, like he was taking his own pulse. After a few seconds, he scowled and dropped his hands to his side. *One hundred twenty beats per minute. Crap.*

Just then Toby and Bidge ran into the room, breathing hard and barely able to speak.

Mr. Leonard looked first at his Toby, then at Mr. Ott. All other options now exhausted, he ran for the door. The stare that he gave Toby on the way out the door was pure evil. It was the kind of look that said, without words, "You *will* regret this." Toby shuddered and then walked briskly to the window overlooking the parking lot.

Mr. Leonard flew down the stairs, out the front door and jumped back into his Porsche.

Splat. He plopped into another pile of chocolate pudding that Toby had placed in the driver's seat just before entering the building.

The scream of frustration that left Mr. Leonard's lungs at that moment became a Choate legend. All over campus, birds burst out of the trees, forming a huge cloud in the sky, black as Mr. Leonard's soul. The board of trustees heard the scream loudest, being only thirty yards away. They recognized the voice, of course, and hoped that Mr. Leonard perhaps had been physically wounded.

Gathering his wits, Mr. Leonard started the engine and sped down Christian Street for the last time.

Meanwhile, back in the conference room, Marc at last emerged from under the conference table. He had stayed down there during the whole exchange, displaying his more typical level of courage. The three friends exchanged high-fives. Operation Pantalones II had been a success. It was now 3:38 pm, twenty-two minutes until market close.

▲ ▲ ▲

"Toby Gold, I presume?" Mr. Ott walked briskly over to where the kids were standing with an outstretched hand. Toby shook it. "My name is Jerry Ott. I am the executive director of the board of trustees."

"Nice to meet you."

"We've just seen the video you sent. On behalf of the board and Choate Rosemary Hall, let me extend my deepest apologies for what Mr. Leonard has attempted to do to you."

"Apology accepted. It wasn't the school's fault — it was Mr. Leonard's. I should have known better than to trust a man with fancy cufflinks." Mr. Ott looked down at the cuffs on his sleeves, which happened to be held together by a couple of fancy looking cufflinks. Toby noticed this and immediately felt embarrassed, since he had only been referring to Mr. Leonard with that last statement.

The temporarily festive mood was interrupted when two police officers appeared at the door, both of them fat, but one considerably taller than the other. "We were called about a disturbance," the shorter one stated, hands on his hips, looking around the room suspiciously.

Mr. Ott stepped forward and put his hands on Toby's shoulders. "Yes," he replied, "the man you want is Jack Leonard. He committed a major financial crime against this school then attempted to kill this young man to cover it up. We are all willing to give statements on the matter, but right now he is getting away, so you might want to go catch him."

"You heard the man," the short cop said to the tall one. "Let's roll!" He turned again to Mr. Ott. "Umm, what kind of car is he driving?"

"Some kind of sports car. A convertible I think --"

"It's a silver 1955 Porsche 356 Speedster with red leather interior," interrupted Toby.

"Shaaweet," said the tall cop.

"And he has a gun," Toby added.

"Good to know. We'll be back as soon as we can to take your statements. Nobody leaves the building, okay?" There were nods all around the room. The two officers speed-waddled out the door, and the occupants of the conference room could hear one say into his police radio, 'We have an attempted murder suspect fleeing the scene of a crime at the Choate campus. He's driving a

222

silver antique Porsche convertible. Suspect is armed and danger-ous…"

Mr. Ott took a deep breath and turned his attention to Toby. "I've been looking forward to meeting you, Toby. I wish it had been under better circumstances. We've heard a great deal about you. Apparently you are a young man of extraordinary talents."

"So they tell me."

"Well, I'm hoping that we might utilize those talents right now. Do you have online access to Choate's investment ac-counts?"

"Yes, sir. I know the account number and password."

"Good. Would you mind sitting down here at the computer and accessing the account? We need to know the extent of the damage that Mr. Leonard has done today."

"No problem." Toby sat down and logged into the Choate account at Legio Investments. The conference room projector displayed the account summary page on a nine-foot screen on the wall.

There were many groans from the trustees. "Toby, you're familiar with our accounts. Tell me, how much have we actually lost today?"

Toby hesitated. This was going to be bad. "Just over twenty-eight million dollars, sir."

Several of the board members slumped into their chairs. Mr. Ott frowned and thought for a moment. "Toby," he asked, "is there any way you could reverse the damage that Mr. Leonard has done here today?"

Toby looked at the clock on the wall. It was 3:40 pm, twenty minutes to market close. "Well, that depends. By manipulating the market myself in the opposite direction, I'm pretty sure I could definitely do it, but I think that would be just as illegal as what Mr. Leonard did."

"You're absolutely right, Toby. And we don't want any more laws broken today. Is there any way to reverse the damage *without* market manipulation?"

"I can't be totally sure, sir, but I think that maybe I can."

Mr. Ott turned to the other board members seated around the table. "I move that we authorize Mr. Toby Gold to make stock trades in the Choate account in order to attempt to reverse the losses that Jack Leonard has perpetrated against us today. Does anyone second that motion?"

"I second it," came the response from one of the directors on the opposite side of the table.

"All those in favor, say 'Aye,'" continued Mr. Ott.

"Aye," responded six of the nine directors.

"Any opposed, say 'Nay.'"

"Nay." Only one of the directors opposed the motion, a stern-looking woman named Irene Jensen. The other two remaining directors abstained from the vote. They were justifiably too scared to be on the record for letting a thirteen-year-old kid trade stocks in the name of the school.

"The 'Ayes' have it. Motion approved. Toby, get to work." It was 3:41 pm.

"Does that TV over there have cable?" Toby asked. There was a television in the corner of the room mounted to the ceiling.

"Satellite," responded Mrs. Krebbs.

"That'll work. Can someone please turn on the financial news channel?"

Mrs. Krebbs picked up the remote, turned on the TV, and flipped through the channels until the right one appeared. The stock ticker came into view, streaming across the bottom of the screen like a magnificent dancing red ribbon.

From the sea of red color on the screen, Toby immediately knew that the market had taken losses that day, and those losses were severe. The good news for Toby was that the downward momentum felt as though it had nearly slowed to a stop. So Toby took the plunge and entered his first buy order. It was a small one, buying back some of the shares of one of the companies that Choate had held at the beginning of the day. A little green blip appear on the ticker, as the price nudged upwards in order to fill his order.

Toby sat back and let the new ticker data swirl through his head. The market still held a lot of uncertainty. It was as though the market was hoping that things were starting to turn around, but was hesitating, not quite sure what to believe.

Toby was careful to make each stock purchase small enough that his orders did not influence the market price. Otherwise, he would have been manipulating the market, just like Jack Leonard had done earlier, only in the opposite direction. Instead, his orders were just gentle nudges, after which he relied on the subsequent trends and momentum to take him where he needed to go.

He entered another series of small buy orders, this time for a different stock that had been in Choate's portfolio earlier, but had been sold by Mr. Leonard.

The market was starting to turn around. More and more green appeared on the ticker and a smile came across Toby's face. He entered more buy orders, slowly building the Choate portfolio back to the way it had been.

Then Toby began to be concerned, but for a totally different reason. "Mr. Ott, this may sound like a strange question…do you want Choate to make a profit today, take a loss, or just break even?" It was 3:50 pm, only ten minutes to market close.

Mr. Ott was surprised at the question. He had hoped that Toby might be able to recover some of the losses, but hadn't considered that a profit was possible. The idea that this tragedy might

turn into a success was tremendously appealing. His face bright-
ened for a moment, but then the scowl returned.

"Toby, if you can, we need to come as close to breaking even
as possible. What Jack Leonard did today was blatantly illegal.
Furthermore, to tell you the truth, I'm not sure if what we're doing right now is totally okay or not. But what I *am* sure about is
that if Choate makes a profit from today's events, it will make the
school look quite bad… like we were in on the whole scheme. So
I think the best course of action is to just do our best to reverse
the illegal actions of our rogue director to the best of our abilities in order to protect the investments of the school. Therefore, a
small loss today would be the ideal outcome."

Toby nodded and turned his attention back to the computer
screen.

Mr. Ott leaned down and whispered in Toby's ear. "Just try to
make that loss as small as possible, okay?"

Toby smiled and nodded again. His eyes darted back and
forth from the TV to the computer screen. He still had a lot more
stock to buy back, but now he had to wait a little longer for the
market to go higher. Otherwise he would be buying at too low a
price and the school would end up with a highly suspicious profit
at the end of the day. So he mostly waited, picking up shares here
and there, slowly reversing Mr. Leonard's losses without accidentally driving the prices up too high. The market rally began to lose
momentum.

Rat Snacks, Toby thought as he started to panic. He focuses
all his energy on the market song and the swirling numbers in
his head. Toby entered the last round of purchase orders for the
remaining stocks he needed to restore the portfolio to its original
condition, but he couldn't to press the *Enter* key until the market
was right. It was 3:59 p.m. He was *so* close he could taste it.

Toby doubled his focus. His brow became furrowed and sweaty, then closed his eyes for one last ditch mental push. *Up, Up, Up,* Toby thought desperately. *You have to go up NOW!*

Toby opened his eyes, but could no longer see the conference room. For a brief second, he was standing on the trading floor of the New York stock exchange. He looked down at his hands, turning them over, then back again, in confusion. These were *not* his hands. He was somehow seeing through someone else's eyes!

Then, in the next moment, he could see the trading floor from a different person's perspective, from the opposite side of the room. But the view from the first person was still there, just overlaid by the second view. It was very disorienting. In the brief second that it took to get accustomed to seeing two points of view at the same time, it became four. Then eight. The doubling continued until he found himself in the minds of hundreds of traders simultaneously. It was like watching every channel on cable at the same time. The noise of all their thoughts at once was deafening, creating an overwhelming buzz in his head. As the last moments of the trading day ticked by, Toby became ever dizzier as he tried to force himself to stay conscious. He felt his mind being squashed by the force of so many other competing minds in his head.

Just as he felt himself slipping away into unconsciousness, he mustered one more force of will. "UP!" he screamed to all the other people occupying his head. Back in the conference room, the scream had been out loud. The whites of Toby's eyes fluttered back in his head as he hit the *Enter* key and fell unconscious to the floor.

▲ ▲ ▲

CLANG CLANG CLANG. The closing bell for the New York Stock Exchange rang out, signaling the end of trading for the day. Bidge and Marc knelt beside Toby on the floor, trying to shake him awake.

"Toby…TOBY! Are you okay?" Bidge appeared frantic. Toby was completely out, but still breathing. Bidge's shaking of his shoulders was having no apparent effect, however.

Mr. Ott was wringing his hands and looking around the table at the other members of the finance committee. "Should we call an ambulance or something?"

"No, I'm okay." Toby slowly opened his eyes, hoping that he would only be seeing through his own eyes. To his great relief, he was. As he was giving himself a quick once-over to check for injuries, a small drop of blood emerged from his right nostril, hesitated briefly, then quickly traveled the remaining distance down to his upper lip where it paused again. Toby wiped it unceremoniously on his sleeve.

"You gave us quite a scare there, young man," Mr. Ott said. "Are you sure you don't want us to call a doctor?"

"No, really. I feel fine now." Toby tried his best to sound reassuring. "So, how did we do?" Toby asked, attempting to change the subject and deflect attention from his embarrassing fainting spell.

All eyes in the room then turned to the computer screen near Toby.

"To be honest, we're not sure," Mr. Ott replied. "We were kind of waiting for you to tell us."

Toby got back up from the floor and sat back down in his chair. He looked down at the computer screen, doing some quick calculations in his head. "The way I figure it, when all is said and done, we ended up taking a loss of seven hundred and twenty-six dollars, give or take."

A deafening cheer went up from around the conference table. He could have sworn that a couple of them were even crying with joy. Mr. Ott was the first to embrace Toby. "Young man," he said, "you just saved Choate."

One by one each member of the board of trustees came to Toby, except for Irene Jensen. She was in the corner talking on her cell phone. They exuberantly shook his hand, not with regular handshakes, but those two-handed handshakes that men do when they're really happy to see each other. They made comments to him like "great job," "thank you so much" and "that was truly amazing."

All the attention was rather embarrassing for Toby. He was accustomed to being socially invisible, so his sudden hero status was uncomfortable, like wearing a new wool sweater on bare skin. Even if it's a really expensive high-quality sweater, it still feels itchy. He just wanted to get out of there.

Bidge and Marc were the last to approach him.

"Looks like we're all alive," Toby said.

"Barely," Marc responded, trying to sound annoyed.

"That was pretty incredible what you just did in there," Bidge said. "How did you do that?"

"I don't know really. I just sort of absorb the market data and then I know what to do. This is the first time I've actually traded stocks. It was fun."

"Probably would have been even more fun without a room full of stressed out directors staring at the back of your head," Marc added.

Mr. Ott cleared his throat loudly. "I think that we should adjourn the meeting for today. I need to go make some phone calls and alert the Securities and Exchange Commission about Mr. Leonard's actions. Everyone just sit tight until the police come back to do their investigation. I'll have Mrs. Krebbs order some food for everyone."

Mrs. Krebbs nodded and left the room.

Mr. Ott walked over to where the three kids were standing. He spoke first to Bidge and Marc. "I want to thank you both for what you did today, it was quite brave and it showed great loyalty to your friend."

"You're welcome, sir," Bidge said.

"Anytime," Marc added.

He then turned to Toby. "Toby, if you don't mind, please go ahead and change the password on our investment account and log off. We don't want Mr. Leonard getting back in there."

"Sure, no problem." Toby quickly changed the password to *BidgeRocks1* and then logged off.

"Also, if you have a few minutes, would you mind coming down to my office?"

"Okay." Toby and Mr. Ott left the conference room and went down the hall to the third office on the right. It was much larger than Mr. Leonard's. Brighter, too. The office faced west, so the afternoon sunshine poured into the room through the large window, bathing everything in a radiant golden glow.

"Sit down, Toby." Mr. Ott smiled and motioned to one of the big leather chairs in front of his desk. Toby sat down in the one on the left. Mr. Ott, instead of sitting in his own chair behind the desk, sat down in the other guest chair right beside Toby.

"I just wanted to thank you again for what you did for Choate today. It could have been a real disaster for us if you hadn't come to the rescue."

Toby blushed. He was uncomfortable with all this praise. There hadn't been much of it in his life up until today. "Glad I could help" was the only thing he could think of to say. Toby thought about the twenty-eight million dollars for a moment, then realized something bad. "Mr. Ott, you're probably not aware of this, but today is not the first time Mr. Leonard has done illegal trading on Choate's accounts. The whole reason that I dug into

230

his files and uncovered his plan was because I was trying to figure out how he was earning fourteen percent returns on Choate's portfolio. He's been manipulating the market for at least three years."

Mr. Ott's face fell. "Well, Toby, it is what it is. Thanks for telling me. I'll pass that along to the SEC. We may end up paying fines for what he did, but the important thing is to get this behind us. When the police and the government investigators get statements from you, just tell them everything you can remember about the whole incident. If there's any issue with the government about the stock trading you did for us this afternoon, I will back you up and tell them that we asked you to do it to try to undo Jack Leonard's trades — since you were the only one familiar with the accounts. I think it's best that we don't mention your special *talent* with financial data. That will only confuse matters and draw more attention to you. I will suggest to the other board members that they consider exercising similar discretion with regard to your privacy. Ultimately, what they say will be entirely up to them though."

Toby just nodded in agreement.

Mr. Ott continued. "Again, on behalf of the school, I sincerely apologize for all this. We feel quite fortunate that a young man of your talents and abilities will be joining our student body next year. I promise that your future here at Choate will be much less dangerous than today!" Toby knew that Mr. Ott had no way of keeping that promise, but it was an admirable gesture anyway.

"I'm really anxious to get started here this Summer."

"Good. I'm glad this experience hasn't affected your opinion of the school." Mr. Ott laughed and patted Toby on the knee. He seemed relieved that Toby was still coming. "On a more serious note, though, you saved the school twenty-eight million dollars today. We owe you a tremendous debt of gratitude. So if there is ever anything we can do for you, anything at all, you just let me know. Okay?"

"Anything?"

"ANYTHING," Mr. Ott replied. Then he thought better of it and added with a grin, "Well, anything that is legal and within my power, that is."

Toby sat back and thought for a minute. Then he leaned toward Mr. Ott with a glimmer in his eye. "Well, now that you mention it, there *is* something you can do for me…"

▲ ▲ ▲

Toby, Bidge and Marc spent the rest of that afternoon and evening in the conference room answering questions from the police. All the parents, and foster parents, had to be called. One by one they arrived, in various stages of hysteria. Marc's parents were the worst. His mom was a complete basket case, but was overjoyed that her little boy was safe from the homicidal maniac. She couldn't stop kissing his forehead, much to his embarrassment and the intense amusement of Toby and Bidge, who took a picture of the effusive mother-son affection with her cell phone. Bidge's mom simply hugged her daughter, asked her if she was okay, and then took her home, glaring at Toby on her way out of the room. She clearly was displeased that he had mixed her up in this whole situation.

When FM10 came to pick up Toby, he could tell that she had been crying. She hugged him and said, "I came home early today to check on you to see if you were feeling better. You weren't home and I was worried sick about you."

Toby felt like a jerk for lying to her earlier. "I'm really sorry I lied to you. I would never have done it if I wasn't being black-mailed."

"I know, Toby. Mr. Ott already called me and explained what happened. "I'm very proud of you, but *never* do anything like that again, okay?"

"I'll try," replied Toby.

She scowled at him.

As they walked toward the car, Toby said, "Can I ask you a favor?"

"Anything, sweetie," she replied.

"I need to open a savings account at the bank. Would you mind co-signing the application with me?"

CHAPTER 25

Am I in Trouble?

TOBY NEEDED TO TALK to Earl, so he decided to take the bus to school the next day instead of walking. As he shuffled out to the bus stop, Toby mulled over the many questions he had that remained unanswered. So much had happened, yet he still felt almost completely in the dark about what was really going on.

With its big red lights flashing, the bus pulled up to the curb and the door opened. There was Earl, as usual, with a big warm grin on his face. Today he was wearing a blue jumpsuit instead of his typical tan one. Toby figured it must be a special occasion.

"Hello there, young man. Hop aboard!"

Toby climbed onto the bus and took the first seat, directly to Earl's right. There were only ten other students on the bus, all gathered in the back.

Earl broke the silence. "That was some impressive work you did yesterday. We're all very proud of you," he said in a hushed tone.

Toby replied, "I thought you told me the other day that you were assigned to protect me. Where *were* you yesterday?"

234

"Oh, I was around. If things had gotten any more hairy, I might have stepped in. You seemed to be handling it just fine without me."

"Right. Mr. Leonard's gun was certainly no match for my chocolate pudding," replied Toby, his words dripping with sarcasm.

"You were very resourceful. You're a lot like your dad that way."

"You know my dad?" Toby asked. He leaned forward on his seat.

"Knew," Earl replied, lowering his voice. "Toby, your father is dead. He was murdered by Jack Leonard in Manhattan that same night you were found on the train."

"What about my mom? Is she alive?"

Earl looked uncomfortable. "I've already said too much. Too much knowledge is a dangerous thing for you still."

"*Angela* is my mother, isn't she?"

"You'll have to take that up with Angela the next time you meet," Earl said. "The night you were found, Jack Leonard shot your mother and threw her from the train. As far as Legio knows, she died that night. We wouldn't want them thinking any different, now, would we?"

▲ ▲ ▲

The story of Toby's police incident had spread around quickly via the middle school rumor mill. There were several versions of the story, all of them inaccurate, and each more fantastic than the next. Toby's favorite version was that his real father was a mafia boss who had finally made contact and had involved him in a scheme to blackmail the headmaster at Choate. Nobody dared to actually ask him what the real story was, so he just kept quiet and let everyone's imagination run wild. Even the eighth graders seemed a little scared of him. He liked that.

He sat with Bidge and Marc at lunch, just like old times.

"I just wish I could have seen his face when he sat in the pudding the second time," Marc said. "That was a nice touch, Toby. You really have a good eye for detail."

"Well, when Bidge and I got there on our bikes, I still had two pudding cups in my jacket. I figured I might as well put them to good use."

They all laughed and made plans for the weekend.

Later that day, when Toby arrived home from school, there were two investigators from the Securities and Exchange Commission waiting inside with FM10. One of the agents was middle-aged and mostly bald. The other was younger, sort of military-looking with a blond buzz cut.

"Sit down Toby," the bald agent said. He was smiling. Toby took that as a good sign.

"Have you caught Mr. Leonard yet?" Toby asked hopefully.

"Unfortunately, no," replied the bald agent. "His car was found at JFK airport, but there was no sign of Jack Leonard, and no record of him as a passenger on any flight. The only clue was a gate attendant in the international terminal that kept saying 'these are not the droids we're looking for.' A flight to Brazil had left from that gate twenty minutes earlier."

"So he's still out there? Am I in danger? What if he comes back for me?"

"We think it's unlikely that he'll come back here where he'd be recognized. And with all the evidence you collected against him, we could get a conviction even without your direct testimony, so there's really no good reason for him to kill you now."

"Oh. That makes me feel much better," Toby said, trying unsuccessfully to hide his insincerity. "So am I in any trouble?"

"Should you be?" The buzz-cut agent raised one blond eyebrow inquisitively.

Toby shook his head.

"We just need to take a statement from you — and ask you a few questions. We've reviewed the video you emailed to us. You really should have contacted us before, rather than put yourself in danger like that."

"I was afraid that you'd believe him and not me. He told me you wouldn't, and I didn't have any evidence that could prove my innocence."

Toby told them the whole story from start to finish. He gave them the folder in his backpack that contained all of the brokerage statement copies, including the one in Toby's name.

"Just one more question," the bald agent asked, "why on earth did the board of trustees ask a thirteen-year-old kid to reverse Mr. Leonard's stock trades?"

Toby became a bit nervous and his voice was shaky. "I suppose it's because the market was about to close, and I was the only one in the room that was familiar with the accounts and with the trades that Mr. Leonard had made. I guess with only a few minutes left of trading, I was their only option."

"You got pretty lucky. Your school came out relatively undamaged by the whole thing."

My school. Toby liked the sound of that. He hadn't started thinking of Choate as *his* school yet. "That's what they tell me, sir. I'm just glad I was able to help."

CHAPTER 26

A Surprise for Bidge

OVER THE NEXT DAYS and weeks, life mostly returned to normal for the kids of Wallingford, both at Choate and at Dag Hammarskjold. But for Bidge, it would never be quite normal again. She had been practicing her telepathy skills with Toby and was starting to really enjoy the feeling. It made her feel powerful.

Exactly two weeks later, though, her life changed yet again. Bidge was just getting home from school when the phone rang.

"I'll get it!" she yelled sarcastically. Her brothers never answered the phone, and her mom normally just let the answering machine pick it up, unless it happened to ring during a commercial.

"Hello?"

"Hello, may I speak to Bridget Donnelly please?" The voice on the other end was deep and professional-sounding.

"Speaking."

"This is Ed Stanis. I'm the head coach of the girls' basketball team here at Choate. We've been very impressed with your playing this season. We'd like to set up a meeting to talk about you joining us here next year."

"You've seen me play?" Bidge was stunned. She dropped into a nearby kitchen chair.

"We sure have. My assistant coach scouts around at the local junior high games looking for talent. We were both at your game against Moran Middle School. Are you interested in talking to us about it?"

"Yes, of course I'm interested. You've got a great team. But..."

"Is there a problem?" Coach Stanis asked.

Bidge was a little embarrassed. "My dad died two years ago. We don't have money for private school."

"We have ways of dealing with that kind of financial situation. Tomorrow is Friday. Can you and your mother meet me at the admissions office at 3:00 p.m.?"

"Sure," she replied.

"Great. It was nice speaking with you, Bidge. I look forward to meeting you in person tomorrow."

"Me, too. Bye." Bidge was physically shaking when she hung up the phone. Nothing good had happened to her since her dad and sister had died. She barely dared to hope that her luck might be changing.

▲　▲　▲

After school the next afternoon, Toby was out on the lawn in front of the Choate admissions office, waiting with hands in pockets for Bidge and her mom as they left the building after their meeting. Bidge was wearing a dark green dress. Toby had never seen her in a dress before. She almost looked like a girl. She was beaming from ear to ear. Even her mom was smiling, which was an event in itself.

Bidge saw Toby and waved excitedly. She turned to her mom and said, "You go ahead home, Mom. I'm going to stay here a while with Toby, if that's okay. We'll walk back."

Her mom gave her a hug. "I'll see you later on. I'll make dinner tonight, okay?" Her mom hadn't made dinner in over two years.

Bidge became misty-eyed and gave her mom another hug. "Sure. I'd like that."

Toby and Bidge walked toward the flagpole in silence. Bidge was looking around the campus as if for the first time, different now that she was no longer an outsider. They both lay down on the grass face up, with feet pointed in opposite directions but with their heads only about a foot apart. The clouds meandered slowly across the sky like a sparse herd of gigantic, lazy sheep.

Bidge was the first to speak. "You're the one behind all this, right?"

"The trustees were very grateful for your help." Toby paused for a moment. "But you realize that if you become a Choatie like me, the smell will be unbearable…"

Bidge blushed, being reminded of her earlier opposition to Toby's change of schools. "Yeah, sorry about that one."

"Already forgotten," Toby said dismissively with a wave of the hand.

Bidge was silent for several seconds, then smiled and said, "Eight."

Toby had just been calculating the cube root of five hundred twelve in his head. "Yup. You're getting good. And you weren't even making eye contact."

Toby's hand accidentally brushed against hers. She grabbed it and held it tight. "You know that you're the most amazing friend ever, don't you?"

Toby just smiled and didn't answer for a few seconds. "You, too, Bidge. And welcome to Choate."

"Thanks. I feel bad that Marc's not coming here, too."

"I tried. Choate offered him a scholarship and everything."

"Was it his dad?"

"Yup. Being a public school teacher, it would have looked bad to send his son to a private school. The PTA gets bugged about stuff like that."

Bidge got a sad look on her face. "It would have been cool if it had been all three of us here next year."

"Yeah."

Just then a man in a navy blue blazer walked up to them. "Mr. Gold?"

"Oh, hi Mr. Sheehan," Toby replied. It was the headmaster. "It's okay for us to be here, isn't it?"

"Of course. Is this Miss Donnelly?"

"Yes, it is." Suddenly remembering his manners, Toby made the introduction. "Bridget Donnelly, this is Mr. Sheehan, the headmaster here at Choate."

"It's a pleasure to meet you, Mr. Sheehan."

"The pleasure is mine. I've heard lots of wonderful things about you."

Bidge just blushed and looked down at her feet.

"If you two have a few minutes, I have something to show you back at my house."

The headmaster's house was just a short walk across campus. As they arrived at the front door, two energetic golden retrievers greeted them.

Toby recognized them at once. "Max and Ginnie!" He immediately dropped to the floor and hugged his old friends. Max dropped a slimy tennis ball at Toby's knees. Toby looked up at Mr. Sheehan. "But how—"

"The Leonards apparently left town without the dogs. The police found them in the backyard after the neighbors complained about the barking, so they were taken to the city dog pound. I knew from the police reports that you had been walking them every day this past year. I figured you wouldn't want them destroyed by Animal Control."

Toby was horrified at the idea that Max and Ginnie might have been killed if no one had claimed them. "What's going to happen to them now?"

"My wife and I were thinking that we might keep them here with us," Mr. Sheehan replied. "That's assuming, of course, that you are available to walk them every day, Mr. Gold."

"That won't be any problem at all!" Toby gave the dogs another hug. Ginnie responded by licking his ear enthusiastically.

"Then it's all settled," said Mr. Sheehan, smiling and putting his hand on Toby's shoulder. "There's just one more item that I need to discuss with you, Mr. Gold. Miss Donnelly, would you mind waiting here while I speak to Toby a moment in my study?"

"Of course not," Bidge replied politely.

Toby and Mr. Sheehan stepped into his study. Mr. Sheehan shut the door and they sat down.

"Is something wrong?"

"On the contrary, Mr. Gold. I actually have some interesting news for you. Do you recall the online brokerage account that Jack Leonard set up in your name?"

"Sure, what about it?"

"As it turns out, that account was never used for criminal purposes. He didn't use it on the day of the crime. The police don't even have any real evidence that Jack Leonard opened the account."

"Of course he opened it. It even had the same password as the other fake accounts. The only reason he didn't use it that day is because I changed the password so he couldn't."

"Lucky thing you did that. Given your circumstances as an orphan, and that the account is in your name and isn't directly linked to the crimes, the Connecticut District Attorney's office and the SEC have agreed that the account is legally yours. Consider it an unintentional gift from Jack Leonard."

"Mine? For real? There's two hundred and fifty thousand dollars in that account."

"For real. You deserve it. The only catch is that you are still a minor and as such are not allowed to have an account like that solely in your own name."

"So what does that mean?"

"The account has been closed and I've worked with your county caseworker and your current guardians to set up a trust fund for you. No one can touch it except you, as soon as you turn eighteen. Until then, you will receive a monthly income of four hundred dollars from the interest. The remaining balance should become an excellent college fund for you. You have a very bright future ahead of you, Mr. Gold."

Tears welled up in Toby's eyes. He was sufficiently overwhelmed that all he could say was, "Thanks."

Mr. Sheehan handed him a tissue and led him back out to where Bidge was waiting. He opened the door and shook both their hands. "Nice meeting you, Miss Donnelly. I'll see you at Matriculation this fall."

"Nice meeting you, too."

As soon as Mr. Sheehan closed the door, Bidge turned to Toby. "You know, for someone who's supposed to be a headmaster, he looks *nothing* like Dumbledore."

"Yeah, I thought the same thing when I met him." Toby seemed distracted.

"What's wrong, Toby? What did he say to you?"

Toby smiled. "Nothing's wrong. Absolutely nothing."

"Do you want to tell me voluntarily, or I should I just read your mind?" Bidge teased.

"C'mon," Toby replied. "Let's go to the Tuck Shop and I'll buy you a double sundae." Toby was suddenly feeling generous. "It's good news. I'll tell you all about it."

"Yummy." Bidge smacked her lips.

Toby paused and looked at Bidge. "Three," he said matter-of-factly.

"What?" Bidge replied.

"Three. You were thinking of the number three."

Bidge gasped, her eyes growing wide. "How did you know that?"

"Can't say. It's a secret."

"You know you can't hide anything from me. I am the Great Bidgini…" Bidge stared into Toby's eyes, rubbing her temples menacingly with her index fingers while failing to suppress a giggle.

Toby just smirked and silently recited *Mary Had a Little Lamb* in his mind.

THE END

EPILOGUE

While he and Bidge were at the Tuck Shop, Toby's television sat unwatched at home, tuned to the financial news. Just before the market closed for the day, seven stocks with the same first letter appeared on the ticker crawling across the bottom of the screen. These seven stocks were followed by quotes for twenty additional stocks — the very last ones of the day:

XNR 3.8K@4.28 ▲0.09 PAA 6.8K@50.44 ▼0.25
TCO 1.7K@51.35 ▲0.18 AKS 8.0K@16.30 UNCH
BCE 2.4K@26.33 ▲0.53 ZQK 6.3K@15.31 ▲0.28
OXM 5.0K@50.46 ▼0.70 SKS 1.1K@18.26 ▲0.18
AKR 2.5K@25.35 UNCH OXY 0.9K@46.45 ▲2.11
Q 8.6K@8.26 ▲0.04 NCI 6.5K@20.35 ▲0.29 SNP
4.5K@90.40 ▲1.84 DPZ 9.9K@28.26 ▲0.04 BBV
7.2K@24.30 ▲0.72 USG 6.7K@53.27 ▼0.89 ARG
2.0K@40.40 UNCH IRS 4.6K@17.33 ▼0.43 FNM
3.4K@59.31 ▼0.47 QTM 2.4K@2.44 ▲0.01

DISCUSSION GUIDE

1. When Toby first becomes the Fruit Snack Tycoon, he calculates the return on investment (ROI) for his first deal as 100%. After purchasing the package of fruit snacks for 25 cents, if Toby had instead sold them for 40 cents, what would his ROI have been?

2. What does it mean to be gifted? When Toby meets Angela at the train station, he learns that everyone is born with a gift. In real life, what are some different ways that people can be gifted?

3. Toby feels helpless when his foster brother Eddie bullies him. Other than Operation Pantalones, what are some other ideas for how Toby could have dealt with his bully problem?

4. Operation Pantalones was a success because Toby, Bidge and Marc worked together as a team. Could Toby have succeeded alone? Why or why not? How does teamwork and trust lead to success in real life?

5. To get a permanent allowance of five dollars per week (or $260 per year) at 4% interest, Toby needed to save $6,500. How much money would he have needed to save if the interest rate had been 6% instead?

6. Toby received secret messages in the stock ticker data. The first ticker quote he received was **IDTC 8.2K@13.34 ▼0.37**. What does **IDTC** stand for? What is the meaning of **8.2K@13.34**? What is the significance of the arrow that points up and the number that immediately follows it (for example **▼0.37**)?

8. The secret messenger asks Toby to "Tell No One." In real life, what should you do if an adult says or does something, then asks you *not* to tell anyone?

9. Toby is exhorted by the messenger to use his gift wisely. What are some ways that we can use our gifts wisely? What is an example of using a gift *unwisely*?

10. At Bidge's big basketball game, the principal confiscated signs that said rude things about the other team. Do you agree that those signs demonstrated poor sportsmanship? Why is good sportsmanship important?

11. Suppose Marc has $120 dollars in the bank, a computer worth $400, and a bike worth $75. He owes Toby $13. Bidge owes Marc $5. What is Marc's net worth today?

12. Why was finding the baby bird on the ground so upsetting to Toby?

13. Bidge and her mom dealt with the death of Bidge's dad in very different ways. Why don't people in the same family necessarily react to tragedy in the same way?

14. Who was Karl Marx and why is he famous? How about Adam Smith and David Hume?

15. Toby discovers that even though everyone is born with a gift, very few people develop their gift fully. What are some ways we can develop our natural gifts?

16. What is market manipulation? Why do you think it's illegal?

17. Toby was able to successfully undo Choate's stocks losses due to Mr. Leonard's market manipulation. Was that the right thing to do?

18. By the end of the book, Bidge becomes more skilled at reading Toby's mind. How would you feel if one of your best friends could read your mind? Would it be a good thing or a bad thing?

AUTHOR'S NOTE

Wallingford, Connecticut is a real place, the Vermonter is a real train and Choate is a real school. Many other places, business and institutions mentioned in the book are also real. Notwithstanding, the reader should note that none of the events depicted in this book ever actually occurred. In particular, no one should be given the impression that any of the staff, faculty, administration or trustees of Choate Rosemary Hall has ever been involved in any adventures such as the ones depicted in this book. This is purely a work of fiction.

While historical figures mentioned in this work bear the names of actual people, their actions have been imagined by the author. Having said that, Benjamin Franklin and Adam Smith did indeed meet in Paris, but their forming of a secret society is a product of the author's imagination.

Regarding the financial content, sophisticated readers will recognize that in certain passages I took some liberties in the name of simplification. The balance sheet in chapter 14 is a good example of this. In some parts of the book, I made assumptions which could not be incorporated fluidly into the story. Examples include the calculation of the probability of Toby's first ticker message appearing by happenstance. I assumed 27 letters in the alphabet (a space being the 27th letter) and random letter draws with replacement.

Toby's calculation of total income replacement in fifteen years by investing half of his income is based on 7.5% average annual return (very much achievable over the long-term with a market index fund), as well as an assumption of no taxes - which seems a reasonable assumption for teenager with a modest income. When calculating his required endowment, he assumes a money market account interest rate of 4%. I have actually seen this kind of rate during my lifetime, but at the time of this publication, Toby would probably need to buy corporate bonds to get an interest rate that high.

Any other 'errors' that you may find in this book were of course *completely* intentional — just to make sure you were paying attention.

Save Half!

ACKNOWLEDGMENTS

I would like to acknowledge that sometimes I get grumpy when interrupted. I also acknowledge that I am seemingly incapable of getting mad at a puppy — thus far anyway. Perhaps someday I will meet my puppy nemesis.

My first and trusted readers deserve many thanks. Several of them happen to also be members of my immediate and extended family. They are the ones that read the book well before it had attained any measure of quality, so they are the ones that unfortunately experienced the most pain in the process. So I'd like to thank my trusted readers: Sandee Roe Everett, Jessica Everett, William Everett, Anna Everett, Janet Alsup, Jody Rolnick, Phoebe Wihtol, Nanette Stucki and Ally Condie. Stacy Whitman deserves special recognition for providing very detailed editorial feedback that helped me get the manuscript ready for publisher scrutiny. Christine Witthohn provided very valuable comments and suggestions that helped prepare the manuscript for publication.

My local Wallingford research was assisted immeasurably by real estate expert Lynn Smith and by my colleague and Choate alumnus Nathan Cho.

I have taken several liberties with some features of Wallingford and Choate. Thus, I acknowledge that there is actually no flagpole in front of Archbold.

I acknowledge both Israel's and Palestine's right to exist. I also acknowledge the District of Columbia's right to exist, but not as a state. "State of Columbia" makes no sense to me, mostly because we already have a state with the abbreviation SC — which reminds me…I acknowledge South Carolina's right to exist.

I'd also like to thank the members of my various writers' circles who have given my valuable input. Some of them I only know by their screen names: Wendy Elliott, Chrissy (Chrissygra), Matt (Stryder), Vicky Campagna, Damiansmom, Gillian Grey, Pamela Daniell, Isabel Mcfarland.

And last but certainly not least, I'd like to give very special thanks to the following people for making this project possible: Antonio Macias, Bill Stone, Brett Hopper, Camden and Colin Ness, Carolyn and Nick Atkins, Cynthia and Lola May, Dale Lutz, Daron Fraley, David Ebdon, Doug Turner, Douglas Clark, Edward Schaefer, Holly Pressman, Jack Warchol, James Aldous, Jill Blaszkowsky, Joe Baldacci, Judi Roe, Julia Babcock, Levi Alley, Levon Ellen Blue, Loretta Allen, Marla Mac, Marty Fernandi, Michelle and Allie, Milton Maldonado, Nabeel Khan, The Nixon Family, Noah Perlis, The Orens Family, Peter Dawes, Phillip & Joanie, Rachel Friendly, Rick Gibson, Rob Roe, Ryan McGauley, Sandra Resnick, Sarah Kageyama, Sean Ryan, Stephen McKeon, Susan Lee MacPhetres, The DiGiovanni Family, The Kattermans, and William Cohen-Pratt.